ANAÏS NIN

DELTA OF VENUS

PENGUIN BOOKS

PENGUIN BOOKS

Published by the Penguin Group
Penguin Books Ltd, 80 Strand, London WC2R 0RL, England
Penguin Putnam Inc., 375 Hudson Street, New York, New York 10014, USA
Penguin Books Australia Ltd, 250 Camberwell Road, Camberwell, Victoria 3124, Australia
Penguin Books Canada Ltd, 10 Alcorn Avenue, Toronto, Ontario, Canada M4V 3B2
Penguin Books India (P) Ltd, 11 Community Centre, Panchsheel Park, New Delhi – 110 017, India
Penguin Books (NZ) Ltd, Cnr Rosedale and Airborne Roads, Albany, Auckland, New Zealand
Penguin Books (South Africa) (Pty) Ltd, 24 Sturdee Avenue, Rosebank 2196, South Africa

Penguin Books Ltd, Registered Offices: 80 Strand, London WC2R 0RL, England

www.penguin.com

First published in Great Britain by W. H. Allen & Co. 1978
Published in Penguin Books 1990
Reprinted in Penguin Classics 2000

022

Printed in England by Clays Ltd, St Ives plc

ISBN-13: 978–0–14–118284–1
ISBN-10: 0–14–118284–9

www.greenpenguin.co.uk

ALWAYS LEARNING   **PEARSON**

..., of Spanish origin, Anaïs Nin was also of Cuban, French and Danish descent. She was born in Paris and spent her childhood in various parts of Europe. Her father left the family for another woman, which shocked Anaïs profoundly and was the reason for her mother to take her and her two brothers to live in the United States. Later Anaïs Nin moved to Paris with her husband, and they lived in France from 1924 to 1939, when Americans left on account of the war. She was analysed in the 1930s by René Allendy and subsequently by Otto Rank, with whom she also studied briefly in the summer of 1934. She became acquainted with many well-known writers and artists, and wrote a series of novels and stories.

Her first book – a defence of D. H. Lawrence – was published in the 1930s. Her prose poem, *House of Incest* (1936), was followed by the collection of three novellas, *Winter of Artifice* (1939). The quality and originality of her work were evident at an early stage but, as is often the case with *avant-garde* writers, it took time for her to achieve wide recognition. The international publication of her *Journals* won her new admirers in many parts of the world, particularly among young people and students. Her novels, *Ladders to Fire*, *Children of the Albatross*, *The Four-Chambered Heart*, *A Spy in the House of Love* and *Seduction of the Minotaur*, were first published in the United States between the 1940s and the 1960s, and eventually gathered in *Cities of the Interior*. She also wrote a collection of short stories, *Under a Glass Bell*. In the 1940s she began to write erotica for an anonymous client, and these pieces are collected in *Delta of Venus* and *Little Birds* (both published posthumously). Penguin also publish *A Woman Speaks*, a collection of lectures and interviews; *Journal of a Wife*, the third volume of *The Early Diary of Anaïs Nin, 1923–1927*; *In Favour of the Sensitive Man and Other Essays*; and, most recently, *The Early Diary 1927–1931*, which is the fourth volume of her diary. *Henry and June*, a chronicle of her passionate involvement with Henry Miller and his wife June Mansfield, and *Incest* are the new volumes of the 'un-expurgated diary' of Anaïs Nin, distinguishable from her previously published volumes by the references to both her husband and her love life. Her books have been translated into twenty-six languages around the world.

During her later years Anaïs Nin lectured frequently at universities throughout the USA. In 1973 she received an honorary doctorate from Philadelphia College of Art and in 1974 was elected to the National Institute of Arts and Letters. She died in Los Angeles in 1977.

CONTENTS

Preface*

A book collector offered Henry Miller a hundred dollars a month to write erotic stories. It seemed like a Dantesque punishment to condemn Henry to write erotica at a dollar a page. He rebelled because his mood of the moment was the opposite of Rabelaisian, because writing to order was a castrating occupation, because to be writing with a voyeur at the keyhole took all the spontaneity and pleasure out of his fanciful adventures.

[December, 1940]

Henry told me about the collector. They sometimes had lunch together. He bought a manuscript from Henry and then suggested that he write something for one of his old and wealthy clients. He could not tell much about his client except that he was interested in erotica.

Henry started out gaily, jokingly. He invented wild stories which we laughed over. He entered into it as an experiment, and it seemed easy at first. But after a while it palled on him. He did not want to touch upon any of the material he planned to write about for his real work, so he was condemned to force his inventions and his mood.

He never received a word of acknowledgment from the strange patron. It could be natural that he would not want to disclose his identity. But Henry began to tease the collector. Did this patron really exist? Were these pages for the collector himself, to heighten his own melancholy life? Were they one and the same person? Henry and I discussed this at length, puzzled and amused.

At this point, the collector announced that his client was

* Adapted from *The Diary of Anaïs Nin*, Volume III

coming to New York and that Henry would meet him. But somehow this meeting never took place. The collector was lavish in his descriptions of how he sent the manuscripts by airmail, how much it cost, small details meant to add realism to the claims he made about his client's existence.

One day he wanted a copy of *Black Spring* with a dedication.

Henry said, 'But I thought you told me he had all my books already, signed editions?'

'He lost his copy of *Black Spring*.'

'Who should I dedicate it to?' said Henry innocently.

'Just say "to a good friend", and sign your name.'

A few weeks later Henry needed a copy of *Black Spring* and none could be found. He decided to borrow the collector's copy. He went to the office. The secretary told him to wait. He began to look over the books in the bookcase. He saw a copy of *Black Spring*. He pulled it out. It was the one he had dedicated to the 'Good Friend'.

When the collector came in, Henry told him about this, laughing. In equally good humour, the collector explained: 'Oh, yes, the old man got so impatient that I sent him my own copy while I was waiting to get this one signed by you, intending to exchange them later when he comes to New York again.'

Henry said to me when we met, 'I'm more baffled than ever.'

When Henry asked what the patron's reaction to his writing was, the collector said, 'Oh, he likes everything. It is all wonderful. But he likes it better when it is a narrative, just storytelling, no analysis, no philosophy.'

When Henry needed money for his travel expenses he suggested that I do some writing in the interim. I felt I did not want to give anything genuine, and decided to create a mixture of stories I had heard and inventions, pretending they were from the diary of a woman. I never met the collector. He was to read my pages and to let me know what he thought. Today I received a telephone call. A voice said, 'It is fine. But leave out the poetry and descriptions of anything but sex. Concentrate on sex.'

So I began to write tongue-in-cheek, to become outlandish, inventive, and so exaggerated that I thought he would realize I was caricaturing sexuality. But there was no protest. I spent days in the library studying the *Kama Sutra*, listened to friends' most extreme adventures.

'Less poetry,' said the voice over the telephone. 'Be specific.'

But did anyone ever experience pleasure from reading a clinical description? Didn't the old man know how words carry colors and sounds into the flesh?

Every morning after breakfast I sat down to write my allotment of erotica. One morning I typed: 'There was a Hungarian adventurer . . .' I gave him many advantages: beauty, elegance, grace, charm, the talents of an actor, knowledge of many tongues, a genius for intrigue, a genius for extricating himself from difficulties, and a genius for avoiding permanence and responsibility.

Another telephone call: 'The old man is pleased. Concentrate on sex. Leave out the poetry.'

This started an epidemic of erotic 'journals'. Everyone was writing up their sexual experiences. Invented, overheard, researched from Krafft-Ebing and medical books. We had comical conversations. We told a story and the rest of us had to decide whether it was true or false. Or plausible. Was this plausible? Robert Duncan would offer to experiment, to test our inventions, to confirm or negate our fantasies. All of us needed money, so we pooled our stories.

I was sure the old man knew nothing about the beatitudes, ecstasies, dazzling reverberations of sexual encounters. Cut out the poetry was his message. Clinical sex, deprived of all the warmth of love – the orchestration of all the senses, touch, hearing, sight, palate; all the euphoric accompaniments, background music, moods, atmosphere, variations – forced him to resort to literary aphrodisiacs.

We could have bottled better secrets to tell him, but such secrets he would be deaf to. But one day when he reached saturation, I would tell him how he almost made us lose interest in passion by his obsession with the gestures empty of their emotions, and how we reviled him, because he almost caused us to take vows of chastity, because what he wanted us to exclude was our own aphrodisiac – poetry.

PREFACE

I received one hundred dollars for my erotica. Gonzalo needed cash for the dentist, Helba needed a mirror for her dancing, and Henry money for his trip. Gonzalo told me the story of the Basque and Bijou and I wrote it down for the collector.

[February, 1941]

The telephone bill was unpaid. The net of economic difficulties was closing in on me. Everyone around me irresponsible, unconscious of the shipwreck. I did thirty pages of erotica.

I again awakened to the consciousness of being without a cent and telephoned the collector. Had he heard from his rich client about the last manuscript I sent? No, he had not, but he would take the one I had just finished and pay me for it. Henry had to see a doctor. Gonzalo needed glasses. Robert came with B. and asked me for money to go to the movies. The soot from the transom window fell on my typing paper and on my work. Robert came and took away my box of typing paper.

Wasn't the old man tired of pornography? Wouldn't a miracle take place? I began to imagine him saying, 'Give me everything she writes, I want it all, I like all of it. I will send her a big present, a big check for all the writing she has done.'

My typewriter was broken. With a hundred dollars in my pocket I recovered my optimism. I said to Henry, 'The collector says he likes simple, unintellectual women – but he invites me to dinner.'

I had a feeling that Pandora's box contained the mysteries of woman's sensuality, so different from man's and for which man's language was inadequate. The language of sex had yet to be invented. The language of the senses was yet to be explored. D. H. Lawrence began to give instinct a language, he tried to escape the clinical, the scientific, which only captures what the body feels.

[October, 1941]

When Henry came he made several contradictory statements. That he could live on nothing, that he felt so good he could even

x

take a job, that his integrity prevented him from writing scenarios in Hollywood. At the last I said, 'And what of the integrity of doing erotica for money?'

Henry laughed, admitted the paradox, the contradictions, laughed and dismissed the subject.

France has had a tradition of literary erotic writing, in fine, elegant style. When I first began to write for the collector I thought there was a similar tradition here, but found none at all. All I had seen was shoddy, written by second-rate writers. No fine writer seemed ever to have tried his hand at erotica.

I told George Barker how Caresse Crosby, Robert, Virginia Admiral and others were writing. It appealed to his sense of humor. The idea of my being the madam of this snobbish literary house of prostitution, from which vulgarity was excluded.

Laughing, I said, 'I supply paper and carbon, I deliver the manuscript anonymously, I protect everyone's anonymity.'

George Barker felt this was much more humorous and inspiring than begging, borrowing or cajoling meals out of friends.

I gathered poets around me and we all wrote beautiful erotica. As we were condemned to focus only on sensuality, we had violent explosions of poetry. Writing erotica became a road to sainthood rather than to debauchery.

Harvey Breit, Robert Duncan, George Barker, Caresse Crosby, all of us concentrating our skills in a *tour de force*, supplying the old man with such an abundance of perverse felicities, that now he begged for more.

The homosexuals wrote as if they were women. The timid ones wrote about orgies. The frigid ones about frenzied fulfillments. The most poetic ones indulged in pure bestiality and the purest ones in perversions. We were haunted by the marvelous tales we could not tell. We sat around, imagined this old man, talked of how much we hated him, because he would not allow us to make a fusion of sexuality and feeling, sensuality and emotion.

[December, 1941]

George Barker was terribly poor. He wanted to write more erotica. He wrote eighty-five pages. The collector thought they were too surrealistic. I loved them. His scenes of lovemaking were disheveled and fantastic. Love between trapezes.

He drank away the first money, and I could not lend him anything but more paper and carbons. George Barker, the excellent English poet, writing erotica to drink, just as Utrillo painted paintings in exchange for a bottle of wine. I began to think about the old man we all hated. I decided to write to him, address him directly, tell him about our feelings.

'Dear Collector: We hate you. Sex loses all its power and magic when it becomes explicit, mechanical, overdone, when it becomes a mechanistic obsession. It becomes a bore. You have taught us more than anyone I know how wrong it is not to mix it with emotion, hunger, desire, lust, whims, caprices, personal ties, deeper relationships that change its color, flavor, rhythms, intensities.

'You do not know what you are missing by your microscopic examination of sexual activity to the exclusion of aspects which are the fuel that ignites it. Intellectual, imaginative, romantic, emotional. This is what gives sex its surprising textures, its subtle transformations, its aphrodisiac elements. You are shrinking your world of sensations. You are withering it, starving it, draining its blood.

'If you nourished your sexual life with all the excitements and adventures which love injects into sensuality, you would be the most potent man in the world. The source of sexual power is curiosity, passion. You are watching its little flame die of asphyxiation. Sex does not thrive on monotony. Without feeling, inventions, moods, no surprises in bed. Sex must be mixed with tears, laughter, words, promises, scenes, jealousy, envy, all the spices of fear, foreign travel, new faces, novels, stories, dreams, fantasies, music, dancing, opium, wine.

'How much do you lose by this periscope at the tip of your sex, when you could enjoy a harem of distinct and never-repeated wonders? No two hairs alike, but you will not let us waste words on a description of hair; no two odors, but if we expand on this you cry Cut the poetry. No two skins with the same texture, and never the same light, temperature, shadows, never the same gesture; for a lover, when he is aroused by true love, can run the gamut of centuries of love lore. What a range, what changes of age, what variations of maturity and innocence, perversity and art . . .

'We have sat around for hours and wondered how you look. If you have closed your senses upon silk, light, color, odor, character, temperament, you must be by now completely shriveled up. There are so many minor senses, all running like tributaries into the mainstream of sex, nourishing it. Only the united beat of sex and heart together can create ecstasy.'

POSTSCRIPT

At the time we were all writing erotica at a dollar a page, I realized that for centuries we had had only one model for this literary genre – the writing of men. I was already conscious of a difference between the masculine and feminine treatment of sexual experience. I knew that there was a great disparity between Henry Miller's explicitness and my ambiguities – between his humorous, Rabelaisian view of sex and my poetic descriptions of sexual relationships in the unpublished portions of the diary. As I wrote in Volume III of the *Diary*, I had a feeling that Pandora's box contained the mysteries of woman's sensuality, so different from man's and for which man's language was inadequate.

Women, I thought, were more apt to fuse sex with emotion, with love, and to single out one man rather than be promiscuous. This became apparent to me as I wrote the novels and the *Diary*, and I saw it even more clearly when I began to teach. But although women's attitude towards sex was quite distinct from that of men, we had not yet learned how to write about it.

Here in the erotica I was writing to entertain, under pressure from a client who wanted me to 'leave out the poetry', I believed that my style was derived from a reading of men's works. For this reason I long felt that I had compromised my feminine self. I put the erotica aside. Rereading it these many years later, I see that my own voice was not completely suppressed. In numerous passages I was intuitively using a woman's language, seeing sexual experience from a woman's point of view. I finally decided to release the erotica for publication because it shows the beginning efforts of a woman in a world that had been the domain of men.

If the unexpurgated version of the *Diary* is ever published, this feminine point of view will be established more clearly. It will show that women (and I, in the *Diary*) have never separated sex from feeling, from love of the whole man.

Anaïs Nin
Los Angeles
September, 1976

The Hungarian Adventurer

There was a Hungarian adventurer who had astonishing beauty, infallible charm, grace, the powers of a trained actor, culture, knowledge of many tongues, aristocratic manners. Beneath all this was a genius for intrigue, for slipping out of difficulties, for moving smoothly in and out of countries.

He traveled in grandiose style, with fifteen trunks of the finest clothes, with two Great Danes. His air of authority had earned him the nickname the Baron. The Baron was seen in the most luxurious hotels, at watering places and horse races, on world tours, excursions to Egypt, trips through the desert into Africa.

Everywhere he became the center of attraction for women. Like the most versatile of actors, he passed from one role to another to please the taste of each of them. He was the most elegant dancer, the most vivacious dinner partner, the most decadent of entertainers in tête-à-têtes; he could sail a boat, ride, drive. He knew each city as though he had lived there all his life. He knew everyone in society. He was indispensable.

When he needed money he married a rich woman, plundered her and left for another country. Most of the time the women did not rebel or complain to the police. The few weeks or months they had enjoyed him as a husband left a sensation that was stronger than the shock of losing their money. For a moment they had known what it was to live with strong wings, to fly above the heads of mediocrity.

He took them so high, whirled them so fast in his series of enchantments, that his departure still had something of the flight. It seemed almost natural – no partner could follow his great eagle sweeps.

The free, uncapturable adventurer, jumping thus from one golden branch to another, almost fell into a trap, a trap of human love, when one night he met the Brazilian dancer Anita at a Peruvian theater. Her elongated eyes did not close as other women's eyes did, but like the eyes of tigers, pumas and leopards, the two lids meeting lazily and slowly; and they seemed slightly sewn together towards the nose, making them narrow, with a lascivious, oblique glance falling from them like the glance of a woman who does not want to see what is being done to her body. All this gave her an air of being made love to, which aroused the Baron as soon as he met her.

When he went backstage to see her, she was dressing among a profusion of flowers; and for the delight of her admirers who sat around her, she was rouging her sex with her lipstick without permitting them to make a single gesture toward her.

When the Baron came in she merely lifted her head and smiled at him. She had one foot on a little table, her elaborate Brazilian dress was lifted, and with her jeweled hands she took up rouging her sex again, laughing at the excitement of the men around her.

Her sex was like a giant hothouse flower, larger than any the Baron had seen, and the hair around it abundant and curled, glossy black. It was these lips that she rouged as if they were a mouth, very elaborately so that they became like blood-red camellias, opened by force, showing the closed interior bud, a paler, fine-skinned core of the flower.

The Baron could not persuade her to have supper with him. Her appearance onstage was only the prelude to her work at the theater. Now followed the performance for which she was famed all through South America, when the boxes in the theater, deep, dark and half-curtained, filled with society men from all over the world. Women were not brought to this high-class burlesque.

She had dressed herself all over again in the full-petticoated costume she wore onstage for her Brazilian songs, but she wore no shawl. Her dress was strapless, and her rich, abundant breasts, compressed by the tight-waisted costume, bulged upwards, offering themselves almost in their entirety to the eye.

In this costume, while the rest of the show continued, she made her round of the boxes. There, on request, she knelt before a man, unbuttoned his pants, took his penis in her jeweled hands, and with a neatness of touch, an expertness, a subtlety few women had ever developed, sucked at it until he was satisfied. Her two hands were as active as her mouth.

The titillation almost deprived each man of his senses. The elasticity of her hands; the variety of rhythms; the change from a hand grip of the entire penis to the lightest touch of the tip of it, from firm kneading of all the part to the lightest teasing of the hair around it – all this by an exceptionally beautiful and voluptuous woman while the attention of the public was turned toward the stage. Seeing the penis go into her magnificent mouth between her flashing teeth, while her breasts heaved, gave men a pleasure for which they paid generously.

Her presence on the stage prepared them for her appearance in the boxes. She provoked them with her mouth, her eyes, her breasts. And to have their satisfaction, along with music and light and singing in a dark, half-curtained box above the audience, was an exceptionally piquant form of amusement.

The Baron almost fell in love with Anita and stayed with her for a longer time than with any woman. She fell in love with him and bore him two children.

But after a few years he was off again. The habit was too strong; the habit of freedom and change.

He traveled to Rome and took a suite at the Grand Hotel. The suite happened to be next to that of the Spanish Ambassador, who was staying there with his wife and two small daughters. The Baron charmed them, too. The Ambassador's wife admired him. They became so friendly and he was so delightful with the children, who did not know how to amuse themselves in this hotel, that soon it became a habit of the two little girls, upon getting up in the morning, to go and visit the Baron and awaken him with laughter and teasing, which they were not permitted to lavish upon their more solemn father and mother.

One little girl was about ten, the other twelve. They were both beautiful, with huge velvet-black eyes, long silky hair and golden skin. They wore short white dresses and short white socks. Shrieking, the two little girls would run into the Baron's room and playfully throw themselves over his big bed. He would tease them, fondle them.

Now the Baron, like many men, always awakened with a

peculiarly sensitive condition of the penis. In fact, he was in a most vulnerable state. He had no time to rise and calm the condition by urinating. Before he could do this the two little girls had run across the shining floor and thrown themselves over him, and over his prominent penis, which the big pale blue quilt somewhat concealed.

The little girls did not mind how their skirts flew upward and their slender dancers' legs got tangled and fell over his penis lying straight in the quilt. Laughing, they turned over on him, sat on him, treated him like a horse, sat astride him and pushed down on him, urging him to swing the bed by a motion of his body. With all this, they would kiss him, pull at his hair, and have childish conversations. The Baron's delight in being so treated would grow into excruciating suspense.

One of the girls was lying on her stomach, and all he had to do was to move a little against her to reach his pleasure. So he did this playfully, as if he meant to finally push her off the bed. He said, 'I am sure you will fall off if I push this way.'

'I won't fall off,' said the little girl, holding on to him through the covers while he moved as if he would force her to roll over the side of the bed. Laughing, he pushed her body up, but she lay close to him, her little legs, her little panties, everything, rubbing against him in her effort not to slide off, and he continued his antics while they laughed. Then the second girl, wishing to even the strength of the game, sat astride him in front of the other one, and now he could move even more wildly with the weight of both on him. His penis, hidden in the thick quilt, rose over and over again between the little legs, and it was like this that he came, with a strength he had rarely known, surrendering the battle, which the girls had won in a manner they never suspected.

Another time when they came to play with him he put his hands under the quilt. Then he raised the quilt with his forefinger and dared them to catch it. So with great eagerness, they began to chase the finger, which disappeared and reappeared in different parts of the bed, catching it firmly in their hands. After a moment it was not the finger but the penis they caught over and over again, and seeking to extricate it, he made them grasp it more strongly than ever. He would disappear under the covers completely, and taking his penis in his hand suddenly thrust it upward for them to catch.

He pretended to be an animal, sought to catch and bite them, sometimes quite near where he wanted to, and they took great delight in this. With the 'animal' they also played hide-and-seek. The 'animal' was to spring at them from some hidden corner. He hid in the closet on the floor and covered himself with clothes. One of the little girls opened the closet. He could see under her dress; he caught her and bit her playfully on the thighs.

So heated were the games, so great were the confusion of the battle and the abandon of the little girls at play, that very often his hand went everywhere he wanted it to go.

Eventually the Baron moved on again, but his high trapeze leaps from fortune to fortune deteriorated when his sexual quest became stronger than his quest for money and power. It seemed as though the strength of his desire for women was no longer under control. He was eager to rid himself of his wives, so as to pursue his search for sensation throughout the world.

One day he heard that the Brazilian dancer he had loved had died of an overdose of opium. Their two daughters were grown to the ages of fifteen and sixteen and wanted their father to take care of them. He sent for them. He was then living in New York with a wife by whom he had had a son. The woman was not happy at the thought of his daughters' arrival. She was jealous for her son, who was only fourteen. After all his expeditions, the Baron now wanted a home and a rest from difficulties and pretenses. He had a woman he rather liked and three children. The idea of meeting his daughters again interested him. He received them with great demonstrations of affection. One was beautiful, the other, less so but piquant. They had been brought up to witness their mother's life and were not restrained or prudish.

The beauty of their father impressed them. He, on the other hand, was reminded of his games with the two little girls in Rome, only his daughters were a little older, and it added a great attraction to the situation.

They were given a large bed for themselves, and later, when

they were still talking of their voyage and of meeting their father again, he came into the room to bid them goodnight. He stretched out at their side and kissed them. They returned his kisses. But as he kissed them, he slipped his hands along their bodies, which he could feel through their nightgowns.

The caresses pleased them. He said, 'How beautiful you are, both of you. I am so proud of you. I cannot let you sleep alone. It is such a long time since I have seen you.'

Holding them in a fatherly way, with their heads on his chest, caressing them protectively, he let them fall asleep, one on each side of him. Their young bodies, with their small breasts barely formed, affected him so that he did not sleep. He fondled one and then the other, with catlike movements, so as not to disturb them, but after a moment his desire was so violent that he awakened one and began to force himself on her. The other did not escape either. They resisted and wept a little, but they had seen so much of this during their life with their mother that they did not rebel.

But this was not to be an ordinary case of incest, for the Baron's sexual fury was increasing and had become an obsession. Being satisfied did not free him, calm him. It was like an irritant. From his daughters he would go to his wife and take her.

He was afraid his daughters would abandon him, run away, so he spied on them and practically imprisoned them.

His wife discovered this and made violent scenes. But the Baron was like a madman now. He no longer cared about his dressing, his elegance, his adventures, his fortune. He stayed at home and thought only of the moment when he could take his daughters together. He had taught them all the caresses imaginable. They learned to kiss each other in his presence until he was excited enough to possess them.

But his obsession, his excesses, began to weigh on them. His wife deserted him.

One night when he had taken leave of his daughters, he wandered through the apartment, still a prey to desire, to erotic fevers and fantasies. He had exhausted the girls. They had fallen asleep. And now his desire was tormenting him again. He was blinded by it. He opened the door to his son's room. His son was calmly sleeping, lying on his back, with his mouth slightly open. The

Baron watched him, fascinated. His hard penis continued to torment him. He fetched a stool and placed it near the bed. He kneeled on it and he put his penis to his son's mouth. The son awakened choking and struck at him. The girls also awakened.

Their rebellion against their father's folly mounted, and they abandoned the now frenzied, aging Baron.

Mathilde

Mathilde was a hat maker in Paris and barely twenty when she was seduced by the Baron. Although the affair did not last more than two weeks, somehow in that short time she became, by contagion, imbued with his philosophy of life and his seven-leagued way of solving problems. She was intrigued by something the Baron had told her casually one night: that Parisian women were highly prized in South America because of their expertness in matters of love, their vivaciousness and wit, which was quite a contrast to many of the South American wives, who still cherished a tradition of self-effacement and obedience, which diluted their personalities and was due, possibly, to men's reluctance to make mistresses out of their wives.

Like the Baron, Mathilde developed a formula for acting out life as a series of roles – that is, by saying to herself in the morning while brushing her blond hair, 'Today I want to become this or that person,' and then proceeding to be that person.

One day she decided she would like to be an elegant representative of a well-known Parisian modiste and go to Peru. All she had to do was to act the role. So she dressed with care, presented herself with extraordinary assurance at the house of the modiste, was engaged to be her representative and given a boat ticket to Lima.

Aboard ship, she behaved like a French missionary of elegance. Her innate talent for recognizing good wines, good perfumes, good dressmaking, marked her as a lady of refinement. Her palate was that of a gourmet.

Mathilde had piquant charms to enhance this role. She laughed perpetually, no matter what happened to her. When a valise was mislaid, she laughed. When her toe was stepped on, she laughed.

It was her laugh that attracted the Spanish Line representative, Dalvedo, who invited her to sit at the captain's table. Dalvedo looked suave in his evening suit, carried himself like a captain, and had many anecdotes to share. The next night he took her to a dance. He was fully aware that the trip was not long enough for the usual courtship. So he immediately began to court the little mole on Mathilde's chin. At midnight he asked if she liked cactus figs. She had never tasted them. He said that he had some in his cabin.

But Mathilde wanted to heighten her value by resistance, and she was on her guard when they entered the cabin. She had easily rebuffed the audacious hands of the men she brushed against when marketing, the sly buttock pats by the husbands of her clients, the pinching of her nipples by male friends who invited her to the movies. None of this stirred her. She had a vague but tenacious idea of what could stir her. She wanted to be courted with mysterious language. This had been determined by her first adventure, as a girl of sixteen.

A writer, who was a celebrity in Paris, had entered her shop one day. He was not looking for a hat. He asked if she sold luminous flowers that he had heard about, flowers which shone in the dark. He wanted them, he said, for a woman who shone in the dark. He could swear that when he took her to the theater and she sat back in the dark loges in her evening dress, her skin was as luminous as the finest sea shells, with a pale pink glow to it. And he wanted these flowers for her to wear in her hair.

Mathilde did not have them. But as soon as the man left she went to look at herself in the mirror. This was the kind of feeling she wanted to inspire. Could she? Her glow was not of that nature. She was much more like fire than light. Her eyes were ardent, violet in color. Her hair was dyed blond but it shed a copper shadow around her. Her skin was copper-toned, too, firm and not at all transparent. Her body filled her dresses tightly, richly. She did not wear a corset, but her body had the shape of the woman who did. She arched so as to throw the breasts forward and the buttocks high.

The man had come back. But this time he was not asking for anything to buy. He stood looking at her, his long finely carved face smiling, his elegant gestures making a ritual out of lighting a cigarette, and said, 'This time I came back just to see you.'

Mathilde's heart beat so swiftly that she felt as if this were the moment she had expected for years. She almost stood up on her toes to hear the rest of his words. She felt as if she were the luminous woman sitting back in the dark box receiving the unusual flowers. But what the polished gray-haired writer said in his aristocratic voice was, 'As soon as I saw you, I was stiff in my pants.'

The crudity of the words was like an insult. She reddened and struck at him.

This scene was repeated on several occasions. Mathilde found that when she appeared, men were usually speechless, deprived of all inclination for romantic courtship. Such words as these fell from them each time at the mere sight of her. Her effect was so direct that all they could express was their physical disturbance. Instead of accepting this as a tribute, she resented it.

Now she was in the cabin of the smooth Spaniard, Dalvedo. Dalvedo was peeling some cactus figs for her, and talking. Mathilde was regaining confidence. She sat on the arm of a chair in her red velvet evening dress.

But the peeling of the figs was interrupted. Dalvedo rose and said, 'You have the most seductive little mole on your chin.' She thought that he would try to kiss her. But he didn't. He unbuttoned himself quickly, took his penis out and, with the gesture of an apache to a woman of the streets, said, 'Kneel.'

And Mathilde again struck, then moved towards the door.

'Don't go,' he begged, 'you drive me crazy. Look at the state you put me in. I was like this all evening when I danced with you. You can't leave me now.'

He tried to embrace her. As she struggled to elude him, he came all over her dress. She had to cover herself with her evening cape to regain her cabin.

As soon as Mathilde arrived in Lima, however, she attained her dream. Men approached her with flowery words, disguising their intent with great charm and adornments. This prelude to the sexual act satisfied her. She liked a little incense. In Lima she received much of it, it was a part of the ritual. She was raised on a pedestal of poetry so that her falling into the final embrace might seem more of a miracle. She sold many more of her nights than hats.

Lima at that time was strongly influenced by its large Chinese population. Opium-smoking was prevalent. Rich young men traveled in bands from bordello to bordello, or they spent their nights in the opium dens, where prostitutes were available, or they rented absolutely bare rooms in prostitute quarters, where they could take drugs in groups, and the prostitutes visited them there.

The young men liked to visit Mathilde. She turned her shop into a boudoir, full of *chaises-longues*, lace and satin, curtains and pillows. Martinez, a Peruvian aristocrat, initiated her to opium. He brought his friends there to smoke. At times they spent two or three days lost to the world, to their families. The curtains were kept closed. The atmosphere was dark, slumberous. They shared Mathilde among them. The opium made them more voluptuous than sensual. They could spend hours caressing her legs. One of them would take one of her breasts, another would sink his kisses into the soft flesh of her neck, pressing her with the lips only, because the opium heightened every sensation. A kiss could throw shivers throughout her body.

Mathilde would lie naked on the floor. All the movements were slow. The three or four young men lay back among the pillows. Lazily one finger would seek her sex, enter it, lie there between the lips of the vulva, not moving. Another hand would seek it out too, content itself with circles around the sex, seek another orifice.

One man would offer his penis to her mouth. She would suckle at it very slowly, every touch magnified by the drug.

Then for hours they might lie still, dreaming.

Erotic images would form again. Martinez saw the body of a woman, distended, headless, a woman with the breasts of a Balinese woman, the belly of an African woman, the high buttocks of a Negress; all this confounded itself into an image of a mobile flesh, a flesh that seemed to be made of elastic. The taut breasts would swell towards his mouth, and his hand would extend towards them, then other parts of the body would stretch, become prominent, hang over his own body. The legs would part in an inhuman, impossible way, as if they were severed from the woman, to leave the sex exposed, open, as if one had taken a tulip in the hand and opened it completely by force.

This sex was also mobile, moving like rubber, as if invisible hands stretched it, curious hands that wanted to dismember the body to get at the interior of it. Then the ass would be turned fully toward him and begin to lose its shape, as if drawn apart. Every movement tended to open the body completely until it would tear. Martinez was taken with a fury because other hands were handling this body. He would half sit up and seek Mathilde's breast, and if he found a hand on it, or a mouth suckling it, he would seek her belly, as if it were still the image that haunted his opium dream, and then fall lower upon her body so that he could kiss her between parted legs.

Mathilde's pleasure in caressing the men was so immense, and their hands passed over her body and fondled her so completely, so continuously, that she rarely had an orgasm. She would only become aware of this fact after the men had left. She awakened from her opium dreams with her body still restless.

She would lie filing her nails and covering them with lacquer, doing her refined toilette for future occasions, brushing her blond hair. Sitting in the sun, using little cotton wads of peroxide, she dyed her pubic hair to match.

Left to herself, memories of the hands over her body haunted her. Now she felt one under her arm, sliding down to her waist. She remembered Martinez, his way of opening the sex like a bud, the flicks of his quick tongue covering the distance from the pubic hair to the buttocks, ending on the dimple at the end of her spine. How he loved this dimple, which led his fingers and his tongue to follow the downward curve and vanish between the two full mounts of flesh.

Thinking of Martinez, Mathilde would feel passionate. And she could not wait for his return. She looked down at her legs. From living so much indoors they had become white, very alluring, like the chalk-white complexion of the Chinese women, the morbid hothouse paleness that men, and particularly the dark-skinned Peruvians, loved. She looked at her belly, without fault, without a single line that should not be there. The pubic hair shone red-gold now in the sun.

'How do I look to him?' she asked herself. She got up and brought a long mirror toward the window. She stood it on the floor against a chair. Then she sat down in front of it on the rug and, facing it, slowly opened her legs. The sight was enchanting. The skin was flawless, the vulva, roseate and full. She thought it was like the gum plant leaf with its secret milk that the pressure of the finger could bring out, the odorous moisture that came like the moisture of the sea shells. So was Venus born of the sea with this little kernel of salty honey in her, which only caresses could bring out of the hidden recesses of her body.

Mathilde wondered if she could bring it out of its mysterious core. With her fingers she opened the two little lips of the vulva, and she began stroking it with catlike softness. Back and forth she stroked it as Martinez did with his more nervous dark fingers. She remembered his dark fingers on her skin, such a contrast to her skin, and the thickness of them seeming to promise to hurt the skin rather than arouse pleasure by their touch. How delicately he touched it, she thought, how he held the vulva between his fingers, as if he were touching velvet. She held it now as he did, in her forefinger and thumb. With the other free hand she continued the caresses. She felt the same dissolving feeling that she felt under Martinez's fingers. From somewhere a salty liquid was coming, covering the wings of her sex; between these it now shone.

Then Mathilde wanted to know how she looked when Martinez told her to turn over. She lay on her left side and exposed her ass to the mirror. She could see her sex now from another side. She moved as she moved for Martinez. She saw her own hand appear over the little hill formed by the ass, which she began to stroke. Her other hand went between her legs and showed in the mirror from behind. This hand stroked her sex back and forth. Then a forefinger was inserted and she began to rub against it. Now she was taken with the desire to be taken from both sides, and she inserted her other forefinger into the ass hole. Now when she moved forwards she felt her finger in the front, and when she lurched back she felt the other finger, as she sometimes felt Martinez and a friend when they both caressed her at once. The approach of the orgasm excited her, she went into convulsive gestures, as if to pull away the ultimate fruit from a branch, pulling, pulling at the branch to bring down everything into a wild orgasm, which came while she watched herself in the mirror, seeing the hands move, the honey shining, the whole sex and ass shining wet between the legs.

After seeing her movements in the mirror she understood the story told to her by a sailor – how the sailors on his ship had made a rubber woman for themselves to while away the time and satisfy the desires they felt during their six or seven months at sea. The woman had been beautifully made and gave them a perfect illusion. The sailors loved her. They took her to bed with them. She was made so that each aperture could satisfy them. She had the quality that an old Indian had once attributed to his young wife. Soon after their marriage, his wife was the mistress of every young man in the hacienda. The master called the old Indian to inform him of the scandalous conduct of his young wife and advised him to watch over her better. The Indian shook his head skeptically and answered, 'Well, I don't see why I should worry my head so much. My wife is not made of soap, she will not wear out.'

So it was with the woman made of rubber. The sailors found her untiring and yielding – truly a marvelous companion. There were no jealousies, no fights between them, no possessiveness. The rubber woman was very much loved. But in spite of her innocence, her pliant good nature, her generosity, her silence, in spite of her faithfulness to her sailors, she gave them all syphilis.

Mathilde laughed as she remembered the young Peruvian sailor who had told her this story, how he had described lying over her as if she were an air mattress, and how she made him bounce off her sometimes by sheer resilience. Mathilde felt exactly like this rubber woman when she took opium. How pleasurable was the feeling of utter abandon! Her only occupation was to count the money that her friends left her.

One of them, Antonio, did not seem content with the luxury of her room. He was always begging her to visit him. He was a prizefighter and looked like the man who knows how to make women work for his living. He had at once the necessary elegance to make women proud of him, a groomed air of the man of leisure and a suave manner that, one felt, could turn to violence at the necessary moment. And in his eyes he had the look of the cat who inspires a desire to caress but loves no one, who never feels he must respond to the impulses he arouses.

He had a mistress who matched him well, who was equal to his strength and vigor, able to take blows lustily; a woman who wore her femaleness with honor and who did not demand pity from men; a real woman who knew that a vigorous fight was a marvelous stimulant to the blood (pity only dilutes the blood) and that the best reconciliations could come only after combat. She knew that when Antonio was not with her he was at the Frenchwoman's taking opium, but she did not mind that as much as not knowing where he was at all.

Today he had just finished brushing his mustache with satisfaction and was preparing himself for an opium feast. To placate his mistress he started to pinch and pat her buttocks. She was an unusual-looking woman with some African blood in her. Her breasts were higher than any woman's he had ever seen, placed almost parallel with the shoulder line, and they were absolutely round and big. It was these breasts which had first attracted him. Their being placed so provocatively, so near the mouth, pointing upwards, somehow awakening in him a direct response. It was as if his sex had a peculiar affinity with these breasts, and as soon as they showed themselves in the whorehouse where he had found her, his sex raised itself to challenge them on equal terms.

Every time he had gone into the whorehouse, he experienced the same condition. He finally took the woman out of the house and lived with her. At first he could only make love to her breasts. They haunted him, obsessed him. When he inserted his penis into her mouth they seemed to be pointing hungrily toward it, and he would rest it between her breasts, holding them against the penis with his hands. The nipples were large and would harden like a fruit pip in his mouth.

Aroused by his caresses, she was left with the lower half of her body completely disregarded. Her legs would shake, begging violence, the sex would open, but he gave no attention to it. He filled his mouth with her breasts and rested his penis there; he liked to see the sperm spraying them. The rest of her body would writhe in space, legs and sex curling like a leaf at each caress, beating the air, and finally she would put her own hands there and masturbate.

This morning as he was about to leave, he repeated his caresses.

He bit into her breasts. She offered her sex to him but he would not have it. He made her kneel before him and take his penis into her mouth. She rubbed her breasts against him. Sometimes this made her come. Then he went out and walked leisurely to Mathilde's place. He found the door partially open. He walked in with his catlike steps, which made no sound on the carpet. He found Mathilde lying on the floor in front of a mirror. She was on her hands and knees and looking between her legs at the mirror.

He said, 'Don't move, Mathilde. That's a pose I love.'

He crouched over her like a giant cat, and his penis went into her. He gave Mathilde what he would not give his mistress. His weight finally made her sink down and sprawl on the rug. He raised her ass with his two hands and fell on her again and again. His penis seemed made of hot iron. It was long and narrow, and he moved it in all directions, and leaped inside of her with an agility she had never known. He quickened his gestures even more and said hoarsely, 'Come now, come now, come, I tell you. Give it all to me, now. Give it to me. Like you never did before. Give yourself now.' At these words she began to fling herself against him, furiously, and the orgasm came like lightning striking them together.

The others found them still entangled on the rug. They laughed at seeing the mirror which had witnessed the embrace. They began to prepare their opium pipes. Mathilde was languid. Martinez began his dream of distended, open-sexed women. Antonio retained his erection and asked Mathilde to sit over him, which she did.

When this opium feast was over and all but Antonio had gone, he repeated his request that she accompany him to his special den. Mathilde's womb still burned from his plowing and churnings, and she yielded, for she wanted to be with him and to repeat this embrace.

They walked in silence through the little streets of Chinatown. Women from all over the world smiled at them from open windows, stood on the doorsteps inviting them in. Some of the rooms were exposed to the street. Only a curtain concealed the beds. One could see couples embracing. There were Syrian women wearing their native costume, Arabian women with jewelry

covering their half-naked bodies, Japanese and Chinese women
beckoning slyly, big African women squatting in circles, chatting
together. One house was filled with French whores wearing short
pink chemises and knitting and sewing as if they were at home.
They always hailed the passers-by with promises of specialities.

The houses were small, dimly lit, dusty, foggy with smoke, filled
with dusky voices, the murmurs of drunkards, of love-making.
The Chinese adorned the setting and made it more confused with
screens and curtains, lanterns, burning incense, Buddhas of gold.
It was a maze of jewels, paper flowers, silk hangings, and rugs,
with women as varied as the designs and colors, inviting men who
passed by to sleep with them.

It was in this quarter that Antonio had a room. He took
Mathilde up the shabby stairway, opened a door that was almost
worn away, and pushed her in. There was no furniture in it. On
the floor there was a Chinese mat, and on this lay a man in rags, a
man so gaunt, so diseased-looking, that Mathilde drew back.

'Oh, you're here,' said Antonio rather irritably.

'I had nowhere to go.'

'You can't stay here you know. The police are after you.'

'Yes, I know.'

'I suppose you're the one who stole that cocaine the other day?
I knew it must be you.'

'Yes,' the man talked sleepily, indifferently.

Then Mathilde saw that his body was covered with scratches
and small wounds. The man made an effort to sit up. He held an
ampoule in one hand, in the other hand, a fountain pen and a penknife.

She watched him with horror.

He broke the top of the ampoule with his finger, shaking off
the broken bits. Then, instead of inserting a hypodermic syringe,
he inserted the fountain pen and drew the liquid out. With his
penknife he made a slit in his arm that was already covered with
old wounds and more recent ones, and in this slit he inserted the
fountain pen and pushed the cocaine into his flesh.

'He's too poor to get an injection needle,' said Antonio. 'And I
did not give money to him because I thought I could save him
from stealing it. But that's what he has found to do.'

Mathilde wanted to go. But Antonio would not let her. He wanted her to take cocaine with him. The man was lying back with his eyes closed. Antonio took out a needle and gave Mathilde an injection.

They lay on the floor and she was taken with an overpowering numbness. Antonio said to her, 'You feel dead, don't you?' It was as if she had been given ether. His voice seemed to come from so far. She motioned to him that she felt as if she were fainting. He said, 'It will pass.'

There began a nightmarish dream. Far away there was the figure of the prostrate man, lying back on the mat, then the figure of Antonio, very large and black. Antonio took the penknife and bent over Mathilde. She felt his penis inside of her, and it was soft and pleasurable, she moved in a slow, relaxed, wavering gesture. The penis was taken out. She felt it swinging out over the silky moisture between her legs, but she had not been satisfied and she was making a gesture as if to retrieve it. Next in the nightmare Antonio held the penknife open and he bent over her parted legs, and he touched her with the tip of it, pushed it slightly in. Mathilde felt no pain, no energy to move, she was hypnotized by this open knife. Then she became wildly conscious of what was happening – that it was not a nightmare. Antonio was watching the penknife tip touching the entrance of her sex. She screamed. The door opened. It was the police, who had come to fetch the cocaine thief.

Mathilde was rescued from the man who had so often slashed at the sexual opening of the whores, and who for this reason would never touch his mistress there. He had been safe only when he lived with her, when the provocativeness of her breasts kept his attention diverted from the sex, the morbid attraction to what he called 'woman's little wound', which he was so violently tempted to enlarge.

The Boarding School

This is a story of life in Brazil many years ago, far from the city, where the customs of strict Catholicism still prevailed. Boys of good birth were sent to boarding schools run by the Jesuits, who continued the severe habits of the Middle Ages. The boys slept on beds of wood, rose at dawn, attended mass without breakfast, confessed every day and were constantly watched and spied upon. The atmosphere was austere and inhibiting. The priests ate their meals apart and created an aura of sainthood around themselves. They were stylized in their gestures and speech.

Among them was a very dark-skinned Jesuit who had some Indian blood, the face of a satyr, large ears glued to his head, piercing eyes, a loose-lipped mouth that was always watering, thick hair and the smell of an animal. Under his long brown robe the boys had often noticed a bulge which the younger boys could not explain and which older boys laughed at behind his back. This bulge would appear unexpectedly at any hour – while the class read *Don Quixote* or Rabelais, or sometimes while he merely watched the boys, and one boy in particular, the only fair-haired one in all the school, with the eyes and skin of a girl.

He liked to get this boy off by himself and show him books from his private collection. These contained reproductions of Inca pottery on which there were often depictions of men standing against each other. The boy would ask questions which the old priest had to answer elusively. Other times the prints were quite clear; a long member came out of the middle of one man and penetrated the other from behind.

At confession this priest plied the boys with questions. The more innocent they appeared to be, the closer he questioned them in the darkness of the little confessional box. The kneeling boys were unable to see the priest, who was sitting inside. His low voice came through a small grilled window, asking, 'Have you ever had sensual fantasies? Have you thought about women?

Have you tried to imagine a woman naked? How do you behave at night in bed? Have you ever touched yourself? Have you ever fondled yourself? What do you do in the morning upon rising? Do you have an erection? Have you ever tried to look at other boys while they dress? Or at the bath?'

The boy who did not know anything would soon learn what was expected of him and be tutored by these questions. The boy who knew took pleasure in confessing in detail his emotions and dreams. One boy dreamed every night. He did not know what a woman looked like, how she was made. But he had seen the Indians making love to the vicuña, which resembled a delicate deer. And he dreamed about making love to vicuñas and awakened all wet every morning. The old priest encouraged these confessions. He listened with endless patience. He imposed strange punishments. A boy who masturbated continuously was ordered to go into the Chapel with him when no one was around, dip his penis in the holy water, and thus be purified. This ceremony was carried out in great secrecy at night.

There was one very wild boy who looked like a little Moorish prince, black-faced, with noble features, a royal carriage, and a beautiful body so smooth that no bones ever showed, lean and polished as a statue. This boy rebelled against the customary wearing of nightgowns. He was used to sleeping naked and the nightgown choked him, stifled him. So every night he put it on like the other boys, and then he would secretly take it off under his covers, and finally fall asleep without it.

Every night the old Jesuit would make his rounds, watching that no boy visited another in his bed, or masturbated, or talked in the dark to his neighbor. When he reached the bed of the undisciplined one, he would slowly and cautiously lift the cover and look at his naked body. If the boy awakened he would scold him. 'I came to see if you were sleeping without a nightgown again!' But if the boy did not awaken he was content with a long lingering glance at the youthful body asleep.

Once during anatomy class when he stood on the teacher's platform, and the girlish blond boy sat staring at him, the prominence under his priest's robe became obvious to everyone.

He asked the blond boy, 'How many bones does man have in his body?'

The blond boy answered meekly, 'Two hundred and eight.'

Another boy's voice came from the back of the classroom, 'But Father Dobo has two hundred and nine!'

It was soon after this incident that the boys were taken on a botanical excursion. Ten of them lost their way. Among them was the delicate blond boy. They found themselves in a forest, far from the teachers and the rest of the school. They sat down to rest and decide upon a course of action. They began eating berries. How it began, no one knew, but after a while the blond boy was thrown on the grass, undressed, turned on his stomach, and the other nine boys all passed over him, taking him as they would a prostitute, brutally. The experienced boys penetrated his anus to satisfy their desire, while the less experienced used friction between the legs of the boy, whose skin was as tender as a woman's. They spat on their hands and rubbed saliva over their penises. The blond boy screamed and kicked and wept, but they all held him and used him until they were satiated.

The Ring

In Peru it is the custom among the Indians to exchange rings for a betrothal, rings that have been in their possession for a long time. These rings are sometimes in the shape of a chain.

A very handsome Indian fell in love with a Peruvian woman of Spanish descent, but there was violent opposition on the part of her family. The Indians were purported to be lazy and degenerate, and to produce weak and unstable children, particularly when married to Spanish blood.

In spite of the opposition, the young people carried out their engagement ceremony among their friends. The girl's father came in during the festivities and threatened that, if he ever met the Indian wearing the chain ring the girl had already given him, he would tear it from his finger in the bloodiest manner, and if necessary cut his finger off. The festivities were spoiled by this incident. Everybody went home, and the young people separated with promises to meet secretly.

They met one evening after many difficulties, and kissed fervently for a long while. The woman was exalted by his kisses. She was ready to give herself, feeling that this might be their last moment together, for her father's anger was growing every day. But the Indian was determined to marry her, determined not to possess her in secrecy. Then she noticed that he did not have the ring on his finger. Her eyes questioned him. He said in her ear, 'I am wearing it, but not where it can be seen. I am wearing it where no one can see it, but where it will prevent me from taking you or any other woman until we are married.'

'I don't understand,' said the woman. 'Where is the ring?'

Then he took her hand, led it to a certain place between the legs. The woman's fingers felt his penis first of all, and then he guided her fingers and she felt the ring there at the base of it. At the touch of her hand, however, the penis hardened and he cried out, because the ring pressed into it and gave him excruciating pain.

The woman almost fainted with horror. It was as if he wanted to kill and mutilate the desire in himself. And at the same time the thought of this penis bound and encircled by her ring roused her sexually, so that her body became warm and sensitive to all kinds of erotic fantasies. She continued to kiss him, and he begged her not to, because it brought him greater and greater pain.

A few days later the Indian was again in agony, but he could not get the ring off. The doctor had to be called, and the ring filed away.

The woman came to him and offered to run away with him. He accepted. They got on horses and traveled for a whole night together to a nearby town. There he concealed her in a room and went out to get work on an hacienda. She did not leave the room until her father tired of searching for her. The night watchman of the town was the only one aware of her presence. The watchman was a young man and had helped to conceal her. From her window she could see him walking back and forth carrying the keys of the houses, and calling, 'The night is clear and all is well in the town.'

When someone came home late he would clap his hands together and call for the watchman. The watchman would open the door. While the Indian was away at work the watchman and the woman chatted together innocently.

He told her about a crime that had recently taken place in the village. The Indians who left the mountain and their work on the haciendas and went down to the jungle became wild and beast-like. Their faces changed from lean, noble contours to bestial grossness.

Such a transformation had just taken place in an Indian who had once been the handsomest man of the village, gracious, silent, with a strange humor and a reserved sensuality. He had gone down to the jungle and made money hunting. Now he had returned. He was homesick. He came back poor and wandered about homeless. No one recognized or remembered him.

Then he had caught a litle girl on the road and ripped her sexual parts with a long knife used for skinning animals. He had not violated her, but had taken the knife and inserted it into her sex, and belabored her with it. The whole village was in a turmoil. They could not decide how to punish him. A very old Indian practice was to be revived for his sake. His wounds would be parted and wax, mixed with a biting acid the Indians knew of, inserted into them so that the pain would be doubled. Then he was to be flogged to death.

As the watchman told this story to the woman, her lover returned from his work. He saw her leaning out of the window and looking at the watchman. He rushed up to her room and appeared before her with his black hair wild around his face, his eyes full of lightning bolts of anger and jealousy. He began to curse her and torture her with questions and doubts.

Ever since the accident with the ring his penis had remained sensitive. The lovemaking was accompanied with pain, and so he could not indulge in it as often as he wanted. His penis would swell and hurt him for days. He was always afraid he was not satisfying his mistress and that she might love another. When he saw the tall watchman talking to her, he was sure they were carrying on an affair behind his back. He wanted to hurt her, he wanted her to suffer bodily in some way, as he had suffered for her. He forced her to go downstairs with him to the cellar where the wines were kept in vats under beamed ceilings.

He tied a rope to one of the beams. The woman thought he was going to beat her. She could not understand why he was preparing a pulley. Then he tied her hands and began pulling on the rope so that her body was raised in the air and the whole weight of it hung on her wrists, and the pain was great.

She wept and swore that she had been faithful, but he was insane. When she fainted as he pulled the rope again, he came to his senses. He took her down and began embracing her and caressing her. She opened her eyes and smiled at him.

He was overcome with desire for her and he threw himself on her. He thought that she would resist him, that after the pain she had endured she would be angry. But she made no resistance. She continued to smile at him. And when he touched her sex he found that she was wet. He took her with fury, and she responded with the same exaltation. It was the best night they ever had together, lying there on the cold cellar floor in the darkness.

Mallorca

I was spending the summer in Mallorca, in Deya, near the monastery where George Sand and Chopin stayed. In the early morning we would get on small donkeys and travel the hard, difficult road to the sea, down the mountain. It would take about an hour of slow travail, through the red earth paths, the rocks, the treacherous boulders, through the silver olive trees, down to the fishing villages, made of huts built against the mountain flanks.

Every day I went down to the cove, where the sea came into a small round bay of such transparency that one could swim to the bottom and see the coral reefs and unusual plants.

A strange story was told of the place by the fishermen. The Mallorcan women were very inaccessible, puritanical and religious. When they swam they wore the long skirted bathing suits and black stockings of years ago. Most of them did not believe in swimming at all and left this to the shameless European women who spent the summers there. The fishermen also condemned the modern bathing suits and obscene behavior of Europeans. They thought of Europeans as nudists, who waited for only the slightest opportunity to get completely undressed and lie naked in the sun like pagans. They also looked with disapproval on the midnight bathing parties innovated by Americans.

One evening some years ago, a fisherman's daughter of eighteen was walking along the edge of the sea, leaping from rock to rock, her white dress clinging to her body. Walking thus and dreaming and watching the effects of the moon on the sea, the soft lapping of the waves at her feet, she came to a hidden cove where she noticed that someone was swimming. She could see only the head moving and occasionally an arm. The swimmer was quite far away. Then she heard a light voice calling out to her, 'Come in and swim. It's beautiful.' It was said in Spanish with a foreign accent. 'Hello, Maria,' it called, so the voice knew her. It must have been one of the young American women who bathed there during the day.

She answered, 'Who are you?'

'I'm Evelyn,' said the voice, 'come and swim with me!'

It was very tempting. Maria could easily take off her white dress and wear only her short white chemise. She looked everywhere. There was no one around. The sea was calm and speckled with moonlight. For the first time Maria understood the European love of midnight bathing. She took off her dress. She had long black hair, a pale face, slanted green eyes, greener than the sea. She was beautifully formed, with high breasts, long legs, a stylized body. She knew how to swim better than any other woman on the island. She slid into the water and began her long easy strokes toward Evelyn.

Evelyn swam under the water, came up to her and gripped her legs. In the water they teased each other. The semidarkness and the bathing cap made it difficult to see the face clearly. American women had voices like boys.

Evelyn wrestled with Maria, embraced her under the water. They came up for air, laughing, swimming nonchalantly away and back to each other. Maria's chemise floated up around her shoulders and hampered her movements. Finally it came off altogether and she was left naked. Evelyn swam under and touched her playfully, wrestling and diving under and between her legs.

Evelyn would part her legs so that her friend could dive between them and reappear on the other side. She floated and let her friend swim under her arched back.

Maria saw that she was naked too. Then suddenly she felt Evelyn embracing her from behind, covering her whole body with hers. The water was lukewarm, like a luxuriant pillow, so salty that it bore them, helped them to float and swim without effort.

'You're beautiful, Maria,' said the deep voice, and Evelyn kept her arms around her. Maria wanted to float away, but she was held by the warmth of the water, the constant touch of her friend's body. She let herself be embraced. She did not feel breasts on her friend, but, then, she knew young American women she had seen did not have breasts. Maria's body was languid, and she wanted to close her eyes.

Suddenly what she felt between her legs was not a hand but something else, something so unexpected, so disturbing that she screamed. This was no Evelyn but a young man, Evelyn's younger brother, and he had slipped his erect penis between her legs. She screamed but no one heard, and her scream was only something she had been trained to expect of herself. In reality his embrace seemed to her as lulling and warming and caressing as the water. The water and the penis and the hands conspired to arouse her body. She tried to swim away. But the boy swam under her body, caressed her, gripped her legs, and then mounted her again from behind.

In the water they wrestled, but each movement affected her only more physically, made her more aware of his body against hers, of his hands upon her. The water swung her breasts back and forth like two heavy water lilies floating. He kissed them. With the constant motion he could not really take her, but his penis touched her over and over again in the most vulnerable tip of her sex, and Maria was losing her strength. She swam toward shore, and he followed. They fell on the sand. The waves still lapped them as they lay there panting, naked. The boy then took the girl, and the sea came and washed over them and washed away the virgin blood.

From that night they met only at this hour. He took her there in the water, swaying, floating. The wavelike movements of their bodies as they enjoyed each other seemed part of the sea. They found a foothold on a rock and stood together, caressed by the waves, and shaking from the orgasm.

When I went down to the beach at night, I often felt as though I could see them, swimming together, making love.

Artists and Models

One morning I was called to a studio in Greenwich Village, where a sculptor was beginning a statuette. His name was Millard. He already had a rough version of the figure he wanted and had reached the stage where he needed a model.

The statuette was wearing a clinging dress, and the body showed through in every line and curve. The sculptor asked me to undress completely because he could not work otherwise. He seemed so absorbed by the statuette and looked at me so absently that I was able to undress and take the pose without hesitation. Although I was quite innocent at that time, he made me feel as if my body were no different than my face, as if I were the same as the statuette.

As Millard worked, he talked about his former life in Montparnasse, and the time passed quickly. I didn't know if his stories were meant to affect my imagination, but he showed no signs of being interested in me. He enjoyed recreating the atmosphere of Montparnasse for his own sake. This is one of the stories he told me:

'The wife of one of the modern painters was a nymphomaniac. She was tubercular, I believe. She had a chalk-white face, burning black eyes deeply sunk in her face, with eyelids painted green. She had a voluptuous figure, which she covered very sleekly in black satin. Her waist was small in proportion to the rest of her body. Around her waist she wore a huge Greek silver belt, about six inches wide, studded with stones. The belt was fascinating. It was like the belt of a slave. One felt that deep down she *was* a slave – to her sexual hunger. One felt that all one had to do was to grip the belt and open it for her to fall into one's arms. It was very much like the chastity belt they showed in the Musée Cluny, which the crusaders were said to have put on their wives, a very

28

wide silver belt with a hanging appendage that covered the sex and locked it up for the duration of their crusades. Someone told me the delightful story of a crusader who had put a chastity belt on his wife and left the key in care of his best friend in case of his death. He had barely ridden away a few miles when he saw his friend riding furiously after him, calling out, "You gave me the wrong key!"

'Such were the feelings that the belt of Louise inspired in everyone. Seeing her arrive at a café, her hungry eyes looking us over, searching for a response, an invitation to sit down, we knew she was out on a hunt for the day. Her husband could not help knowing about this. He was a pitiful figure, always looking for her, being told by his friends that she was at another café and then another, where he would go, which gave her time to steal off to a hotel room with someone. Then everyone would try to let her know where her husband was looking for her. Finally, in desperation, he began to beg his best friends to take her, so that at least she would not fall into strangers' hands.

'He had a fear of strangers, of South Americans in particular, and of Negroes and Cubans. He had heard remarks about their extraordinary sexual powers and felt that, if his wife fell into their hands, she would never return to him. Louise, however, after having slept with all his best friends, finally did meet one of the strangers.

'He was a Cuban, a tremendous brown man, extraordinarily handsome, with long, straight hair like a Hindu's and beautifully full, noble features. He would practically live at the Dome until he found a woman he wanted. And then they would disappear for two or three days, locked up in a hotel room, and not reappear until they were both satiated. He believed in making such a thorough feast of a woman that neither one wanted to see the other again. Only when this was over would he be seen sitting in the café again, conversing brilliantly. He was, in addition, a remarkable fresco painter.

'When he and Louise met, they immediately went off together. Antonio was powerfully fascinated by the whiteness of her skin, the abundance of her breasts, her slender waist, her long, straight, heavy blond hair. And she was fascinated by his head and powerful body, by his slowness and ease. Everything made him laugh. He gave one the feeling that the whole world was now shut out and only this sensual feast existed, that there would be no tomorrows, no meetings with anyone else – that there was only this room, this afternoon, this bed.

'When she stood by the big iron bed, waiting, he said, "Keep your belt on." And he began by slowly tearing her dress from around it. Calmly and with no effort, he tore it into shreds as if it were made of paper. Louise was trembling at the strength of his hands. She stood naked now except for the heavy silver belt. He loosened her hair over her shoulders. And only then did he bend her back on the bed and kiss her interminably, his hands over her breasts. She felt the painful weight both of the silver belt and of his hands pressing so hard on her naked flesh. Her sexual hunger was rising like madness to her head, blinding her. It was so urgent that she could not wait. She could not even wait until he undressed. But Antonio ignored her movements of impatience. He not only continued to kiss her as if he were drinking her whole mouth, tongue, breath, into his big dark mouth, but his hands mauled her, pressed deeply into her flesh, leaving marks and pain everywhere. She was moist and trembling, opening her legs and trying to climb over him. She tried to open his pants.

'"There is time," he said. "There is plenty of time. We are going to stay in this room for days. There is a lot of time for both of us."

'Then he turned away and got undressed. He had a golden-brown body, a penis as smooth as the rest of his body, big, firm as a polished wood baton. She fell on him and took it into her mouth. His fingers went everywhere, into her anus, into her sex; his tongue, into her mouth, into her ears. He bit at her nipples, he kissed and bit her belly. She was trying to satisfy her hunger by rubbing against his leg, but he would not let her. He bent her as if she were made of rubber, twisted her into every position. With his two strong hands he took whatever part of her he was hungry for and brought it up to his mouth like a morsel of food, not caring how the rest of her body fell into space. Just so, he took her ass between his two hands, held it to his mouth, and bit and kissed her. She begged, "Take me, Antonio, take me, I can't wait!" He would not take her.

'By this time the hunger in her womb was like a raging fire. She thought that it would drive her insane. Whatever she tried to do to bring herself to an orgasm, he defeated. If she even kissed him too long he would break away. As she moved, the big belt made a clinking sound, like the chain of a slave. She was now indeed the slave of this enormous brown man. He ruled like a king. Her pleasure was subordinated to his. She realized she could do nothing against his force and will. He demanded submission. Her desire died in her from sheer exhaustion. All the tautness left her body. She became as soft as cotton. Into this he delved with greater exultancy. His slave, his possession, a broken body, panting, malleable, growing softer under his fingers. His hands searched every nook of her body, leaving nothing untouched, kneading it, kneading it to suit his fancy, bending it to suit his mouth, his tongue, pressing it against his big shining white teeth, marking her as his.

'For the first time, the hunger that had been on the surface of her skin like an irritation, retreated into a deeper part of her body. It retreated and accumulated, and it became a core of fire that waited to be exploded by his time and his rhythm. His touching was like a dance in which the bodies turned and deformed themselves into new shapes, new arrangements, new designs. Now they were cupped like twins, spoon-fashion, his penis against her ass, her breasts undulating like waves under his hands, painfully awake, aware, sensitive. Now he was crouching over her prone body like some great lion, as she placed her two fists under her ass to raise herself to his penis. He entered her for the first time and filled her as none other had, touching the very depths of the womb.

'The honey was pouring from her. As he pushed, his penis made little sucking sounds. All the air was drawn from the womb, the way his penis filled it, and he swung in and out of the honey endlessly, touching the tip of the womb, but as soon as her breathing hastened, he would draw it out, all glistening, and take up another form of caress. He lay back on the bed, legs apart, his penis raised, and he made her sit upon it, swallow it up to the hilt, so that her pubic hair rubbed against his. As he held her, he made her dance circles around his penis. She would fall on him and rub her breasts against his chest, and seek his mouth, then straighten up again and resume her motions around the penis. Sometimes she raised herself a little so that she kept only the head of the penis in her sex, and she moved lightly, very lightly, just enough to keep it inside, touching the edges of her sex, which were red and swollen, and clasped the penis like a mouth. Then suddenly moving downwards, engulfing the whole penis, and gasping with the joy, she would fall over his body and seek his mouth again. His hands remained on her ass all the time, gripping her to force her movements so that she could not suddenly accelerate them and come.

'He took her off the bed, laid her on the floor, on her hands and knees, and said, "Move." She began to crawl about the room, her long blond hair half-covering her, her belt weighing her waist down. Then he knelt behind her and inserted his penis, his whole body over hers, also moving on its iron knees and long arms. After he had enjoyed her from behind, he slipped his head under her so that he could suckle at her luxuriant breasts, as if she were an animal, holding her in place with his hands and mouth. They were both panting and twisting, and only then did he lift her up, carry her to the bed, and put her legs around his shoulders. He took her violently and they shook and trembled as they came together. She fell away suddenly and sobbed hysterically. The orgasm had been so strong that she had thought she would go insane, with a hatred and a joy like nothing she had ever known. He was smiling; panting they lay back and fell asleep.'

The next day Millard told me about the artist Mafouka, the man-woman of Montparnasse.

'No one knew exactly what she was. She dressed like a man. She was small, lean, flat-chested. She wore her hair short, straight. She had the face of a boy. She played billiards like a man. She drank like a man, with her foot on the bar railing. She told obscene stories like a man. Her drawing had a strength not found in a woman's work. But her name had a feminine sound, her walk was feminine, and she was said not to have a penis. The men did not know quite how to treat her. Sometimes they slapped her on the back with fraternal feelings.

'She lived with two girls in a studio. One of them was a model, the other, a nightclub singer. But no one knew what relationship there was among them. The two girls seemed to have a relationship like that of a husband and a wife. What was Mafouka to them? They would never answer any questions. Montparnasse always liked to know such things, and in detail. A few homosexuals had been attracted to Mafouka and had made advances toward her or him. But she had repulsed them. She quarreled willingly and struck out with force.

'One day I was quite a little drunk and I dropped into Mafouka's studio. The door was open. As I entered I heard giggling up on the balcony. The two girls were obviously making love. The voices would get soft and tender, then violent and unintelligible, and become moans and sighs. Then there would be silences.

'Mafouka came in and found me with my ear cocked, listening. I said to her, "Please let me go and see them."

'"I don't mind," said Mafouka. "Come up after me, slowly. They won't stop if they think it is just me. They like me to watch them."

'We went up the narrow stairs. Mafouka called, "It's I." There was no interruption of the noises. As we went up, I bent over so that they could not see me. Mafouka went to the bed. The two girls were naked. They were pressing their bodies against each other and rubbing together. The friction gave them pleasure. Mafouka leaned over them, caressed them. They said, "Come on, Mafouka, lie with us." But she left them and took me downstairs again.

'"Mafouka," I said, "what are you? Are you a man or a woman? Why do you live with these two girls? If you are a man, why don't you have a girl of your own? If you are a woman, why don't you have a man occasionally?"

'Mafouka smiled at me.

'"Everybody wants to know. Everybody feels that I am not a boy. The women feel it. The men don't know for sure. I am an artist."

'"What do you mean, Mafouka?"

'"I mean that I am, like many artists, bisexual."

'"Yes, but the bisexuality of artists is in their nature. They may be a man with the nature of a woman, but with such an equivocal physique as you have."

'"I have an hermaphrodite's body."

'"Oh, Mafouka, let me see your body."

'"You won't make love to me?"

'"I promise."

'She took her shirt off first and showed a young boy's torso. She had no breasts, just the nipples, marked as they would be on a young boy. Then she slipped down her slacks. She was wearing a woman's panties, flesh-colored, with lace. She had a woman's legs and thighs. They were beautifully curved, full. She was wearing women's stockings and garters. I said, "Let me take the garters off. I love garters." She handed me her leg very elegantly with the movement of a ballet dancer. I slowly rolled down the garter. I held a dainty foot in my hand. I looked up at her legs, which were perfect. I rolled down the stocking and saw beautiful, smooth, woman's skin. Her feet were dainty and carefully pedicured. Her nails were covered with red lacquer. I was more and more intrigued. I caressed her leg. She said, "You promised you would not make love to me."

'I stood up. Then she slipped down her panties. And I saw below the delicate curled pubic hair, shaped like a woman's, that she carried a small atrophied penis, like a child's. She let me look at her – or at him, as I felt I now should say.

'"Why do you call yourself by a woman's name, Mafouka? You are really like a young boy except for the shape of your legs and arms."

'Then Mafouka laughed, this time a woman's laugh, very light and pleasant. She said, "Come and see." She lay back on the couch, opened her legs and showed me a perfect vulva mouth, rosy and tender, behind the penis.

'"Mafouka!"

'My desire was aroused. The strangest desire. The feeling of wanting to take both a man and woman in one person. She saw the stirring of it in me and sat up. I tried to win her by a caress, but she eluded me.

'"Don't you like men?" I asked her. "Haven't you ever had a man?"

'"I'm a virgin. I don't like men. I feel a desire for women only, but I can't take them as a man could. My penis is like a child's – I cannot have an erection."

'"You are a real hermaphrodite, Mafouka," I said. "That is what our age is supposed to have produced because the tension between the masculine and the feminine has broken down. People are mostly half of one and half of the other. But I have never seen it before – actually, physically. It must make you very unhappy. Are you happy with women?"

'"I desire women, but I do suffer, because I cannot take them like a man, and also because when they have taken me like Lesbians, I still feel some dissatisfaction. But I am not attracted to men. I fell in love with Matilda, the model. But I could not keep her. She found a real Lesbian for herself, one that she feels she can satisfy. This penis of mine gives her the feeling that I am not a real Lesbian. And she knows she has no power over me, even though I was attracted to her. So you see, the two girls have formed another link together. I stand between them, perpetually dissatisfied. Also, I do not like the companionship of women. They are petty and personal. They hang on to their mysteries and secrets, they act and pretend. I like the character of men better."

'"Poor Mafouka."

'"Poor Mafouka. Yes, when I was born they did not know how to name me. I was born in a small village in Russia. They thought I was a monster and should perhaps be destroyed, for my own sake. When I came to Paris I suffered less. I found I was a good artist."'

Whenever I left the sculptor's studio, I would always stop in a coffee shop nearby and ponder all that Millard had told me. I wondered whether anything like this were happening around me, here in Greenwich Village, for instance. I began to love posing, for the adventurous aspect of it. I decided to attend a party one Saturday evening that a painter named Brown had invited me to. I was hungry and curious about everything.

I rented an evening dress from the costume department of the Art Model Club, with an evening cape and shoes. Two of the models came with me, a red-haired girl, Mollie, and a statuesque one, Ethel, who was the favorite of the sculptors.

What was passing through my head all the time were the stories of Montparnasse life told to me by the sculptor, and now I felt that I was entering this realm. My first disappointment was seeing that the studio was quite poor and bare, the two couches without pillows, the lighting crude, with none of the trappings I had imagined necessary for a party.

Bottles were on the floor, along with glasses and chipped cups. A ladder led to a balcony where Brown kept his paintings. A thin curtain concealed the washstand and a little gas stove. At the front of the room was an erotic painting of a woman being possessed by two men. She was in a state of convulsion, her body arched, her eyes showing the whites. The men were covering her, one with his penis inside of her and the other with his penis in her mouth. It was a life-size painting and very bestial. Everyone was looking at it, admiring it. I was fascinated. It was the first picture of the sort I had seen, and it gave me a tremendous shock of mixed feelings.

Next to it stood another which was even more striking. It showed a poorly furnished room, filled by a big iron bed. Sitting on this bed was a man of about forty or so, in old clothes, with an unshaved face, a slobbering mouth, loose eyelids, loose jaws, a completely degenerate expression. He had taken his pants down halfway, and on his bare knees sat a little girl with very short skirts, to whom he was feeding a bar of candy. Her little bare legs rested on his bare hairy ones.

What I felt after seeing these two paintings was what one feels when drinking, a sudden dizziness of the head, a warmth through the body, a confusion of the senses. Something awakens in the body, foggy and dim, a new sensation, a new kind of hunger and restlessness.

I looked at the other people in the room. But they had seen so much of this that it did not affect them. They laughed and commented.

One model was talking about her experiences at an underwear shop:

'I had answered an advertisement for a model to pose in underwear for sketches. I had done this many times before and was paid the normal price of a dollar an hour. Usually several artists sketched me at the same time, and there were many people around – secretaries, stenographers, errand boys. This time the place was empty. It was just an office with a desk, files and drawing materials. A man sat waiting for me in front of his drawing board. I was given a pile of underwear and found a screen placed where I could change. I began by wearing a slip. I posed for fifteen minutes at a time while he made sketches.

'We worked quietly. When he gave the signal, I went behind the screen and changed. They were satin underthings of lovely designs, with lace tops and fine embroidery. I wore a brassière and panties. The man smoked and sketched. At the bottom of the pile were panties and a brassière made entirely of black lace. I had posed in the nude often and did not mind wearing these. They were quite beautiful.

'I looked out of the window most of the time, not at the man sketching. After a while I did not hear the pencil working any longer and I turned slightly towards him, not wanting to lose the pose. He was sitting there behind his drawing board staring at me. Then I realized that he had his penis out and that he was in a kind of trance.

'Thinking this would mean trouble for me since we were alone in the office, I started to go behind the screen and dress.

'He said, "Don't go. I won't touch you. I just love to see women in lovely underwear. I won't move from here. And if you want me to pay you more, all you have to do is wear my favorite piece of underwear and pose for fifteen minutes. I will give you five dollars more. You can reach for it yourself. It is right above your head on the shelf there."

'Well, I did reach for the package. It was the loveliest piece of underwear you ever saw – the finest black lace, like a spider web really, and the panties were slit back and front, slit and edged with fine lace. The brassière was cut in such a way as to expose the nipples through triangles. I hesitated because I was wondering if this would not excite the man too much, if he would attack me.

'He said, "Don't worry. I don't really like women. I never

touch them. I like only underwear. I just like to see women in lovely underwear. If I tried to touch you I would immediately become impotent. I won't move from here."

'He put aside the drawing board and sat there with his penis out. Now and then it shook. But he did not move from his chair.

'I decided to put on the underwear. The five dollars tempted me. He was not very strong and I felt that I could defend myself. So I stood there in the slit panties, turning around for him to see me on all sides.

'Then he said, "That's enough." He seemed unsettled and his face was congested. He told me to dress quickly and leave. He handed me the money in a great hurry, and I left. I had a feeling that he was only waiting for me to leave to masturbate.

'I have known men like this, who steal a shoe from someone, from an attractive woman, so they can hold it and masturbate while looking at it.'

Everyone was laughing at her story. 'I think,' said Brown, 'that when we are children we are much more inclined to be fetishists of one kind or another. I remember hiding inside my mother's closet and feeling ecstasy at smelling her clothes and feeling them. Even today I cannot resist a woman who is wearing a veil or tulle or feathers, because it awakens the strange feelings I had in that closet.'

As he said this I remembered how I hid in the closet of a young man when I was only thirteen, for the same reason. He was twenty-five and he treated me like a little girl. I was in love with him. Sitting next to him in a car in which he took all of us for long rides, I was ecstatic just feeling his leg alongside mine. At night I would get into bed and, after turning out the light, take out a can of condensed milk in which I had punctured a little hole. I would sit in the dark sucking at the sweet milk with a voluptuous feeling all over my body that I could not explain. I thought then that being in love and sucking at the sweet milk were related. Much later I remembered this when I tasted sperm for the first time.

Mollie remembered that at the same age she liked to eat ginger while she smelled camphor balls. The ginger made her body feel warm and languid and the camphor balls made her a little dizzy. She would get herself in a sort of drugged state this way, lying there for hours.

Ethel turned to me and said, 'I hope you never marry a man you don't love sexually. That is what I have done. I love everything about him, the way he behaves, his face, his body, the way he works, treats me, his thoughts, his way of smiling, talking, everything except the sexual man in him. I thought I did, before we married. There is absolutely nothing wrong with him. He is a perfect lover. He is emotional and romantic, he shows great feeling and great enjoyment. He is sensitive and adoring. Last night while I was asleep he came into my bed. I was half-asleep so I could not control myself, as I usually do, because I do not want to hurt his feelings. He got in beside me and began to take me very slowly and lingeringly. Usually it is all over quickly, which makes it possible to bear. I do not even let him kiss me if I can help it. I hate his mouth on mine. I usually turn my face away, which is what I did last night. Well, there he was, and what do you think I did? I suddenly began to strike him with my closed fists, on the shoulder, while he was enjoying himself, to dig my nails into him, and he took it as a sign that I was enjoying it, growing rather wild with pleasure, and he went on. Then I whispered as low as I could, "I hate you." And then I asked myself if he had heard me. What would he think? Was he hurt? As he was himself partly asleep, he merely kissed me good night when it was over and went back to his bed. The next morning I was waiting for what he would say. I still thought perhaps he had heard me say, "I hate you." But no, I must have formed the words without saying them. And all he said was, "You got quite wild last night, you know," and smiled, as if it pleased him.'

Brown started the phonograph and we began to dance. The little alcohol I had taken had gone to my head. I felt a dilation of the whole universe. Everything seemed very smooth and simple. Everything, in fact, ran downward like a snowy hill on which I could slide without effort. I felt a great friendliness, as if I knew all these people intimately. But I chose the most timid of the painters to dance with. I felt that he was pretending somewhat, as

I was, to be very familiar with all of this. I felt that deep down he was a little uneasy. The other painters were caressing Ethel and Mollie as they danced. This one did not dare. I was laughing to myself at having discovered him. Brown saw that my painter was not making any advances, and he cut in for a dance. He was making sly remarks about virgins. I wondered whether he was alluding to me. How could he know? He pressed against me, and I drew away from him. I went back to the timid young painter. A woman illustrator was flirting with him, teasing him. He was equally glad that I came back to him. So we danced together, retreating into our own timidity. All around us people were kissing now, embracing.

The woman illustrator had thrown off her blouse and was dancing in her slip. The timid painter said, 'If we stay here we will soon have to lie on the floor and make love. Do you want to leave?'

'Yes, I want to leave,' I said.

We went out. Instead of making love, he was talking, talking. I was listening to him in a daze. He had a plan for a picture of me. He wanted to paint me as an undersea woman, nebulous, transparent, green, watery except for the very red mouth and the very red flower I was wearing in my hair. Would I pose for him? I did not respond very quickly because of the effects of the liquor, and he said apologetically, 'Are you sorry that I was not brutal?'

'No, I'm not sorry. I chose you myself because I knew you would not be.'

'It's my first party,' he said humbly, 'and you're not the kind of woman one can treat – that way. How did you ever become a model? What did you do before this? A model does not have to be a prostitute, I know, but she has to bear a lot of handling and attempts.'

'I manage quite well,' I said, not enjoying this conversation at all.

'I will be worrying about you. I know some artists are objective while they work, I know all that. I feel that way myself. But there is always a moment before and after, when the model is undressing and dressing, that does disturb me. It's the first surprise of seeing the body. What did you feel the first time?'

'Nothing at all. I felt as if I were a painting already. Or a
statue. I looked down at my own body like some object, some
impersonal object.'

I was growing sad, sad with restlessness and hunger. I felt that
nothing would happen to me. I felt desperate with desire to be a
woman, to plunge into living. Why was I enslaved by this need of
being in love first? Where would my life begin? I would enter each
studio expecting a miracle which did not take place. It seemed to
me that a great current was passing all around me and that I was
left out. I would have to find someone who felt as I did. But
where? Where?

The sculptor was watched by his wife, I could see that. She
came into the studio so often, unexpectedly. And he was frightened. I did not know what frightened him. They invited me to
spend two weeks at their country house where I would continue
to pose – or rather, she invited me. She said that her husband did
not like to stop work during vacations. But as soon as she left he
turned to me and said, 'You must find an excuse not to go. She
will make you miserable. She is not well – she has obsessions. She
thinks that every woman who poses for me is my mistress.'

There were hectic days of running from studio to studio with
very little time for lunch, posing for magazine covers, illustrations
for magazine stories, and advertisements. I could see my face everywhere, even in the subway. I wondered if people recognized me.

The sculptor had become my best friend. I was anxiously
watching his statuette coming to a finish. Then one morning when
I arrived I saw that he had ruined it. He said that he had tried to
work on it without me. But he did not seem unhappy or worried.
I was quite sad, and to me it looked very much like sabotage,
because it seemed spoiled with such awkwardness. I saw that he
was happy to be beginning it all over again.

It was at the theater that I met John and discovered the power
of a voice. It rolled over me like the tones of a pipe organ, making
me vibrate. When he repeated my name and mispronounced it, it
sounded to me like a caress. It was the deepest, richest voice I had
ever heard. I could scarcely look at him. I knew that his eyes were

big, of an intense, magnetic blue, that he was large, rather restless. His foot moved nervously like that of a racehorse. I felt his presence blurring everything else – the theater, the friend sitting at my right. And he behaved as if I had enchanted him, hypnotized him. He talked on, looking at me, but I was not listening. In one moment I was no longer a young girl. Every time he spoke, I felt myself falling into some dizzy spiral, falling into the meshes of a beautiful voice. It was truly a drug. When he had finally 'stolen' me, as he said, he hailed a taxi.

We did not say another word until we reached his apartment. He had not touched me. He did not need to. His presence had affected me in such a way that I felt as if he had caressed me for a long time.

He merely said my name twice, as if he thought it sufficiently beautiful to repeat. He was tall, glowing. His eyes were so intensely blue that when they blinked, for a second it was like some tiny flash of lightning, giving one a sense of fear, a fear of a storm that would completely engulf one.

Then he kissed me. His tongue went around mine, around and around, and then it stopped to touch the tip only. As he kissed me he slowly lifted my skirt. He unrolled my garters, my stockings. Then he lifted me up and carried me to the bed. I was so dissolved that I felt he had already penetrated me. It seemed to me that his voice had opened me, opened my whole body to him. He sensed this, and so he was amazed by the resistance to his penis that he felt.

He stopped to look at my face. He saw the great emotional receptiveness, and then he pressed harder. I felt the tear and the pain, but the warmth melted everything, the warmth of his voice in my ear saying, 'Do you want me as I want you?'

Then his pleasure made him groan. His whole weight upon me, pressing against my body, the shaft of pain vanished. I felt the joy of being opened. I lay there in a semidream.

John said, 'I hurt you. You did not enjoy it.' I could not say, 'I want it again.' My hand touched his penis. I caressed it. It sprung up, so hard. He kissed me until I felt a new wave of desire, a desire to respond completely. But he said, 'It will hurt now. Wait a little while. Can you stay with me, all night? Will you stay?'

I saw that there was blood on my leg. I went to wash it off. I felt that I had not been taken yet, that this was only a small part of the breaking through. I wanted to be possessed and know blinding joys. I walked unsteadily and fell on the bed again.

John was asleep, his big body still curved as when he was lying against me, his arm thrown out where my head had been resting. I slipped in at his side and fell half-asleep. I wanted to touch his penis again. I did so gently, not wanting to wake him. Then I slept and was awakened by his kisses. We were floating in a dark world of flesh, feeling only the soft flesh vibrating, and every touch was a joy. He gripped my hips tautly against him. He was afraid to wound me. I parted my legs. When he inserted his penis it hurt, but the pleasure was greater. There was a little outer rim of pain and, deeper in, a pleasure at the presence of his penis moving there. I pressed forwards, to meet it.

This time he was passive. He said, 'You move, you enjoy it now.' So as not to feel the pain, I moved gently around his penis. I put my closed fists under my backside to raise myself toward him. He placed my legs on his shoulders. Then the pain grew greater and he withdrew.

I left him in the morning, dazed, but with a new joy of feeling that I was growing nearer to passion. I went home and slept until he telephoned.

'When are you coming?' he said. 'I must see you again. Soon. Are you posing today?'

'Yes, I must. I'll come after the pose.'

'Please don't pose,' he said, 'please don't pose. It makes me desperate to think of it. Come and see me first. I want to talk to you. Please come and see me first.'

I went to him. 'Oh,' he said, burning my face with the breath of his desire. 'I can't bear to think of you posing now, exposing yourself. You can't do that anymore. You must let me take care of you. I cannot marry you because I have a wife and children. Let me take care of you until we know how we can escape. Let me get a little place where I can come and see you. You should not be posing. You belong to me.'

So I entered a secret life, and when I was supposed to be posing for everyone else in the world, I was really waiting in a beautiful room for John. Each time he came, he brought a gift, a book, colored stationery for me to write on. I was restless, waiting.

The only one who was taken into the secret was the sculptor because he sensed what was happening. He would not let me stop posing, and he questioned me. He had predicted how my life would be.

The first time I felt an orgasm with John, I wept because it was so strong and so marvelous that I did not believe it could happen over and over again. The only painful moments were the ones spent waiting. I would bathe myself, spread polish on my nails, perfume myself, rouge my nipples, brush my hair, put on a negligée, and all the preparations would turn my imagination to the scenes to come.

I wanted him to find me in the bath. He would say he was on his way. But he would not arrive. He was often detained. By the time he arrived I would be cold, resentful. The waiting wore out my feelings. I would rebel. Once I would not answer when he rang the doorbell. Then he knocked gently, humbly, and that touched me, so I opened the door. But I was angry and wanted to hurt him. I did not respond to his kiss. He was hurt until his hand slipped under my negligée and he found that I was wet, in spite of the fact that I kept my legs tightly closed. He was joyous again and he forced his way.

Then I punished him by not responding sexually and he was hurt again, for he enjoyed my pleasure. He knew by the violent heartbeats, by the changes in the voice, by the contraction of my legs, how I had enjoyed him. And this time I lay like a whore. That really hurt him.

We could never go out together. He was too well known, as was his wife. He was a producer. His wife was a playwright.

When John discovered how angry it would make me to wait for him, he did not try to remedy it. He came later and later. He would say that he was arriving at ten o'clock and then come at midnight. So one day he found that I was not there when he came. This put him in a frenzy. He thought I would not come back. I felt that he was doing this deliberately, that he liked my being angry. After two days he pleaded with me and I returned. We were both very keyed up and angry.

He said, 'You've gone back to pose. You like it. You like to show yourself.'

'Why do you make me wait so long? You know that it kills my desire for you. I feel cold when you come late.'

'Not so very cold,' he said.

I closed my legs tightly against him, he could not even touch me. But then he slipped in quickly from behind and caressed me. 'Not so cold,' he said.

On the bed he pushed his knee between my legs and forced them open. 'When you are angry,' he said, 'I feel that I am raping you. I feel then that you love me so much you cannot resist me, I see that you are wet, and I like your resistance and your defeat too.'

'John, you will make me so angry that I will leave you.'

Then he was frightened. He kissed me. He promised not to repeat this.

What I could not understand was that, despite our quarrels, being made love to by John made me only more sensitive. He had awakened my body. Now I had even a greater desire to abandon myself to all whims. He must have known this because the more he caressed me, awakened me, the more he feared that I would return to posing. Slowly, I did return. I had too much time to myself, I was too much alone with my thoughts of John.

Millard particularly was happy to see me. He must have spoiled the statuette again, purposely I knew now, so he could keep me in the pose he liked.

The night before, he had smoked marijuana with friends. He said, 'Did you know that very often it gives people the feeling that they are transformed into animals? Last night there was a woman who was completely taken by this transformation. She fell on her hands and knees and walked around like a dog. We took her clothes off. She wanted to give milk. She wanted us to act like puppies, sprawl on the floor and suckle at her breasts. She kept on her hands and knees and offered her breasts to all of us. She wanted us to walk like dogs – after her. She insisted on our taking her in this position, from behind, and I did, but then I was terribly tempted to bite her as I crouched over her. I bit into her shoulder harder than I have ever bitten anyone. The woman did not get frightened. I did. It sobered me. I stood up and then saw that a friend of mine was following her on his hands and knees, not caressing her or taking her, but merely smelling exactly as a dog would do, and this reminded me so much of my first sexual impression that it gave me a painful hard-on.

'As children we had a big servant girl in the country who came from Martinique. She wore voluminous skirts and a colored kerchief on her head. She was a rather pale mulatto, very beautiful. She would make us play hide-and-seek. When it was my turn to hide she would hide me under her skirt, sitting down. And there I was, half-suffocated, hiding between her legs. I remember the sexual odor that came from her and that stirred me even as a boy. Once I tried to touch her, but she slapped my hand.'

I was posing quietly and he came over to measure me with an instrument. Then I felt his hand on my thighs, caressing me so lightly. I smiled at him. I stood on the model's stand, and he was caressing my legs now, as if he were modeling me out of clay. He kissed my feet, he ran his hands up my legs again and again, and around my ass. He leaned against my legs and kissed me. He lifted me up and brought me down to the floor. He held me tightly against him, caressing my back and shoulders and neck. I shivered a little. His hands were smooth and supple. He touched me as he touched the statuette, so caressingly, all over.

Then we walked towards the couch. He lay me there on my stomach. He took his clothes off and fell on me. I felt his penis against my ass. He slipped his hands around my waist and lifted me up slightly so that he could penetrate me. He lifted me up toward him rhythmically. I closed my eyes to feel him better and to listen to the sound of the penis sliding in and out of the moisture. He pushed so violently that it made tiny clicks, which delighted me.

His fingers dug into my flesh. His nails were sharp and hurt. He aroused me so much with his vigorous thrusts that my mouth opened and I was biting into the couch cover. Then at the same time we both heard a sound. Millard rose swiftly, picked up his clothes and ran up the ladder to the balcony where he kept his sculpture. I slipped behind the screen.

There came a second knock on the studio door, and his wife came in. I was trembling, not with fear, but the shock of having stopped in the middle of our enjoyment. Millard's wife saw the studio empty and left. Millard came out dressed. I said, 'Wait for me a minute,' and began to dress too. The moment was destroyed. I was still wet and shivering. When I slipped on my panties the silk touch affected me like a hand. I could not bear the tension and desire any longer. I put my two hands over my sex as Millard had done and pressed against it, closing my eyes and imagining Millard was caressing me. And I came, shaking from head to foot.

Millard wanted to be with me again, but not in his studio where we might be surprised by his wife, so I let him find another place. It belonged to a friend. The bed was set in a deep alcove and there were mirrors above the bed and small dim lamps. Millard wanted all the lights out, he said he wanted to be in the dark with me.

'I have seen your body and I know it so well, now I want to feel it, with my eyes closed, just to feel the skin and the softness of the flesh. Your legs are so firm and strong, but so soft to the touch. I love your feet with the toes free and set apart like the fingers of a hand, not cramped – and the toenails so beautifully lacquered – and the down on your legs.' He passed his hand all over my body, slowly, pressing into the flesh, feeling every curve. 'If my hand stays here between the legs,' he said, 'do you feel it, do you like it, do you want it nearer?'

'Nearer, nearer,' I said.

'I want to teach you something,' said Millard. 'Do you want to let me do it?'

He inserted his finger inside my sex. 'Now, I want you to contract around my finger. There is a muscle there that can be made to contract and expand around the penis. Try.'

I tried. His finger there was tantalizing. Since he was not moving it, I tried to move inside of my womb, and I felt the muscle that he mentioned, weakly at first, opening and closing around the finger.

Millard said, 'Yes, like that. Do it stronger, stronger.'

So I did, opening, closing, opening, closing. It was like a little mouth inside, tightening around the finger. I wanted to take it in, suckle at it, so I continued to try.

Then Millard said that he would insert his penis and not move and that I should continue to move inside. I tried with more and more strength to clutch at him. The motion was exciting me, and I felt that at any moment I would reach the orgasm, but after I had clutched at him several times, sucking his penis in, he suddenly groaned with pleasure and began to push quickly, as he himself could not hold back the orgasm. I merely continued the inner motion and I felt the orgasm, too, in the most marvelous deep way, deep inside of the womb.

He said, 'Did John ever show you this?'

'No.'

'What has he shown you?'

'This,' I said. 'You kneel over me and push.'

Millard obeyed. His penis did not have much strength, for it was too soon after the first orgasm, but he slipped it in, pushing it with his hand. Then I reached out with my two hands and caressed the balls and put two fingers at the base of the penis and rubbed as he moved. Millard was instantly aroused, his penis hardened, and he began to move in and out again. Then he stopped himself.

'I must not be so demanding,' he said in a strange tone. 'You will be tired out for John.'

We lay back and rested, smoking. I was wondering if Millard had felt more than sensual desire, whether my love for John weighed on him. But although there was always a hurt sound to his words, he continued to ask me questions.

'Did John have you today? Did he take you more than once? How did he take you?'

In the weeks to come, Millard taught me many things I had not done with John, and as soon as I learned them I tried them with John. Finally he became suspicious of where I was learning new positions. He knew I had not made love before I met him. The first time I tightened my muscles to clutch at the penis, he was amazed.

The two secret relationships became difficult for me, but I enjoyed the danger and the intensity.

Lilith

Lilith was sexually cold, and her husband half knew it, in spite of her pretenses. This led to the following incident.

She never took sugar because she did not want to grow plumper than she was, and she used a sugar substitute, tiny white pills which she carried in her handbag all the time. One day she ran out of them and asked her husband to buy some on his way home. So he brought her a little vial like the one she had ordered, and she put two of the pills into her coffee after dinner.

They were sitting there together and he was looking at her with an expression of mellow tolerance, which he often had in face of her nervous explosions, her crises or egotism, of self-blame, of panic. To all her dramatic behavior he responded with an unwavering good humor and patience. She was always storming alone, being angry alone, going through vast emotional upheavals in which he did not take part.

Possibly this was a symbol of the tension which did not take place between them sexually. He refused all her primitive, violent challenges and hostilities, he refused to enter this emotional arena with her and respond to her need of jealousies, of fears, of battles.

Perhaps if he had taken up her challenges and played the games that she liked to play, perhaps then she might have felt his presence with more of a physical impact. But Lilith's husband did not know the preludes to sensual desire, did not know any of the stimulants that certain jungle natures require, and so, instead of answering her as soon as he saw her hair grow electric, her face more vivid, her eyes like lightning, her body restless and jerky like a racehorse's, he retired behind this wall of objective understanding, this gentle teasing and acceptance of her, just as one watches an animal in the zoo and smiles at his antics, but is not drawn into his mood. It was this which left Lilith in a state of isolation – indeed, like a wild animal in an absolute desert.

When she stormed and when her temperature rose, her husband

was nowhere to be seen. He was like some bland sky looking down at her and waiting for her storm to spend itself. If he, like an equally primitive animal, had appeared at the other end of this desert, facing her with the same electric tension of hair, skin, and eyes, if he had appeared with the same jungle body, treading heavily and wanting some pretext to leap out, embrace in fury, feel the warmth and strength of his opponent, then they might have rolled down together and the biting might have become of another sort, and the bout might have turned into an embrace, and the hair-pulling might have brought their mouths together, their teeth together, their tongues together. And out of the fury their genitals might have rubbed against each other, drawing sparks, and the two bodies would have had to enter each other to end this formidable tension.

And so tonight he sat back with this expression in his eyes, and she sat under the lamp furiously painting some object as if after she had painted it, she would devour it whole. Then he said, 'You know, that was not sugar that I brought you and that you took for dinner. It was Spanish fly, a powder that makes one passionate.'

Lilith was astounded. 'And you gave me that to take?'

'Yes, I wanted to see how it would affect you, I thought it might be very pleasant for both of us.'

'Oh, Billy,' she said, 'what a trick to play on me. And I promised Mabel that we'd go to the movies together. I can't disappoint her. She's been shut in at home for a week. Suppose it begins to affect me at the movies.'

'Well, if you promised, you must go. But I'll be waiting up for you.'

So, in a state of fever and high tension, Lilith went to fetch Mabel. She did not dare confess what her husband had done to her. She remembered all the stories that she had heard about Spanish fly. In the eighteenth century in France, men had made great use of it. She remembered the story of a certain aristocrat who, at the age of forty, when he was already a little weary from his assiduous lovemaking to all the attractive women of his time, fell so violently in love with a dancer who was only twenty years old that he spent three full days and nights with her in sexual intercourse – with the help of Spanish fly. Lilith tried to imagine what such an experience might be, how it would take her at some unexpected moment and she would have to run home and confess her desire to her husband.

As she sat in the darkened cinema, she could not watch the screen. Her head was in chaos. She sat taut on the edge of her seat, trying to sense the effects of the drug. She pulled herself up with a start when she noticed first of all that she had sat with her legs far apart, her skirt up on her knees.

She thought this was an expression of her already growing sexual fever. She tried to remember whether she had ever sat in this position before at the movies. She saw the parted legs as the most obscene position ever imagined, and realized that the person sitting in the row in front of her, which was set so much lower, would be able to see up her skirt and regale himself with the spectacle of her fresh new panties and new garters that she had bought only that day. Everything seemed to conspire for this night of orgy. Intuitively she must have foreseen it all when she went to buy herself panties with a fine lace ruffle on them, and garters of a deep coral color, which were very becoming to her smooth dancer's legs.

She brought her legs together in anger. She thought that if this wild sexual mood took hold of her just then, she would not know what to do. Would she get up suddenly and say she had a headache and leave? Or could she turn toward Mabel – Mabel had always adored her. Would she dare turn to Mabel and caress her? She had heard of women caressing each other in the movies. A friend of hers had sat this way in the darkness of the movies, and very slowly her companion's hand had unhooked the side opening of her skirt, slipped a hand to her sex and fondled her for a long time until she had come. How often this friend had repeated the delight of sitting still, controlling the upper half of her body, sitting straight and still, while a hand was caressing in the dark, secretly, slowly, mysteriously. Is this what would happen to Lilith now? She had never caressed a woman. She had some-times thought to herself how marvelous it must be to caress a woman, the roundness of the ass, the softness of the belly, that particularly soft skin between the legs, and she had tried caressing herself in her bed in the dark, just to imagine how it must feel to touch a woman. She had often caressed her own breasts, imagining that they were those of another woman.

Closing her eyes now, she recalled Mabel's body in a bathing suit, Mabel with her very round breasts almost bursting from the bathing suit, her thick, soft laughing mouth. How wonderful it would be! But still, between her own legs, there was no warmth of such nature to cause her to lose control and stretch her hand toward Mabel. The pills had not taken effect yet. She was cool, even constrained, between her legs; there was a tightness there, a tension. She could not relax. If she touched Mabel now, she would not have followed with a bolder gesture. Was Mabel wearing a skirt that fastened on the side, would Mabel like to be caressed? Lilith was growing restless. Every time she forgot herself, her legs stretched open again, in that pose that seemed to her so obscene, so inviting, like those gestures she had seen in the Balinese dancers, stretching out and away from the sex, leaving it unprotected.

The movie came to an end. Lilith drove her car silently along the dark roads. Her headlights fell on a car parked on the side of the road and suddenly illumined a couple not caressing in the usual sentimental way. The woman was sitting on the man's knees with her back to him, he was raising himself tautly toward her, his whole body in a pose of a man reaching a sexual climax. He was in such a state that he could not stop when the lights fell on him. He stretched himself taut so as to feel the woman sitting over him, and she moved like a person half-faint from pleasure.

Lilith gasped at the sight, and Mabel said, 'We certainly caught them at the best moment.' And laughed. So Mabel knew this climax which Lilith had not known and wanted to know. Lilith wanted to ask her, 'What is it like?' But soon she would know. She would be impelled to let loose all those desires usually experienced only in fantasies, in long daydreams that filled her hours when she was alone in the house. She would sit painting and think: Now a man with whom I am very much in love enters. He enters the room and says, 'Let me undress you.' My husband never undressed me – he gets undressed by himself and then gets into bed and if he wants me he puts out the light. But this man

LILITH

will come and undress me slowly, piece by piece. This will give
me so much time to feel him, his hands about me. He will loosen
the belt first of all and touch my waist with his two hands and
say, 'What a beautiful waist you have, how it curves in, how
slender it is.' And then he will unbutton my blouse very slowly,
and I will feel his hands unbuttoning each button and touching
my breasts little by little, until they come out of the blouse, and
then he will love them and suckle at the nipples like a child,
hurting me a little with his teeth, and I will feel all this creeping
over my whole body, untying each little tight nerve and dissolving
me. He will get impatient with the skirt, tear at it a little. He will
be in such a state of desire. He will not put out the light. He will
keep looking at me with his desire, admiring me, worshiping me,
warming my body with his hands, waiting until I am completely
aroused, every little part of my skin.

Was the Spanish fly affecting her? No, she was languid, with
her fantasy beginning again, over and over again – but that was
all. Yet, the sight of the couple in the automobile, their state of
ecstasy, was something she wanted to know.

When she reached home her husband was reading. He looked
up and smiled at her mischievously. She did not want to confess
that she was not affected. She was immensely disappointed in
herself. What a cold woman she was, whom nothing could affect
– not even this which had once made a nobleman in the eighteenth
century make love for three nights and three days without stopping. What a monster she was. Even her husband must not know.
He would laugh at her. In the end he would look for a more
sensitive woman.

So she began to undress in front of him, walking back and forth
half-naked, brushing her hair in front of the mirror. Usually she
never did this. She did not want him to desire her. She did not
enjoy it. It was something to be done quickly, for his sake. For her
it was a sacrifice. His excitement and his enjoyment that she did
not share were rather repulsive to her. She felt like a whore who
was receiving money for this. She was a whore who had no
feelings, and in exchange for his love and devotion she would
fling this empty, unfeeling body at him. She felt ashamed to be so
dead in her body.

But when she had finally slipped into bed, he said, 'I don't think the Spanish fly has affected you enough. I feel sleepy. You wake me up if . . .'

Lilith tried to sleep, but all of the time she was waiting to go wild with desire. After an hour she got up and went to the bathroom. She took the little tube along and took about ten pills, thinking, 'This will do it now.' And she waited. During the night her husband came into her bed. But she was so tight between her legs that no moisture would come, and she had to wet his penis with saliva.

The next morning she awakened weeping. Her husband questioned her. She told him the truth. Then he laughed. 'But Lilith, it was a prank I played on you. That was not Spanish fly at all. I just played a prank on you.'

But from that moment Lilith was haunted by the idea that there might be ways of arousing herself artificially. She tried all the formulas she had heard about. She tried drinking big cups of chocolate with a great deal of vanilla in it. She tried eating onions. Alcohol did not affect her as it affected other people, because she was on her guard against it from the first. She could not forget herself.

She had heard about small balls that were used as an aphrodisiac in the East Indies. But how to obtain them? Where to ask for them? East Indian women inserted them inside the vagina. They were made of some very soft rubber with a soft, skinlike surface. When they were introduced into the sex they molded themselves to the form of it and then they moved as the woman moved, sensitively shaping themselves to every motion of the muscles, causing a titillation much more exciting than that of the penis or finger. Lilith would have liked to find one, and to keep it inside of herself day and night.

Marianne

I shall call myself the madam of a house of literary prostitution, the madam for a group of hungry writers who were turning out erotica for sale to a 'collector'. I was the first to write, and every day I gave my work to a young woman to type up neatly.

This young woman, Marianne, was a painter, and in the evenings she typed to earn a living. She had a golden halo of hair, blue eyes, a round face, and firm and full breasts, but she tended to conceal the richness of her body rather than set it off, to disguise it under formless Bohemian clothes, loose jackets, school-girl skirts, raincoats. She came from a small town. She had read Proust, Krafft-Ebing, Marx, Freud.

And, of course, she had had many sexual adventures, but there is a kind of adventure in which the body does not really partici-pate. She was deceiving herself. She thought that, having lain down with men, caressed them, and made all the prescribed gestures, she had experienced sexual life.

But it was all external. Actually her body had been numb, unformed, not yet matured. Nothing had touched her very deeply. She was still a virgin. I could feel this when she entered the room. No more than a soldier wants to admit being frightened, did Marianne want to admit that she was cold, frigid. But she was being psychoanalyzed.

I could not help wondering, as I gave her my erotica to type, how it would affect her. Together with an intellectual fearlessness, curiosity, there was in her a physical prudishness which she fought hard not to betray, and it had been revealed to me accidentally by the discovery that she had never taken a sun bath naked, that the very idea of it intimidated her.

What she remembered most hauntingly was an evening with a man she had not at first responded to, and then, just as he was leaving her studio, he had pressed her hard against a wall, lifted one of her legs, and pushed into her. The strange part is that at the time she had not felt anything, but afterwards, every time she remembered this picture, she grew hot and restless. Her legs would relax, she would have given anything to feel again that big body pressing against her, pinning her to the wall, leaving her no escape, then taking her.

One day she was late in bringing me the work. I went to her studio and knocked on the door. No one answered. I pushed the door open. Marianne must have gone out on an errand.

I went to the typewriter to see how the work was going and saw a text I did not recognize. I thought perhaps I was beginning to forget what I wrote. But it could not be. That was not my writing. I began to read. And then I understood.

In the middle of her work, Marianne had been taken with the desire to write down her own experiences. This is what she wrote:

'There are things one reads that make you aware that you have lived nothing, felt nothing, experienced nothing up to that time. I see now that most of what happened to me was clinical, anatomical. Here were the sexes touching, mingling, but without any sparks, wildness, sensation. How can I attain this? How can I begin to *feel* – to *feel*? I want to fall in love in such a way that the mere sight of a man, even a block away from me, will shake and pierce me, will weaken me, and make me tremble and soften and melt between the legs. That is how I want to fall in love, so hard that the mere thought of him will bring on an orgasm.

'This morning while I was painting there was a very gentle knock on the door. I went to open it and there stood a rather handsome young man, but shy, embarrassed, to whom I took an instant liking.

'He slid into the studio, did not look around, kept his eyes fastened on me as if begging, and said, "A friend sent me. You are a painter; I want some work done. I wonder if you would . . . will you?"

'His speech was tangled. He blushed. He was like a woman, I thought.

'I said, "Come in and sit down," thinking that would put him at ease. Then he noticed my paintings. They were abstract. He said, "But you can draw a lifelike figure, can't you?"

' "Of course I can." I showed him my drawings.

' "They are very strong," he said, falling into a trance of admiration for one of my drawings of a muscular athlete.

' "Did you want a portrait of yourself?"

' "Why, yes – yes and no. I want a portrait. At the same time, it is a sort of unusual portrait I want, I don't know if you will . . . consent."

' "Consent to what?" I asked.

' "Well," he blurted out finally, "would you make me this kind of a portrait?" And he held up the naked athlete.

'He expected some reaction from me. I was so accustomed to men's nudity at the art school that I smiled at his shyness. I did not think there was anything odd about his demand, although it was slightly different having a naked model who paid the artist for drawing him. That was all I could see, and I told him so. Meanwhile, with the right to observe that is given to painters, I studied his violet eyes, the fine, gold, downy hair on his hands, the fine hair on the tip of his ears. He had a faunish air and a feminine evasiveness which attracted me.

'Despite his timidity, he looked healthy and rather aristocratic. His hands were soft and supple. He held himself well. I showed a certain professional enthusiasm which seemed to delight and encourage him.

'He said, "Do you want to start right away? I have some money with me. I can bring the rest tomorrow."

'I pointed to a corner of the room where there was a screen hiding my clothes and the washstand. But he turned his violet eyes towards me and said innocently, "Can I undress here?"

'Then I grew slightly uneasy, but I said yes. I busied myself getting drawing paper and charcoal together, moving a chair, and sharpening my charcoal. It seemed to me that he was abnormally slow in undressing, that he was waiting for my attention. I looked at him boldly, as if I were beginning my study of him, charcoal stick in hand.

'He was undressing with amazing deliberateness as if it were a choice occupation, a ritual. Once he looked at me fully in the eyes and smiled, showing his fine even teeth, and his skin was so delicate it caught the light that poured in through the big window and held it like a satin fabric.

'At this moment the charcoal in my hands felt alive, and I thought what a pleasure it would be to draw the lines of this young man, almost like caressing him. He had taken off his coat, his shirt, shoes, socks. There were only the trousers left. He held these as a stripteaser holds the folds of her dress, still looking at me. I still could not understand the gleam of pleasure that animated his face.

'Then he leaned over, unfastened his belt, and the trousers slid down. He stood completely naked before me and in a most obvious state of sexual excitement. When I saw this, there was a moment of suspense. If I protested, I would lose my fee, which I needed so badly.

'I tried to read his eyes. They seemed to say, "Do not be angry. Forgive me."

'So I tried to draw. It was a strange experience. If I drew his head, neck, arms, all was well. As soon as my eyes roved over the rest of his body I could see the effect of it on him. His sex had an almost imperceptible quiver. I was half tempted to sketch the protrusion as calmly as I had sketched his knee. But the defensive virgin in me was troubled. I thought, I must draw attentively and slowly to see if the crisis passes, or he may vent his excitement on me. But no, the young man made no move. He was transfixed and contented. I was the only one disturbed, and I did not know why.

'When I finished, he calmly dressed again, and seemed absolutely self-possessed. He walked up to me, shook my hand politely and said, "May I come tomorow at the same time?"'

Here the manuscript ended, and Marianne entered the studio, smiling.

'Wasn't it a strange adventure?' she asked me.

'Yes, and I would like to know how you felt after he left.'

'Afterwards,' she confessed, 'it was I who was excited all day, remembering his body, and his very beautiful rigid sex. I looked at my drawings, and to one of them I added the complete image of the incident. I was actually tormented with desire. But a man like that, he is only interested in my *looking* at him.'

This might have remained a simple adventure, but to Marianne it became more important. I could see her growing obsessed with the young man. Evidently the second session had duplicated the first. Nothing was said. Marianne revealed no emotion. He did not acknowledge the condition of pleasure he was plunged in by her scrutiny of his body. Each day after that she discovered greater marvels. Every detail of his body was perfect. If only he would evince some small interest in the details of hers, but he didn't. And Marianne was growing thin and perishing with unsatisfied desire.

She was also affected by the continuous copying of other people's adventures, for now everyone in our group who wrote gave his manuscript to her because she could be trusted. Every night little Marianne with the rich, ripe breasts bent over her typewriter and typed fervid words about violent physical happenings. Certain facts affected her more than others.

She liked violence. That is why this situation with the young man was for her the most impossible of all situations. She could not believe that he would stand in a condition of physical excitement and so clearly enjoy the mere fact of her eyes fixed on him, as if she were caressing him.

The more passive and undemonstrative he was, the more she wanted to do violence to him. She dreamed of forcing his will, but how could one force a man's will? Since she could not tempt him by her presence, how could she make him desire her?

She wished that he would fall asleep and she could have a chance to caress him, and that he would take her while he was half-conscious, half-asleep. Or she wished that he would enter the studio while she was dressing and that the sight of her body would arouse him.

Once when she expected him, she tried leaving the door ajar while she was dressing, but he looked away and took up a book.

He was impossible to arouse except by gazing on him. And Marianne was by now in a frenzy of desire for him. The drawing was coming to an end. She knew every part of his body, the color of his skin, so golden and light, every shape of his muscles and, above all, the constantly erect sex, smooth, polished, firm, tempting.

She would approach him to arrange a piece of white cardboard near him that would cast a whiter reflection or more shadows on his body. Then finally she lost control of herself and fell on her knees before the erect sex. She did not touch it, but merely looked and murmured, 'How beautiful it is!'

At this he was visibly affected. His whole sex became more rigid with pleasure. She kneeled very near it – it was almost within reach of her mouth – but again only said, 'How beautiful it is!'

Since he did not move, she came closer, her lips parted slightly, and delicately, very delicately, she touched the tip of his sex with her tongue. He did not move away. He was still watching her face and the way her tongue flicked out caressingly to touch the tip of his sex.

She licked it gently, with the delicacy of a cat, then she inserted a small portion of it in her mouth and closed her lips around it. It was quivering.

She restrained herself from doing more, for fear of encountering resistance. And when she stopped, he did not encourage her to continue. He seemed content. Marianne felt that that was all she should ask of him. She sprang to her feet and returned to her work. Inwardly she was in a turmoil. Violent images passed before her eyes. She was remembering penny movies she had seen once in Paris, of figures rolling on the grass, hands fumbling, white pants being opened by eager hands, caresses, caresses, and pleasure making the bodies curl and undulate, pleasure running over their skins like water, causing them to undulate as the wave of pleasure caught their bellies or hips, or as it ran up their spines or down their legs.

But she controlled herself with the intuitive knowledge a woman has about the tastes of the man she desires. He remained entranced, his sex erect, his body at times shivering slightly, as if pleasure coursed through it at the memory of her mouth parting to touch the smooth penis.

The day after this episode Marianne repeated her worshipful pose, her ecstasy at the beauty of his sex. Again she kneeled and prayed to this strange phallus which demanded only admiration. Again she licked it so neatly and vibrantly, sending shivers of pleasure up from the sex into his body, again she kissed it, enclosing it in her lips like some marvelous fruit, and again he trembled. Then, to her amazement, a tiny drop of a milky-white, salty substance dissolved in her mouth, the precursor of desire, and she increased her pressure and the movements of her tongue.

When she saw that he was dissolved with pleasure, she stopped, divining that perhaps if she deprived him now he might make a gesture towards fulfillment. At first he made no motion. His sex was quivering, and he was tormented with desire, then suddenly she was amazed to see his hand moving towards his sex as if he were going to satisfy himself.

Marianne grew desperate. She pushed his hand away, took his sex into her mouth again, and with her two hands she encircled his sexual parts, caressed him and absorbed him until he came.

He leaned over with gratitude, tenderness, and murmured, 'You are the first woman, the first woman, the first woman . . .'

Fred moved into the studio. But, as Marianne explained, he did not progress from the acceptance of her caresses. They lay in bed, naked, and Fred acted as if she had no sex at all. He received her tributes, frenziedly, but Marianne was left with her desire unanswered. All he would do was to place his hands between her legs. While she caressed him with her mouth his hands opened her sex like some flower and he sought for the pistil. When he felt its contractions, he willingly caressed the palpitating opening. Marianne was able to respond, but somehow this did not satisfy her hunger for his body, for his sex, and she yearned to be possessed by him more completely, to be penetrated.

It occurred to her to show him the manuscripts that she was typing. She thought this might incite him. They lay on the bed and read them together. He read the words aloud, with pleasure. He lingered over the descriptions. He read and reread, and again he took his clothes off and showed himself, but no matter what height his excitement reached he would do no more than this.

Marianne wanted him to be psychoanalyzed. She told him how much her own analysis had liberated her. He listened with interest but resisted the idea. She urged him to write, too, to write out his experiences.

At first he was shy about this, ashamed. Then, almost surreptitiously, he began to write, hiding the pages from her when she came into the room, using a worn pencil, writing as though it were a criminal confession. It was by accident that she read what he had written. He was urgently in need of money. He had pawned his typewriter, his winter coat and his watch, and there was nothing more to be pawned.

He could not let Marianne take care of him. As it was, she tired her eyes out typing, worked late at night and never made more than was necessary for the rent and a very small supply of food. So he went to the collector to whom Marianne delivered manuscripts, and offered his own manuscript for sale, apologizing for its being written by hand. The collector, finding it difficult to read, innocently gave it to Marianne to be typed.

So Marianne found herself with her lover's manuscript in her hands. She read avidly before typing, unable to control her curiosity, in search of the secret of his passivity. This is what she read:

'Most of the time the sexual life is a secret. Everybody conspires to make it so. Even the best of friends do not tell each other the details of their sexual lives. Here with Marianne I live in a strange atmosphere. What we talk about, read about and write about is the sexual life.

'I remember an incident I had completely forgotten about. It happened when I was about fifteen and still sexually innocent. My family had taken an apartment in Paris which had many balconies, and doors giving on these balconies. In the summer I used to walk about my room naked. Once I was doing this when the doors were open, and then I noticed that a woman was watching me across the way.

'She was sitting on her balcony watching me, completely unashamed, and something drove me to pretend that I was not noticing her at all. I feared that if she knew I was aware of her she might leave.

'And being watched by her gave me the most extraordinary pleasure. I would walk about or be on my bed. She never moved. We repeated this scene every day for a week, but on the third day I had an erection.

'Could she detect this from across the street, could she see? I began to touch myself, feeling all the time how attentive she was to my every gesture. I was bathed in delicious excitement. From where I lay I could see her very luxuriant form. Looking straight at her now, I played with my sex, and finally got myself so excited that I came.

'The woman never ceased looking at me. Would she make a sign? Did it excite her to watch me? It must have. The next day I awaited her appearance with anxiety. She emerged at the same hour, sat on her balcony and looked toward me. From this distance I could not tell if she was smiling or not. I lay on my bed again.

'We did not try to meet in the street, though we were neighbors. All I remember was the pleasure I derived from this, which no other pleasure ever equaled. At the mere recollection of these episodes, I get excited. Marianne gives me somewhat the same pleasure. I like the hungry way she looks at me, admiring, worshiping me.'

When Marianne read this, she felt she would never overcome his passivity. She wept a little, feeling betrayed as a woman. Yet she loved him. He was sensitive, gentle, tender. He never hurt her feelings. He was not exactly protective, but he was fraternal, responsive to her moods. He treated her like the artist of the family, was respectful of her painting, carried her canvases, wanted to be useful to her.

She was a monitor in a painting class. He loved to accompany her there in the morning with the pretext of carrying her paints. But soon she saw that he had another purpose. He was passionately interested in the models. Not in them personally, but in their experience of posing. He wanted to be a model.

At this Marianne rebelled. If he had not derived a sexual pleasure from being looked at, she might not have minded. But knowing this, it was as if he were giving himself to the whole class. She could not bear the thought. She fought him.

But he was possessed by the idea and finally was accepted as a model. That day Marianne refused to go to the class. She stayed at home and wept like a jealous woman who knows her lover is with another woman.

She raged. She tore up her drawings of him as if to tear his image from her eyes, the image of his golden, smooth, perfect body. Even if the students were indifferent to the models, he was reacting to their eyes, and Marianne could not bear it.

This incident began to separate them. It seemed as if the more pleasure she gave him, the more he succumbed to his vice, and sought it unceasingly.

Soon they were completely estranged. And Marianne was left alone again to type our erotica.

The Veiled Woman

George once went to a Swedish bar he liked, and sat at a table to enjoy a leisurely evening. At the next table he noticed a very stylish and handsome couple, the man suave and neatly dressed, the woman all in black, with a veil over her glowing face and brilliant colored jewelry. They both smiled at him. They said nothing to one another, as if they were very old acquaintances and had no need to talk.

The three of them watched the activity at the bar – couples drinking together, a woman drinking alone, a man in search of adventures – and all seemed to be thinking the same things.

Finally the neatly dressed man began a conversation with George, who now had a chance to observe the woman at length and found her even more beautiful. But just when he expected her to join in the conversation, she said a few words to her companion that George could not catch, smiled, and glided off. George was crestfallen. His pleasure in the evening was gone. Furthermore, he had only a few dollars to spend, and he could not invite the man to drink with him and discover perhaps a little more about the woman. To his surprise, it was the man who turned to him and said, 'Would you care to have a drink with me?'

George accepted. Their conversation went from experiences with hotels in the South of France to George's admission that he was badly in need of money. The man's response implied that it was extremely easy to obtain money. He did not go on to say how. He made George confess a little more.

Now George had a weakness in common with many men; when he was in an expansive mood, he loved to recount his exploits. He did this in intriguing language. He hinted that as soon as he set foot in the street some adventure presented itself, that he was never at a loss for an interesting evening, or for an interesting woman.

His companion smiled and listened.

When George had finished talking, the man said, 'That is what I expected of you the moment I saw you. You are the fellow I am looking for. I am confronted with an immensely delicate problem. Something absolutely unique. I don't know if you have had many dealings with difficult, neurotic women – No? I can see that from your stories. Well, I have. Perhaps I attract them. Just now I am in the most intricate situation. I hardly know how to get out of it. I need your help. You say you need money. Well, I can suggest a rather pleasant way of making some. Listen carefully. There is a woman who is wealthy and absolutely beautiful – in fact, flawless. She could be devotedly loved by anyone she pleased, she could be married to anyone she pleased. But for one perverse accident of her nature – she only likes the unknown.'

'But everybody likes the unknown,' said George, thinking immediately of voyages, unexpected encounters, novel situations.

'No, not in the way she does. She is interested only in a man she has never before and never will see again. And for this man she will do anything.'

George was burning to ask if the woman was the one who had been sitting at the table with them. But he did not dare. The man seemed to be rather unhappy to have to tell, and yet was impelled to tell, this story. He continued, 'I have this woman's happiness to watch over. I would do anything for her. I have devoted my life to satisfying her caprices.'

'I understand,' said George. 'I could feel the same way about her.'

'Now,' said the elegant stranger, 'if you would like to come with me, you could perhaps solve your financial difficulties for a week, and incidentally, perhaps, your desire for adventure.'

George flushed with pleasure. They left the bar together. The man hailed a taxi. In the taxi he gave George fifty dollars. Then he said he was obliged to blindfold him, that George must not see the house he was going to, nor the street, as he was never to repeat this experience.

George was in a turmoil of curiosity now, with visions of the woman he had seen at the bar haunting him, seeing each moment her glowing mouth and burning eyes behind the veil. What he had particularly liked was her hair. He liked thick hair that weighed a face down, a gracious burden, odorous and rich. It was one of his passions.

The ride was not very long. He submitted amiably to all the mystery. The blindfold was taken off his eyes before he came out of the taxi so as not to attract the attention of the taxi driver or doorman, but the stranger had counted wisely on the glare of the entrance lights to blind George completely. He could see nothing but brilliant lights and mirrors.

He was ushered into one of the most sumptuous interiors he had ever seen – all white and mirrored, with exotic plants, exquisite furniture covered in damask and such a soft rug that their footsteps were not heard. He was led through one room after another, each in different shades, all mirrored, so that he lost all sense of perspective. Finally, they came to the last. He gasped slightly.

He was in a bedroom with a canopied bed set on a dais. There were furs on the floor and vaporous white curtains at the windows, and mirrors, more mirrors. He was glad that he could bear these repetitions of himself, infinite reproductions of a handsome man, to whom the mystery of the situation had given a glow of expectation and alertness he had never known. What could this mean? He did not have time to ask himself.

The woman who had been at the bar entered the room, and just as she entered, the man who had brought him to the place vanished.

She had changed her dress. She wore a striking satin gown that left her shoulders bare and was held in place by a ruffle. George had the feeling that the dress would fall from her at one gesture, strip from her like a glistening sheath, and that underneath would appear her glistening skin, which shone like satin and was equally smooth to the fingers.

He had to hold himself in check. He could not yet believe that this beautiful woman was offering herself to him, a complete stranger.

He felt shy, too. What did she expect of him? What was her quest? Did she have an unfulfilled desire?

He had only one night to give all his lover's gifts. He was never to see her again. Could it be he might find the secret to her nature and possess her more than once. He wondered how many men had come to this room.

She was extraordinarily lovely, with something of both satin and velvet in her. Her eyes were dark and moist, her mouth glowed, her skin reflected the light. Her body was perfectly balanced. She had the incisive lines of a slender woman together with a provocative ripeness.

Her waist was very slim, which gave her breasts an even greater prominence. Her back was like a dancer's, and every undulation set off the richness of her hips. She smiled at him. Her mouth was soft and full and half-open. George approached her and laid his mouth on her bare shoulders. Nothing could be softer than her skin. What a temptation to push the fragile dress from her shoulders and expose the breasts which distended the satin. What a temptation to undress her immediately.

But George felt that this woman could not be treated so summarily, that she required subtlety and adroitness. Never had he given to his every gesture so much thought and artistry. He seemed determined to make a long siege of it, and as she gave no sign of hurry, he lingered over her bare shoulders, inhaling the faint and marvelous odor that came from her body.

He could have taken her then and there, so potent was the charm she cast, but first he wanted her to make a sign, he wanted her to be stirred, not soft and pliant like wax under his fingers.

She seemed amazingly cool, obedient but without feeling. Never a ripple on her skin, and though her mouth was parted for kissing, it was not responsive.

They stood there near the bed, without speaking. He passed his hands along the satin curves of her body, as if to become familiar with it. She was unmoved. He slipped slowly to his knees as he kissed and caressed her body. His fingers felt that under the dress she was naked. He led her to the edge of the bed and she sat down. He took off her slippers. He held her feet in his hands.

She smiled at him, gently and invitingly. He kissed her feet, and his hands ran under the folds of the long dress, feeling the smooth legs up to the thighs.

She abandoned her feet to his hands, held them pressed against his chest now, while his hands ran up and down her legs under the dress. If her skin was so soft along the legs, what would it be then near her sex, there where it was always the softest? Her thighs were pressed together so he could not continue to explore. He stood and leaned over her to kiss her into a reclining position. As she lay back, her legs opened slightly.

He moved his hands all over her body, as if to kindle each little part of it with his touch, stroking her again from shoulders to feet, before he tried to slide his hand between her legs, more open now, so that he could almost reach her sex.

With his kisses her hair had become disheveled, and the dress had fallen off her shoulders and partly uncovered her breasts. He pushed it off altogether with his mouth, revealing the breasts he had expected, tempting, taut, and of the finest skin, with roseate tips like those of a young girl.

Her yielding almost made him want to hurt her, so as to rouse her in some way. The caresses roused him but not her. Her sex was cool and soft to his finger, obedient, but without vibrations.

George began to think that the mystery of the woman lay in her not being able to be aroused. But it was not possible. Her body promised such sensuality. The skin was so sensitive, the mouth so full. It was impossible that she should not feel. Now he caressed her continuously, dreamfully, as if he were in no hurry, waiting for the flame to be kindled in her.

There were mirrors all around them, repeating the image of the woman lying there, her dress fallen off her breasts, her beautiful naked feet hanging over the bed, her legs slightly parted under the dress.

He must tear the dress off completely, lie in bed with her, feel her whole body against his. He began to pull the dress down, and she helped him. Her body emerged like that of Venus coming out of the sea. He lifted her so that she would lie fully on the bed, and his mouth never ceased kissing every part of her body.

Then a strange thing happened. When he leaned over to feast his eyes on the beauty of her sex, its rosiness, she quivered, and George almost cried out for joy.

She murmured, 'Take your clothes off.'

He undressed. Naked, he knew his power. He was more at ease naked than clothed because he had been an athlete, a swimmer, a walker, a mountain climber. And he knew then that he could please her.

She looked at him.

Was she pleased? When he bent over her, was she more responsive? He could not tell. By now he desired her so much that he could not wait to touch her with the tip of his sex, but she stopped him. She wanted to kiss and fondle it. She set about this with so much eagerness that he found himself with her full backside near his face and able to kiss and fondle her to his content.

By now he was taken with the desire to explore and touch every nook of her body. He parted the opening of her sex with his two fingers, he feasted his eyes on the glowing skin, the delicate flow of honey, the hair curling around his fingers. His mouth grew more and more avid, as if it had become a sex organ in itself, capable of so enjoying her that if he continued to fondle her flesh with his tongue he would reach some absolutely unknown pleasure. As he bit into her flesh with such a delicious sensation, he felt again in her a quiver of pleasure. Now he forced her away from his sex, for fear she might experience all her pleasure merely kissing him and that he would be cheated of feeling himself inside of her womb. It was as if they both had become ravenously hungry for the taste of flesh. And now their two mouths melted into each other, seeking the leaping tongues.

Her blood was fired now. By his slowness he seemed to have done this, at last. Her eyes shone brilliantly, her mouth could not leave his body. And finally he took her, as she offered herself, opening her vulva with her lovely fingers, as if she could no longer wait. Even then they suspended their pleasure, and she felt him quietly, enclosed.

Then she pointed to the mirror and said, laughing, 'Look, it appears as if we were not making love, as if I were merely sitting on your knees, and you, you rascal, you have had it inside me all the time, and you're even quivering. Ah, I can't bear it any longer, this pretending I have nothing inside. It's burning me up. Move now, move!'

She threw herself over him so that she could gyrate around his erect penis, deriving from this erotic dance a pleasure which made her cry out. And at the same time a lightning flash of ecstasy tore through George's body.

*

Despite the intensity of their lovemaking, when he left, she did not ask him his name, she did not ask him to return. She gave him a light kiss on his almost painful lips and sent him away. For months the memory of this night haunted him and he could not repeat the experience with any woman.

One day he encountered a friend who had just been paid lavishly for some articles and invited him to have a drink. He told George the spectacular story of a scene he had witnessed. He was spending money freely in a bar when a very distinguished man approached him and suggested a pleasant pastime, observing a magnificent love scene, and as George's friend happened to be a confirmed voyeur, the suggestion met with instant acceptance. He had been taken to a mysterious house, into a sumptuous apartment, and concealed in a dark room, where he had seen a nymphomaniac making love with an especially gifted and potent man.

George's heart stood still. 'Describe her,' he said.

His friend described the woman George had made love to, even to the satin dress. He also described the canopied bed, the mirrors, everything. George's friend had paid one hundred dollars for the spectacle, but it had been worthwhile and had lasted for hours.

Poor George. For months he was wary of women. He could not believe such perfidy, and such play-acting. He became obsessed with the idea that the women who invited him to their apartments were all hiding some spectator behind a curtain.

Elena

While waiting for the train to Montreux, Elena looked at the people around her on the quays. Every trip aroused in her the same curiosity and hope one feels before the curtain is raised at the theater, the same stirring anxiety and expectation.

She singled out various men she might have liked to talk with, wondering if they were leaving on her train or merely saying good-bye to other passengers. Her cravings were vague, poetic. If she had been brutally asked what she was expecting she might have answered, '*Le merveilleux*'. It was hunger that did not come from any precise region of her body. It was true, what someone had said about her after she had criticized a writer she had met: 'You cannot see him as he really is, you cannot see anyone as he really is. He will always be disappointing because you are expecting *someone*.'

She was expecting someone – every time a door opened, every time she went to a party, to any gathering of people, every time she entered a café, a theater.

None of the men she had singled out as desirable companions for the trip boarded the train. So she opened the book she was carrying. It was *Lady Chatterley's Lover*.

Afterwards Elena remembered nothing of this trip except a sensation of tremendous bodily warmth, as if she had drunk a whole bottle of the very choicest Burgundy, and a feeling of great anger at the discovery of a secret which it seemed to her was criminally withheld from all people. She discovered first of all that she had never known the sensations described by Lawrence, and second, that this was the nature of her hunger. But there was another truth she was now fully aware of. Something had created in her a state of perpetual defense against the very possibilities of experience, an urge for flight which took her away from the scenes of pleasure and expansion. She had stood many times on the very edge, and then had run away. She herself was to blame for what she had lost, ignored.

It was the submerged woman of Lawrence's book that lay coiled within her, at last exposed, sensitized, prepared as if by a multitude of caresses for the arrival of *someone*.

A new woman emerged from the train at Caux. This was not the place she would have liked to begin her journey. Caux was a mountain top, isolated, looking down upon Lake Geneva. It was spring, the snow was melting, and as the little train panted up the mountain, Elena felt irritation about its slowness, the slow gestures of the Swiss, the slow movement of the animals, the static, heavy landscape, while her moods and her feelings were rushing like newborn torrents. She did not plan to stay very long. She would rest until her new book was ready to be published.

From the station she walked to a chalet that looked like a fairy-tale house, and the woman who opened the door looked like a witch. She stared with coal-black eyes at Elena, and then asked her to come in. It seemed to Elena that the whole house was built for her, with doors and furniture smaller than usual. It was no illusion, for the woman turned to her and said, 'I cut down the legs of my table and chairs. Do you like my house? I call it Casutza – "little house," in Roumanian.'

Elena stumbled on a mass of snow shoes, jackets, fur hats, capes and sticks near the entrance. These things had overflowed from the closet and were left there on the floor. The dishes from breakfast were still on the table.

The witch's shoes sounded like wooden shoes as she walked up the stairs. She had the voice of a man, and a small black rim of hair around her lips, like an adolescent's mustache. Her voice was intense, heavy.

She showed Elena to her room. It opened on a terrace, divided by bamboo partitions, which extended the length of the sunny side of the house, facing the lake. Elena was soon lying exposed to the sun, although she dreaded sun baths. They made her passionate and burningly aware of her whole body. She sometimes caressed herself. Now she closed her eyes and recalled scenes from *Lady Chatterley's Lover*.

During the following days she took long walks. She would always be late for lunch. Then Madame Kazimir would stare at her angrily and not talk as she served her. People came every day to see Madame Kazimir about mortgage payments on the house. They threatened to sell it. It was clear that if she were deprived of her house, her protective shell, her turtle back, she would die. At the same time, she turned out guests she did not like and refused to take in men.

Finally she surrendered at the sight of a family – husband, wife, and a little girl – who arrived one morning straight from the train, captivated by the fantastic appearance of Casutza. Before long they were sitting on the porch next to Elena's and eating their breakfast in the sun.

One day Elena met the man, walking alone up toward the peak of the mountain behind the chalet. He walked fast, smiled at her as he passed, and continued as though pursued by enemies. He had taken his shirt off to receive the rays of the sun fully. She saw a magnificent athlete's torso already golden. His head was youthful, alert, but covered with graying hair. The eyes were not quite human. They had the fixed, hypnotic gaze of an animal tamer, something authoritative, violent. Elena had seen such an expression in the pimps who stood at the corners of the Montmartre district, with their caps and scarves of bright colors.

Apart from his eyes, this man was aristocratic. His movements were youthful and innocent. He swayed as he walked, as though he were a little drunk. All his strength centered in the glance he gave Elena, and then he smiled innocently, easily, and walked on. Elena was stopped by the glance and almost angered by the boldness of it. But his youthful smile dissolved the mordant effect of the eyes and left her with feelings she could not clarify. She turned back.

When she reached Casutza, she was uneasy. She wanted to leave. The desire for flight was already asserting itself. By this she recognized that she was facing a danger. She thought of returning to Paris. In the end, she stayed.

One day the piano, which had been growing rusty downstairs, began to pour out music. The slightly false notes sounded like the pianos of dingy little bars. Elena smiled. The stranger was amusing himself. He was, in fact, playing up to the nature of the piano, and giving it a sound quite alien to its bourgeois staleness, nothing like what had been played on it before by little Swiss girls with long braids.

The house was suddenly gay, and Elena wanted to dance. The piano stopped, but not before winding her up like some mechanical puppet. Alone on the porch, she turned on her feet like a top. Quite unexpectedly a man's voice very near her said, 'There are live people in this house after all!' and laughed.

He was calmly looking through the bamboo slits, and she could see his figure clinging there like that of an imprisoned animal.

'Won't you come for a walk?' he asked her. 'I think this place is a tomb. It is the House of the Dead. Madame Kazimir is the Great Petrifier. She will make stalactites out of us. We shall be allowed one tear an hour, hanging from some cave ceiling, stalactite tears.'

So Elena and the neighbor started out. The first thing he said was, 'You have a habit of turning back, starting a walk and turning back. That is very bad. It is the very first of crimes against life. I believe in audacity.'

'People express audacity in various ways,' said Elena. 'I usually turn back, as you say, and then I go home and write a book which becomes an obsession of the censors.'

'That's a misuse of natural forces,' said the man.

'But then,' said Elena, 'I use my book like dynamite, I place it where I want the explosion to take place, and then I blast my way through with it!'

As she said these words an explosion took place somewhere in the mountain where a road was being made, and they laughed at the coincidence.

'So you are a writer,' he said. 'I am a man of all trades, a painter, a writer, a musician, a vagabond. The wife and child were temporarily rented – for the sake of appearance. I was forced to use the passport of a friend. This friend was forced to lend me the wife and child. Without them I would not be here. I have a gift for irritating the French police. I have not murdered my concierge, though I should have. She has provoked me often enough. I have merely, like some other verbal revolutionaries, exalted the revolution too loudly on too many evenings at the same café, and a plainclothes man was one of my most fervent followers – follower, indeed! My best speeches are always made when I am drunk.

'You were never there,' continued the man, 'you never go to

cafés. The most haunting woman is the one we cannot find in the crowded café when we are looking for her, the one that we must hunt for, and seek out through the disguises of her stories.'

His eyes, smiling, remained on her all the time that he talked. They were fixed on her with the exact knowledge of her evasions and elusiveness, and acted like a catalyst on her, rooting her to the spot where she stood, with the wind lifting her skirt like a ballerina's, inflating her hair as if she would blow away in full sail. He was aware of her capacities for becoming invisible. But his strength was greater, and he could keep her rooted there as long as he wanted. Only when he turned his head away was she free again. But she was not free to escape him.

After three hours of walking, they fell on a bed of pine needles within sight of a chalet. A pianola was playing.

He smiled at her and said, 'It would be a wonderful place to spend the day and night. Would you like it?'

He let her smoke quietly, lying back on the pine needles. She did not answer. She smiled.

Then they walked to the chalet and he asked for a meal and a room. The meal was to be brought up to the room. He gave his orders smoothly, leaving no doubt about his wishes. His decisiveness in small acts gave her the feeling that he would equally wave aside all obstacles to his greatest desires.

She was not tempted to retrace her steps, to elude him. A feeling of exaltation was rising in her, of reaching that pinnacle of emotion which would fling her out of herself for good, which would abandon her to a stranger. She did not even know his name, nor he hers. The nakedness of his eyes on her was like a penetration. On the way upstairs, she was trembling.

When they found themselves alone in the room with its immense, heavily carved bed, she first moved toward the balcony, and he followed her. She felt that the gesture he would make would be a possessive one, one that could not be eluded. She waited. What happened, she had not expected.

It was not she who hesitated, but this man whose authority had brought her here. He stood before her suddenly slack, awkward, his eyes uneasy. He said with a disarming smile, 'You must know, of course, that you are the first real woman I have ever known – a woman I could love, I have forced you here. I want to be sure that you want to be here. I . . .'

At this acknowledgment of his timidity she was immensely moved by tenderness, a tenderness she had never experienced before. His strength was bowing to her, was hesitating before the fulfillment of the dream that had grown between them. The tenderness engulfed her. It was she who moved toward him and offered her mouth.

Then he kissed her, his hands on her breasts. She felt his teeth. He kissed her neck where the veins were palpitating, and her throat, his hands around her neck as if he would separate her head from the rest of her body. She swayed with desire to be taken wholly. As he kissed her he undressed her. The clothes fell around her and they were still standing together kissing. Then without looking at her he carried her to the bed, with his mouth still on her face and throat and hair.

His caresses had a strange quality, at times soft and melting, at other times fierce, like the caresses she had expected when his eyes fixed on her, the caresses of a wild animal. There was something animal-like about his hands, which he kept spread over each part of her body, and which took her sex and hair together as if he would tear them away from the body, as if he grasped earth and grass together.

When she closed her eyes she felt he had many hands, which touched her everywhere, and many mouths, which passed so swiftly over her, and with a wolflike sharpness, his teeth sank into her fleshiest parts. Naked now, he lay his full length over her. She enjoyed his weight on her, enjoyed being crushed under his body. She wanted him soldered to her, from mouth to feet. Shivers passed through her body. He whispered now and then, telling her to raise her legs, as she had never done, until the knees touched her chin; he whispered to her to turn, and he spread her backside with his two hands. He rested inside of her, lay back and waited.

Then she withdrew, half sat up, her hair wild and her eyes drugged, and through a half-mist saw him lying on his back. She slipped down in the bed until her mouth reached his penis. She began kissing all around it. He sighed. The penis shook slightly at each kiss. He was looking at her. His hand was on her head and he pressed it downward so her mouth would fall over the penis. His hand remained on her as she moved up and down and then fell, fell with a sigh of unbearable pleasure, fell on his belly and lay there, with eyes closed, tasting her joy.

She could not look at him as he looked at her. Her eyes were blurred by the violence of her feelings. When she looked at him she was magnetically drawn again to touch his flesh, with her mouth or hands, or with her whole body. She rubbed her whole body against his, with animal luxuriance, enjoying the friction. Then she fell on her side and lay there, touching his mouth as if she were molding it over and over again, like a blind person who wants to discover the shape of the mouth, of the eyes, of the nose, to ascertain his form, the feel of his skin, the length and texture of his hair, the shape of the hair behind his ears. Her fingers were light as she did this, then suddenly they would become frenzied, press deep into the flesh and hurt him, as if violently to assure her of his reality.

These were the external feelings of the bodies discovering each other. From so much touching they grew drugged. Their gestures were slow and dreamlike. Their hands were heavy. His mouth never closed.

How the honey flowed from her. He dipped his fingers in it lingeringly, then his sex, then he moved her so that she lay on him, her legs thrown over his legs, and as he took her, he could see himself entering into her, and she could see him too. They saw their bodies undulate together, seeking their climax. He was waiting for her, watching her movements.

Because she did not quicken her movements, he changed her position, making her lie back. He crouched over so that he could take her with more force, touching the very bottom of her womb, touching the very flesh walls again and again, and then she experienced the sensation that within her womb some new cells awakened, new fingers, new mouths, that they responded to his entrance and joined in the rhythmic motion, that this suction was becoming gradually more and more pleasurable, as if the friction had aroused new layers of enjoyment. She moved quicker to bring the climax, and when he saw this, he hastened his motions inside of her and incited her to come with him, with words, with his hands caressing her, and finally with his mouth soldered to hers, so that the tongues moved in the same rhythm as the womb and penis, and the climax was spreading between her mouth and her sex, in cross-currents of increasing pleasure, until she cried out, half sob and half laughter, from the overflow of joy through her body.

When Elena returned to Casutza, Madame Kazimir refused to speak to her. She carried her stormy condemnation about silently but so intensely that it could be felt all through the house.

Elena postponed her return to Paris. Pierre could not return. They met every day, sometimes staying the whole night away from Casutza. The dream continued unbroken for ten days, until a woman came to call. It was an evening when Elena and Pierre were away. His wife received her. They locked themselves up together. Madame Kazimir tried to listen to what they said but they caught sight of her head at one of the little windows.

The woman was Russian. She was unusually beautiful, with violet eyes and dark hair, an Egyptian cast of features. She did not talk very much. She appeared greatly disturbed. When Pierre arrived in the morning he found her there. He was quite evidently surprised. Elena received a shock of inexplicable anxiety. She feared the woman immediately. She sensed danger for her love. Yet when Pierre met her hours later, he explained it all on the basis of his work. The woman had been sent with orders. He was to move on. He was given work to do in Geneva. He had been rescued from the complications in Paris with the understanding that he was to obey orders from then on. He did not say to Elena, 'Come with me to Geneva.' She waited for his words.

'How long will you be away?'

'I don't know.'

'Are you going with . . . ?' She could not even repeat her name.

'Yes, she is in charge.'

'If I am not to see you any more, Pierre, tell me at least, the truth.'

But neither his expression nor his words seemed to come from the man she knew intimately. He seemed to be saying what he had been made to say, nothing more. He had lost all his personal authority. He was talking as if someone else were listening to him.

Elena was silent. Then Pierre approached her and whispered, 'I am not in love with any woman. I never have been. I am in love with my work. With you I was in great danger. Because we could talk together, because we were so near each other in so many ways, I stayed with you too long. I forgot my work.'

Elena was to repeat these words to herself over and over again. She remembered his face as he talked, his eyes no longer fixed on her with obsessional concentration, but like those of a man obeying orders, not the laws of desire and love.

Pierre, who had done more than any human being to draw her out of the caves of her secret, folded life, now threw her down into deeper recesses of fear and doubt. The fall was greater than she had ever known, because she had ventured so far into emotion and had abandoned herself to it.

She never questioned Pierre's words or considered pursuing him. She left Casutza before he did. On the train she recalled his face as it had been, so open, commanding, yet somewhere, vulnerable and yielding too.

The most terrifying aspect of her feelings was that she was unable to shrink back as before, to shut out the world, to become deaf, colorblind, and to throw herself into some long-drawn-out fantasy, which she had done as a girl to replace reality. She was obsessed with concern for his safety, with anxiety over the dangerous life he led; she realized that he had not only penetrated her body but also her very being. Whenever she thought of his skin, his hair where the sun had bleached it a fine gold, his steady green eyes, flickering only at the moment when he bent over her to take her mouth between his strong lips, then her flesh vibrated, still responded to the image, and she was tortured.

After hours of a pain so vivid and strong that she thought it would shatter her completely, she fell into a strange state of lethargy, a half-sleep. It was as if something had broken inside of her. She ceased to feel pain or pleasure. She was numb. The entire trip became unreal. Her body was dead again.

After eight years of separation, Miguel had come to Paris. Miguel had come but was not bringing Elena any joy or relief, for he himself was the very symbol of her first defeat. Miguel was her first love.

When she first met him they were mere children, two cousins lost at a huge family dinner of many cousins and aunts and uncles. Miguel had been drawn to Elena magnetically, following her like a shadow, listening to her every word, words no one could hear, her voice was so small and transparent.

He wrote her letters from that day on, came to see her now and then during school holidays – a romantic attachment, in which each one used the other as the embodiment of the legend or story or novel they had read. Elena was every heroine; Miguel was every hero.

When they met, they were enveloped in so much unreality that they could not touch each other. They did not even hold hands. They were exalted in each other's presence, they soared together, they were moved by the same sensations. She was the first to experience a deeper emotion.

They went to a dance together, unaware of their beauty. Other people were. Elena saw all the other young girls stare at Miguel and try to attract his attention.

Then she saw him objectively, outside of this warm devotion in which she had enveloped him. He stood a few yards away, a very tall and lithe young man, his movements easy, graceful and strong, his muscles and nerves like those of a leopard, with a gliding walk but in readiness to spring. His eyes were leaf-green, fluid. His skin was luminous, a mysterious sun glow shining through it, like that of some phosphorescent undersea animal. His mouth was full, with a look of sensual hunger in it, with the perfect teeth of a predatory animal.

And for the first time he saw her outside of the legend in which he had enveloped her, saw her pursued by every man, her body never static, always poised in movement, light on its feet, supple, almost evanescent, tantalizing. The quality which set everyone to hunt her down was something in her that was violently sensual, alive, earthy; her full mouth was all the more vivid because of the delicate body that moved with the fragility of tulle.

This mouth, embedded in a face from another world, out of which came a voice which touched the soul directly, so lured

Miguel that he would not let other boys dance with her. At the same time no part of his body touched her except when they danced. Her eyes drew him into her, and into worlds where he was numb, like a drugged person.

But she, as she danced with him, had become aware of her body, as if it had suddenly turned to flesh – ignited flesh, into which each motion of the dance threw a flame. She wanted to fall forward into the flesh of his mouth, abandon herself to a mysterious drunkenness.

Miguel's drunkenness was of another kind. He behaved as if seduced by an unreal creature, a fantasy. His body was dead to hers. The nearer he moved to her, the stronger he felt this taboo surrounding her, and he stood as if he were before a sacred image. As soon as he entered her presence, what he succumbed to was a kind of castration.

As her body warmed to his nearness, he found nothing to say but her name: 'Elena!' At this, his arms and legs and sex were so paralyzed that he stopped dancing. What he was aware of as he uttered her name was his mother, his mother as he had seen her when he was small; that is, a woman larger than other women, immense, abundant, with the curves of her maternity overflowing from her loose white clothes, the breasts from which he had nourished himself and which he had clung to past the age of necessity, until the time when he was becoming conscious of the full dark mystery of flesh.

So each time he saw the breasts of big, full women who resembled his mother, he experienced the desire to suckle, to chew, to bite and even hurt them, to press them against his face, to suffocate under their bursting fullness, to fill his mouth with the nipples, but he felt no desire to possess with sexual penetration.

Now Elena, when he first met her, had the tiny breasts of a girl of fifteen, which aroused in Miguel a certain contempt. She had none of the erotic attributes of his mother. He was never tempted to undress her. He never pictured her as a woman. She was an image, like the images of saints on little cards, the images of heroic women in books, the paintings of women.

Only whores possessed sexual organs. Miguel had seen such

women very early when his older brothers had dragged him to the whorehouses. While his brothers took the women, he caressed their breasts. He filled his mouth with them, hungrily. But he was frightened by what he saw between their legs. To him it looked like a huge, wet, hungry mouth. He felt that he could never satisfy it. He was frightened by the luring crevice, the lips rigid under the stroking finger, the liquid that came like the saliva of a hungry person. He imagined this hunger of women as tremendous, ravenous, insatiable. It seemed to him that his penis would be swallowed forever. The whores he happened to see had big sexes, big, leathery sex lips, big buttocks.

What was there left for Miguel to turn to with his desires? Boys, boys without the gluttonous openings, boys with sexes like his, that did not frighten him, whose desires he could satisfy.

So on the very evening that Elena experienced this dart of desire and warmth in her body, Miguel had discovered the intermediate solution, a boy who aroused him without taboos, fears and doubts.

Elena, completely innocent of the love between boys, went home and sobbed all night because of Miguel's remoteness. She had never been more beautiful; she felt his love, his worship. Then why did he not touch her? The dance had brought them together, but he was not inflamed. What did this mean? What mystery was this? Why was he jealous when others approached her? Why had he watched the other boys who were so eager to dance with her? Why did he not touch even her hand?

Yet he haunted her, and was haunted by her. Her image predominated over all women. His poetry was for her, his creations, his inventions, his soul. The sexual act alone took place away from her. How much suffering would have been spared her had she known, understood. She was too delicate to overtly question him, and he too ashamed to reveal himself.

And now Miguel was here, with his past life known to all, a long train of love affairs with boys, never lasting. He was always in quest, always unsatisfied – Miguel, with the same charm, only enhanced, stronger.

Again she sensed his remoteness, the distance between them. He would not even take her arm, shining brown in the Parisian summer sun. He admired all she wore, her rings, her tinkling bracelets, her dress, her sandals, but without touching her.

Miguel was being analyzed by a famous French doctor. Every time he moved, loved, took someone, it seemed the knots of his life drew closer around his throat. He wanted liberation, liberation to live out his abnormality. This he did not have. Each time he loved a boy, he did so with a sense of crime. The aftermath was guilt. And then he sought to atone with suffering.

Now he could talk about it, and he opened his whole life before Elena, without shame. It caused her no pain. It relieved her doubts about herself. Because he did not understand his nature, he had at first blamed her, put on her the burden of his frigidity toward woman. He said it was because she was intelligent, and intelligent women mixed literature and poetry with love, which paralyzed him; and that she was positive, masculine, in some of her ways, and this intimidated him. She was so young at the time, she had readily accepted this and come to believe that slender, intellectual, positive women could not be desired.

He would say: 'If only you were very passive, very obedient, very very inert, I might desire you. But I always feel in you a volcano about to explode, a volcano of passion, and that frightens me.' Or: 'If you were just a whore, and I could feel that you would not be too exacting, too critical, I might desire you. But I would feel your clever head watching me and looking down on me if I failed, if, for instance, I were suddenly impotent.'

Poor Elena, for years she completely overlooked the men who desired her. Because Miguel was the one she had wanted to seduce, it seemed to her that only Miguel could have proved her power.

Miguel, in his need of someone other than his analyst to confide in, introduced Elena to his lover, Donald. As soon as Elena saw Donald she loved him too, as she would a child, an *enfant terrible*, perverse and knowing.

He was beautiful. He had a slender Egyptian body, wild hair like that of a child who had been running. At times the softness of his gestures made him seem small, but when he stood up, stylized, pure in line, stretched, then he seemed tall. His eyes were in a trance, and he talked flowingly, like a medium.

Elena was so enchanted with him that she began to enjoy subtly and mysteriously Miguel's making love to him – for her. Donald as a woman, being made love to by Miguel, courting his youthful charm, his sweeping eyelashes, his small, straight nose, his faun ears, his strong, boyish hands.

She recognized in Donald a twin brother who used her words, her coquetries, her artifices. He was obsessed with the same words and feelings that obsessed her. He talked continually about his desire to be consumed in love, about his desire for renunciation and for protection of others. She could hear her own voice. Was Miguel aware that he was making love to a twin brother of Elena, to Elena in a boy's body?

When Miguel left them at the café table for a moment, they looked at each other with a stare of recognition. Without Miguel, Donald was no longer a woman. He straightened his body, looked at her unflinchingly, and talked about how he was seeking intensity and tension saying that Miguel was not the father he needed – Miguel was too young, Miguel was just another child. Miguel wanted to offer him a paradise somewhere, a beach where they could make love freely, embrace day and night, a paradise of caresses and lovemaking; but he, Donald, sought something else. He liked the infernos of love, love mixed with great sufferings and great obstacles. He wanted to kill monsters and overcome enemies and struggle like some Don Quixote.

As he talked about Miguel, there came to his face the same expression women have when they have seduced a man, an expression of vain satisfaction. A triumphant, uncontrollable inner celebration of one's power.

Each time Miguel left them for a moment Donald and Elena were acutely aware of the bond of sameness between them, and of a malicious feminine conspiracy to enchant and seduce and victimize Miguel.

With a mischievous glance, Donald said to Elena, 'Talking together is a form of intercourse. You and I exist together in all the delirious countries of the sexual world. You draw me into the marvelous. Your smile keeps a mesmeric flow.'

Miguel returned to them. Why was he so restless? He went for cigarettes. He went for something else. He left them. Each time he returned she saw Donald change, become woman again, tantalizing. She saw them caressing each other with their eyes, and pressing their knees together under the table. There was such a current of love between them that she was taken into it. She saw Donald's feminine body dilating, she saw his face open like a flower, his eyes thirsty, and his lips wet. It was like being admitted into the secret chambers of another's sensual love, and seeing in both Donald and Miguel what would otherwise be concealed from her. It was a strange transgression.

Miguel said, 'You two are exactly alike.'

'But Donald is more truthful,' said Elena, thinking how easily he betrayed the fact that he did not love Miguel wholly, whereas she would have concealed this, out of the fear of hurting the other.

'Because he loves less,' said Miguel. 'He is a narcissist.'

A warmth broke through the taboo between Donald and Elena, and Miguel and Elena. Love now flowed among the three of them, shared, transmitted, contagious, the threads binding them.

She could look with Miguel's eyes at Donald's finely designed body, the narrow waist, the square shoulders of an Egyptian relief figure, the stylized gestures. His face expressed a dissolution so open that it seemed like an act of exhibitionism. Everything was revealed, naked to the eye.

Miguel and Donald spent afternoons together, and then Donald would seek out Elena. With her he asserted his masculinity and felt that she transmitted to him the masculine in her, the strength. She felt this and said, 'Donald, I give you the masculine in my own soul.' In her presence he became erect, firm, pure, serious. A coalescence took place. Then he was the perfect hermaphrodite.

But Miguel could not see this. He continued to treat him as a woman. True, when Miguel was present, Donald's body softened, his hips began to sway, his face became that of the cheap actress, the vamp receiving flowers with a batting of the eyelashes. He was as fluttery as a bird, with a petulant mouth pursed for small kisses, all adornment and change, a burlesque of the little gestures of alarm and promise made by women. Why did men love this travesty of women and yet elude women?

And in contradiction, there was Donald's male fury against

being taken like a woman: 'He overlooks the masculine in me completely,' he complained. 'He takes from behind, he insists on giving it to me through the ass, and treating me like a woman. And I hate him for this. He will make a real fairy out of me. I want something else. I want to be saved from becoming a woman. And Miguel is brutal and masculine with me. I seem to tantalize him. He turns me over by force and takes me as if I were a whore.'

'Is this the first time you have been treated like a woman?'

'Yes, before this I have done nothing but sucking, never this – mouth and penis, that was all – kneeling before the man you love and taking it into your mouth.'

She looked at Donald's small, childish mouth and wondered how he could get it inside. She remembered a night when she had been so frenzied with Pierre's caresses that she had enveloped his penis and balls and hair in her two hands with a kind of gluttony. She had wanted to take it into her mouth, something she had never wanted to do to anyone before, and he had not let her because he liked it so much inside of her womb, and wanted it there for good.

And now she could see so vividly a huge penis – Miguel's blond penis, perhaps, entering Donald's small child's mouth. Her nipples hardened at the image and she turned her eyes away.

'He takes me all day, in front of mirrors, on the floor of the bathroom, while he holds the door with his foot, on the rug. He is insatiable, and he disregards the male in me. If he sees my penis, which is really larger than his, and more beautiful – really, it is – he does not notice it. He takes me from behind, mauls me like a woman, and leaves my penis dangling. He disregards my masculinity. There is no fulfillment between us.'

'It is like the love between women, then,' said Elena. 'There is no fulfillment, no real possession.'

One afternoon Miguel asked Elena to come to his room. When she knocked at the door she heard scurrying. She was about to turn away when Miguel came to the door and said, 'Come in, come in.' But his face was congested, his eyes bloodshot, his hair wild, and his mouth marked by kisses.

Elena said, 'I'll come back later.'

Miguel answered, 'No, come, you can sit in the bathroom for a little while. Donald will be leaving.'

He wanted her to be there! He could have sent her away. But he led her through the little hallways into the bathroom which adjoined the bedroom, and sat her there, laughing. The door remained open. She could hear the groans and the heavy panting. It was as if they were fighting there together in the dark room. The bed creaked rhythmically, and she heard Donald say, 'You hurt me.' But Miguel was panting and Donald had to repeat, 'You hurt me.'

Then the groaning continued, the rhythmic creaking of the bedsprings accelerated, and despite all Donald had told her, she heard his groan of joy. Then he said, 'You're stifling me.'

The scene in the dark affected her strangely. She felt part of herself sharing in it, as a woman, she as a woman within Donald's boy's body, being made love to by Miguel.

She was so affected that, to distract herself, she opened her bag and took out a letter she had found in her letterbox before leaving but had not read yet.

When she opened it, it was like a thunderbolt: 'My elusive and beautiful Elena, I am in Paris again, for you. I could not forget you. I tried. When you gave yourself entirely, you also took me wholly and entirely. Will you see me? You have not retreated and shrunk beyond me for good? I deserve this, but do not do it to me, you will be murdering a deep love, deeper for its struggle against you. I am in Paris . . .'

Elena got up and ran out of the apartment, slamming the door as she left. When she reached Pierre's hotel he was waiting for her, eager. He had no light on in his room. It was as if he wanted to meet her in the darkness, to better feel her skin, her body, her sex.

The separation had made them feverish. In spite of their savage encounter Elena could not have an orgasm. Deep within her was a reserve of fear, and she could not abandon herself. Pierre's pleasure came with such strength that he could not hold it back to wait for her. He knew her so well he sensed the reason for her secret withdrawal, the wound he had dealt her, the destruction of her faith in his love.

She lay back weary from desire and caresses, but without fulfillment. Pierre bent over her and said in a gentle voice, 'I deserve this. You are hiding away, even though you want to meet me. I have lost you forever.'

'No,' said Elena, 'wait. Give me time to believe in you again.'

Before she left Pierre, he tried again to possess her. He again met with that secret, ultimately closed being, she who had attained a wholeness in sexual pleasure the first time she had been caressed by him. Then Pierre bowed his head and sat at the edge of the bed, defeated, sad.

'But you'll come back tomorrow, you'll come back? What can I do to make you trust me?'

He was in France without papers, risking arrest. For greater security Elena hid him at the apartment of a friend who was away. They met every day now. He liked to meet her in the darkness, so that before they could see each other's face, their hands became aware of the other's presence. Like blind people, they felt each other's body, lingering in the warmest curves, making the same trajectory each time; knowing by touch the places where the skin was softest and tenderest and where it was stronger and exposed to daylight; where, on the neck, the heartbeat was echoed; where the nerves shivered as the hand came nearer to the center, between the legs.

His hands knew the fullness of her shoulders so unexpected in her slender body, the tautness of her breasts, the febrile hairs under her arm, which he had asked her not to shave. Her waist was very small, and his hands loved that curve opening wider and wider from the waist to the hips. He followed each curve lovingly, seeking to take possession of her body with his hands, imagining the color of it.

Only once had he looked at her body in full daylight, in Caux, in the morning, and then he had delighted in the color of it. It was pale ivory, and smooth, and only towards the sex this ivory became more golden, like old ermine. Her sex he called 'the little fox', whose hair bristled when his hand reached out for it.

His lips followed his hands; his nose, too, buried in the odors of her body, seeking oblivion, seeking the drug that emanated from her body.

Elena had a little mole hidden away in the folds of secret flesh between the legs. He would pretend to be seeking it when his fingers ran up between the legs and behind the fox's bush, pretend to be wanting to touch the little mole and not the vulva; and as he caressed the mole, it was only accidentally that he touched the vulva, so lightly, just lightly enough to feel the quick plantlike contraction of pleasure which his fingers produced, the leaves of the sensitive plant closing, folding over the excitement, enclosing its secret pleasure, whose vibrato he felt.

Kissing the mole and not the vulva, while sensing how it responded to the kisses given a little space away, traveling under the skin, from the mole to the tip of the vulva, which opened and closed as his mouth came near. He buried his head there, drugged by the sandalwood smells, seashell smells; by the caress of her pubic hair, the fox's bush, one strand losing itself inside of his mouth, another losing itself among the bedclothes, where he found it later, shining, electric. Often their pubic hairs mingled. Bathing afterwards, Elena would find strands of Pierre's hair curled among hers, his hair longer, thicker and stronger.

Elena let his mouth and hands find all kinds of secret shelters and nooks, and rest there, falling into a dream of enveloping caresses, bowing her head over his when he placed his mouth on her throat, kissing the words she could not utter. He seemed to divine where she wanted a kiss to fall next, what part of her body demanded to be warmed. Her eyes fell on her own feet, and then his kisses went there, or below her arm, or in the hollow of her back, or where the belly ran into a valley, where the pubic hairs began, small and light and sparse.

Pierre stretched out his arm as a cat might, to be stroked. He threw his head back at times, closed his eyes, and let her cover him with moth kisses that were only a promise of more violent ones to come. When he could no longer bear the silky light touches, he opened his eyes and offered his mouth like a ripe fruit to bite, and she fell hungrily on it, as if to draw from it the very source of life.

When desire had permeated every little pore and hair of the body, then they abandoned themselves to violent caresses. At times she could hear her bones crack as he raised her legs above his shoulders, she could hear the suction of the kisses, the raindrop sound of the lips and tongues, the moisture spreading in the warmth of the mouth as if they were eating into a fruit which melted and dissolved. He could hear her strange muffled crooning sound, like that of some exotic bird in ecstasy; and she, his breath, which came more heavily as his blood grew denser, richer.

When his fever rose, his breath was like that of some legendary bull galloping furiously to a delirious goring, a goring without pain, a goring which lifted her almost bodily from the bed, raised her sex in the air as if he would thrust right through her body and tear it, leaving her only when the wound was made, a wound of ecstasy and pleasure which rent her body like lightning, and let her fall again, moaning, a victim of too great a joy, a joy that was like a little death, a dazzling little death that no drug or alcohol could give, that nothing else could give but two bodies in love with each other, in love deep within their beings, with every atom and cell and nerve, and thought.

Pierre was sitting at the edge of the bed and had slipped his pants on and was fastening the buckle of his belt. Elena had slipped on her dress but was still coiled around him as he sat. Then he showed her his belt. She sat up to look at it. It had been a heavy, strong leather belt with a silver buckle but was now so completely worn that it looked about to tear. The tip of it was frayed. The places where the buckle fastened were almost as thin as a piece of cloth.

'My belt is wearing out,' Pierre said, 'and it makes me sad because I have had it ten years.' He studied it contemplatively.

As she looked at him sitting there, with his belt not yet fastened, she was sharply reminded of the moment before he unfastened his belt to let his pants down. He never unfastened it until a caress, a tight embrace of their bodies against one another, had aroused his desire so that the confined penis hurt him.

There was always that second of suspense before he loosened his pants and took out his penis for her to touch. Sometimes he let her take it out. If she could not unbutton his underwear quickly enough, then he did it himself. The little snapping sound of the buckle affected her. It was an erotic moment for her, as was, for Pierre, the moment before she took down her panties or loosened her garters.

Though she had been fully satisfied a moment before, she was aroused again. She would have liked to unfasten the belt, let his pants slip down and touch his penis once more. When it first came out of the pants, how alertly it straightened itself to point to her, as if in recognition.

Then suddenly the realization that the belt was so old, that Pierre had always worn it, struck her with a strange, sharp pain. She saw him unfastening it in other places, other rooms, at other hours, for other women.

She was jealous, acutely jealous, with this image repeating itself. She wanted to say, 'Throw the belt away. At least do not carry the same one that you wore for them. I will give you another.'

It was as if his feeling of affection for the belt were a feeling of affection for the past that he could not rid himself of entirely. For her, the belt represented the gestures made in the past. She asked herself if all the caresses had been the same.

For a week or so Elena responded completely to his embraces, almost lost consciousness in his arms, sobbed once with the acuteness of her joys. Then she noticed a change in his mood. He was preoccupied. She did not question him. She interpreted his preoccupation in her own way. He was thinking of his political activity, which he had surrendered for her. Perhaps he was suffering from his inaction. No man could live completely for love as a woman could, could make this the purpose of his life and fill his days with it.

She could have lived for nothing else. In fact, she lived for nothing else. The rest of the time – when she was not with him – she felt and heard nothing clearly. She was absent. She only came to life fully in his room. All day, as she did other things, her thoughts circled around him. Alone in bed, she remembered his expressions, the laughter at the corner of his eyes, the willfulness of his chin, the glittering of his teeth, the shape of his lips as he uttered words of desire.

That afternoon she lay in his arms, noticed the clouds on his face, the clouded eyes, and could not respond to him. Usually they were in rhythm. He felt when her pleasure was mounting, and she, his. In some mysterious way they could hold back the orgasm until the moment when each was ready for it. Usually they were slow in their rhythmic motions, then quicker, then still quicker, in time with the rising temperature of the blood and the mounting waves of pleasure, and they reached the orgasm together, his penis quivering as it spurted semen, and her womb quivering from the darts, which were like flickering tongues of fire inside of her.

Today he waited for her. She moved to meet his thrusts, arching her back, but she did not come. He begged her, 'Come, my darling. Come, my darling. I can't wait any longer. Come, my darling.'

He emptied himself in her and fell on her breast without a sound. He lay there as if she had struck him. Nothing wounded him more than her unresponsiveness.

'You're cruel,' he said. 'Why are you holding back from me now?'

She was silent. She herself was sad that anxiety and doubt could so easily close her being to a possession she wanted. Even if it were to be the last, she wanted it. But because she feared it might be the last, her being closed, and she was deprived of real union with him. And without the orgasm experienced together, there was no union, no absolute communion between the two bodies. Afterwards, she knew, she would be tortured as she had been other times. She would be left unsatisfied, with the imprint of his body on hers.

She would re-enact the scene in her mind, see him bending over her, see how their legs appeared when they were tangled together, see how over and over again his penis penetrated her, how he fell away when it was over, and she would experience the stirring hunger again, and be tormented with desire to feel him deep inside of her body. She knew the tension of unsatisfied desire, the nerves unbearably awake, keen, naked, the blood in turmoil, everything set for a climax that did not take place. Afterwards she could not sleep. She felt cramps along her legs, making her shake like a restless racehorse. Obsessional erotic images pursued her all through the night.

'What are you thinking of?' said Pierre, watching her face.

'Of how sad I will be when I leave you, after not being really yours.'

'There is something else on your mind, Elena, something that was there when you came, something I want to know.'

'I'm concerned about your depression and have asked myself if you missed your activity and were wishing to return to it.'

'Oh, that was it. That was it. You were preparing for my leaving again. But that was not in my mind. On the contrary. I have seen friends who will help me prove that I was not active, that I was only a café revolutionist. Do you remember the character in Gogol? The man who talked day and night but never moved, acted? That is me. That is all I have done – talk. If this can be proved, then I can stay and be free. That is what I am struggling for.'

What an effect these words had on Elena! – as great as her fears had had on her sensual being, arresting her impulses, dominating them. It frightened her. She now wanted to lie on Pierre and have him take her. She knew that his words were sufficient to release her. He may have divined this, for he continued his caresses for a long time, waiting for the touch of his fingers on her moist skin to arouse his desire again. And much later, as they lay in the dark, he took her again, and then she had to hold back the intensity and quickness of her orgasm so as to have it with him, and they both cried out, and she wept with joy.

From then on the struggle of their love was to defeat this coldness which lay dormant in her and which a word, a small wound, a doubt, could bring out to destroy their possession of each other. Pierre became obsessed with it. He was more intent on watching her moods and predispositions than his own. Even as he enjoyed her, his eyes searched her for a sign of that future clouding, always hanging over them. He exhausted himself waiting for her pleasure. He withheld his. He stormed against this unconquerable core of her being, which could close at will against him. He began to understand some of men's perverse devotions to frigid women.

The citadel – the impregnable virgin woman: The conqueror in Pierre, who had never burst forth to carry out a real revolution, gave itself to this conquest, to once and forever break down this barrier that she could erect against him. Their lover's meetings became a secret battle between two wills, a series of ruses.

If they had a quarrel (and he quarreled over her intimate association with Miguel and Donald, because he said they were making love to her through the bodies of each other) then he knew she would withhold her orgasm from him. He stormed and sought to conquer her with the wildest caresses. He treated her brutally at times, as if she were a whore and he could pay for her submission. At other times he tried to melt her with tenderness. He made himself small, almost a child in her arms.

He surrounded her with erotic atmosphere. He made of their room a den, covered with rugs and tapestries, perfumed. He sought to reach her through her response to beauty, luxury, odors. He bought her erotic books, which they read together. This was his latest form of conquest – to arouse a sexual fever in her so potent that she could never resist his touch. As they lay on the couch together and read, their hands wandered over each other's body, to the places described in the book. They exhausted themselves in excesses of all kinds, seeking every pleasure known to lovers, fired by images and words and descriptions of new positions. Pierre believed he had awakened in her such a sexual obsession that she could never control herself again. And Elena did seem corrupted. Her eyes began to shine in an extraordinary way, not with the effulgence of day, but with a disquieting light like that of a tubercular patient, with a fever so intense that it burned rings around them.

Now he ceased to leave the room in darkness. He liked to see her arrive with this fever in her eyes. Her body seemed to have become heavier. Her nipples were always hard, as if she were constantly in a state of erotic excitement. Her skin had become so hypersensitive that as soon as he touched her it rippled under his fingers. A shiver passed through her back, touching every nerve.

They would lie on their stomachs, still dressed, open a new book and read together, with their hands caressing each other. They kissed over erotic pictures. Their mouths, glued together, fell over enormous protruding women's asses, legs open like a compass, men squatting like dogs, with huge members almost dragging the floor.

There was a picture of a tortured woman, impaled on a thick stick which ran into her sex and out of her mouth. It had the appearance of ultimate sexual possession and aroused in Elena a feeling of pleasure. When Pierre took her, it seemed to her that the joy she felt at his penis belaboring her was communicated to her mouth. She opened it, and her tongue protruded, as in the picture, as if she wanted his penis in her mouth at the same time.

For days Elena would respond madly, almost like a woman who was about to lose her reason. But Pierre discovered that a quarrel or a cruel word from him could still arrest her orgasm and kill the erotic flame in her eyes.

When they had exhausted the novelty of erotica, they found a new realm – the realm of jealousy, terror, doubt, anger, hatred, antagonism, of the struggle human beings undergo at times against the bond to one another.

Pierre sought now to make love to the other selves of Elena, the most buried ones, the most delicate ones. He watched her sleep, he watched her dress, he watched her as she combed her hair before the mirror. He sought a spiritual clue to her being, one he could reach with a new form of lovemaking. He no longer spied on her to make certain she had enjoyed an orgasm, for the very simple reason that Elena had now decided to pretend enjoyment even when she did not feel it. She became a consummate actress. She showed all the symptoms of pleasure, the contraction of the vulva, the quickening of the breath, of the pulse, of the heartbeats, the sudden languor, the falling away, the half-fainting fog that followed. She could simulate everything – to her, loving and being loved were so irrevocably mixed with her pleasure that she could achieve a breathless emotional response even if she did not feel physical enjoyment – everything, that is, but the inner palpitation of the orgasm. But this, she knew, was difficult to detect with the penis. She had found Pierre's struggle to always obtain an orgasm from her destructive, and foresaw that it might well end in taking away his confidence in her love and ultimately separate them. She chose the course of pretense.

So now Pierre turned his attention to another kind of courtship. As soon as she entered he noted how she moved, how she took her coat and hat off, how she shook her hair, what rings she wore. He thought that from all these signs he could detect her mood. Then this mood became his ground for conquest. Today she was childlike, pliant, with her hair loose, her head bowing easily with the weight of all her life. She had on less make-up, an innocent expression, she wore a light dress of bright colors. Today he would caress her gently, with tenderness, observing the perfection of her toes, for instance, as free as the fingers of a hand; observing her ankles, on which pale-blue veins showed through; observing the little ink spot forever tattooed below her knee, where, when she was fifteen – a girl in school and wearing black stockings – she had covered a little hole in the stockings with ink. The pen point had broken during the process, wounding her and marking her skin for good. He would look for a broken fingernail so that he might deplore its loss, its pathetic truncated look among her other long, pointed ones. He worried over all her little miseries. He held close to him the little girl in her, whom he would have liked to know. He asked questions: 'So you wore black cotton stockings?'

'We were very poor, and it was also part of the school uniform.'

'What else did you wear?'

'Middy blouses and dark blue skirts, which I hated. I loved finery so.'

'And underneath?' he asked, with such innocence that he might have been asking whether she wore a raincoat in the rain.

'I'm not sure what my underclothes were like then – I liked petticoats with frills on them, I remember. I'm afraid I was made to wear woolen underwear. And in the summer, white slips and bloomers. I did not like the bloomers. They were too full. I dreamed of lace then, and gazed by the hour at the underwear in shop windows, entranced, imagining myself in satin and lace. You would have found nothing entrancing about a little girl's underwear.'

But Pierre thought yes, that no matter if it were white and perhaps shapeless, he could imagine himself very much in love with Elena in her black stockings.

He wanted to know when she had experienced her first sensual tremor. It was while reading, said Elena, and then while coasting on a sled with a boy lying full length over her, and then when she fell in love with men she only knew at a distance, for as soon as they came near her, she discovered some defect that estranged her. She needed strangers, a man seen at a window, a man seen once a day in the street, a man she had seen once in a concert hall. After such encounters, Elena let her hair fall wild, was negligent in her dress, slightly wrinkled, and sat like some Chinese woman concerned with small events and delicate sadnesses.

Then, lying at her side, holding only her hand, Pierre talked about his life, offering her images of himself as a boy, to match those of the little girl she brought him. It was as if in each the older shells of their mature personalities had dissolved, like some added structure, a superimposition, revealing the cores.

As a child, Elena had been what she had suddenly become again for him – an actress, a simulator, someone who lived in her fantasies and roles and never knew what she truly felt.

Pierre had been a rebel. He had been raised among women, without his father, who had died at sea. The woman who mothered him was his nurse, and his mother lived only to find a replacement for the man she had lost. There was no motherhood in her. She was a born mistress. She treated her son like a young lover. She fondled him extravagantly, received him in the morning in her bed, in which he could still detect the recent presence of a man. He shared her lazy breakfast brought by the nurse, who was always incensed to find the boy lying in bed next to his mother, where a moment before her lover had been.

Pierre loved the voluptuousness of his mother, the flesh always appearing through lace, the outline of the body transparent between skirts of chiffon; he loved the sloping shoulders, the fragile ears, the long mocking eyes, the opalescent arms emerging from full-blown sleeves. Her preoccupation was how to make a feast of every day. She eliminated people who were not amusing, anyone who told stories of illness or misfortune. If she went shopping, it was done extravagantly, as if for Christmas, and included everyone in the family, surprises for all; and for herself – caprices and useless things, which accumulated around her until she gave them away.

At ten Pierre was already initiated into all the preparations which a life filled with lovers demanded. He assisted at his mother's toilette, watched her powder herself under the arms and slip the powder puff into her dress, between her breasts. He saw her emerge from the bath half-covered by her kimono, her legs naked, and watched her pull on her very long stockings. She liked her garters to grip her very high, so that the stockings almost touched her hips. As she dressed she talked about the man she was going to meet, extolling to Pierre the aristocratic nature of this one, the charm of another, the naturalness of a third, the genius of a fourth – as if Pierre should some day become all of them for her.

When Pierre was twenty she discouraged all his friendships with women, even his visits to the whorehouse. The fact that he sought women who resembled her did not impress her. In the whorehouses he asked the women to dress up for him, deliberately and slowly, so that he could enjoy an obscure, undefinable joy – the same joy he had experienced in the presence of his mother. For this ceremony he demanded coquetry and particular clothes. The whores laughingly humored him. During these games his desires would suddenly run wild; he tore at the clothes, and his lovemaking resembled a rape.

Beyond this lay the mature regions of his experience which he did not confess to Elena that day. He gave her only the child, his own innocence, his own perversity.

There were days when certain fragments of his past, the most erotic, would rise to the surface, permeate his every movement, give to his eyes the disquieting stare Elena had first seen in him, to his mouth a laxness, an abandon, to his whole face an expression of one whom no experience had eluded. She could then see Pierre and one of his whores together, a willful seeker of poverty, dirt and decay as the only proper accompaniment to certain acts. The apache, the *voyou* appeared in him, the man of vice who could drink for three days and three nights, abandoning himself to every experience as if it were the ultimate one, spending all his desire on some monstrous woman, desiring her because she was unwashed, because so many men had taken her and because her language was charged with obscenities. It was a passion for self-destruction, for baseness, for the language of the street, women of the street, danger. He had been caught in opium raids and arrested for selling a woman.

It was his capacity for anarchy and corruption that gave him at times the expression of a man capable of anything, and that kept awake in Elena a mistrust of him. At the same time, he was fully aware of her own attraction to the demonic and the sordid, to the pleasure of falling, of desecrating and destroying the ideal self. But because of his love for her, he would not let her live out any of this with him. He was afraid to initiate her and lose her to one vice or another, to some sensation he could not give her. So this door upon the corrupt element of their natures was seldom opened. She did not want to know what his body had done, his mouth, his sex. He feared to uncover the possibilities in her.

'I know,' he said, 'that you are capable of many loves, that I will be the first one, that from now on nothing will stop you from expanding. You're sensual, so sensual.'

'You can't love so many times,' she answered. 'I want my eroticism mixed with love. And deep love one does not often experience.'

He was jealous of her future, and she of his past. She became aware that she was twenty-five and he was forty, that he had experienced many things he was already tired of and she had not yet known.

When the silence grew long and Elena did not see on Pierre's face an expression of innocence, but on the contrary, a hovering smile, a certain contempt in the outline of the lips, then she knew he was remembering the past. She lay at his side looking at his long eyelashes.

After a moment he said, 'Until I knew you, I was a Don Juan, Elena. I never wanted to really know a woman. I never wanted to stay with one. My feeling was always that a woman used her charms not for the sake of a passionate relationship but to win from a man some durable relationship – marriage, for instance, or at least companionship – to win, finally, some kind of peace, possession. It was this that frightened me – the sense that behind the *grande amoureuse* lay concealed a little bourgeoise who wanted security in love. What attracts me to you is that you have remained the mistress. You maintain the fervor and the intensity. When you feel unequal to the great battle of love, you stay away. Another thing, it is not the pleasure I can give you which attaches you to me. You repudiate it when you are not emotionally satisfied. But you are capable of all things, of anything. I feel that. You are open to life. I opened you. For the first time I regret my power to open women to life, to love. How I love you when you refuse to communicate with the body, seeking other means to reach into the entire being. You did everything to break down my resistance to pleasure. Yes, at first, I could not bear this power you had to withdraw. It seemed to me that I was losing my power.'

This talk again inspired in Elena a sense of the unstable in Pierre. She never rang his bell without wondering if he might be gone. In an old closet he had discovered a pile of erotic books concealed under blankets by the former occupants of the place. Now he met her every day with a story to make her laugh. He saw that he had saddened her.

He did not know that when the erotic and the tender are mixed in a woman, they form a powerful bond, almost a fixation. She could think only of erotic images in connection with him, his body. If she saw a penny movie on the boulevards that stirred her, she brought her curiosity or a new experiment to their next meeting. She began to whisper certain wishes in his ear.

Pierre was always surprised when Elena was willing to give him pleasure without taking it herself. There were times after their excesses when he was tired, less potent, and yet wanted to repeat the sensation of annihilation. Then he would stir her with caresses, with an agility of the hands that approached masturbation. Meanwhile her own hands would circle around his penis like a delicate spider with knowing fingertips, which touched the most hidden nerves of response. Slowly, the fingers closed upon the penis, at first stroking its flesh shell; then feeling the inrush of dense blood stretching it; feeling the slight swell of the nerves, the sudden tautness of the muscles; feeling as if they were playing upon a stringed instrument. By the degree of tautness Elena knew when Pierre could not sustain sufficient hardness to penetrate her, she knew when he could only respond to her nervous fingers, when he wanted to be masturbated, and soon his own pleasure would slow down the activity of his hands on her. Then he would be drugged by her hands, close his eyes and abandon himself to her caresses. Once or twice he would try, as if in sleep, to continue the motion of his own hands, but then he lay passively, to feel better the knowing manipulations, the increasing tension. 'Now, now,' he would murmur. 'Now.' This meant that her hand must become swifter to keep pace with the fever pulsing within him. Her fingers ran in rhythm with the quickening blood beats, as his voice begged, 'Now, now, now.'

Blind to all but his pleasure, she bent over him, her hair falling, her mouth near his penis, continuing the motion of her hands and at the same time licking the tip of the penis each time it passed within reach of her tongue – this, until his body began to tremble and raised itself to be consumed by her hands and mouth, to be annihilated, and the semen would come, like little waves breaking on the sand, one rolling upon another, little waves of salty foam unrolling on the beach of her hands. Then she enclosed the spent penis tenderly in her mouth, to cull the precious liquid of love.

His pleasure gave her such a joy that she was surprised when he began to kiss her with gratitude, as he said, 'But you, you didn't have any pleasure.'

'Oh, yes,' said Elena, in a voice he could not doubt.

She marveled at the continuity of their exultation. She wondered when their love would enter a period of repose.

Pierre was gaining liberty. He was often out when she telephoned. Meanwhile she was advising an old friend, Kay, who was just back from Switzerland. On the train Kay had met a man who could be described as the younger brother of Pierre. Kay had always so identified with Elena, been so dominated by Elena's personality, that the only thing which could satisfy her was an adventure which, at least in some superficial way, resembled Elena's.

This man also had a mission. What the mission was, he did not confess, but he used it as an excuse, perhaps an alibi, when he went away or when he had to spend a whole day without seeing Kay. Elena suspected that she gave Pierre's double stronger colors than he actually possessed. To begin with, she endowed him with

ELENA

abnormal virility marred only by his habit of falling asleep before
or immediately after the act, without waiting to thank her. He
passed from the middle of a conversation to a sudden desire for
rape. He hated underwear. He taught her not to wear anything
under her dress. His desire was imperative – and unexpected. He
could not wait. With him, she learned hasty departures from
restaurants, wild drives in curtained taxi cabs, séances behind the
trees in the Bois, masturbation in cinemas – never in a bourgeois
bed, in the warmth and comfort of a bedroom. His desire was
distinctly ambulant and bohemian. He liked carpeted floors, even
the cold floors of bathrooms, super-heated Turkish baths, opium
dens, where he did not smoke but where he liked to lie with her
on a narrow mat, and their bones would ache afterwards from
falling asleep. Kay's job was to keep alert enough to follow his
caprices, and to try to catch her own elusive pleasure, in this wild
race, which might have come easier with a little leisure surrounding it.

But no, he enjoyed these sudden tropical outbursts. She followed
him like a somnambulist, giving Elena the feeling that she knocked
against him in a reverie, as against a piece of furniture. Sometimes,
when the scene had happened too swiftly for her to bloom
voluptuously and completely under his rape, she lay at his side
while he slept and invented a more thorough lover. She closed her
eyes and thought: Now his hand is lifting my dress slowly, very
slowly. He is looking at me first. One hand lies over my buttocks,
and the other begins exploring, sliding, circling. Now he dips his
finger there, where it is moist. He touches it like a woman feeling
a piece of silk, to see its quality. Very slowly.

Pierre's double would turn over on his side, and Kay would
hold her breath. If he awakened, he would find her with her
hands in a strange position. Then suddenly, as if he had guessed
her wishes, he would place his hand between her legs and leave it
there, so that she could not move. The presence of his hand
aroused her more than ever. Then she would close her eyes again
and try to imagine that his hand was moving. To create a
sufficiently vivid image for herself, she would begin to contract
and open her vagina, rhythmically, until she felt the orgasm.

*

DELTA OF VENUS

Pierre had nothing to fear from the Elena he knew and had so delicately circumnavigated. But there was an Elena he did not know, the virile Elena. Although she did not wear short hair or a man's suit, ride a horse, smoke cigars or frequent the bars where such women congregate, there was a spiritually masculine Elena, dormant in her for the moment.

In all but matters of love, Pierre was helpless. He could not nail a nail to a wall, hang up a picture, repair a book, discuss technical matters of any kind. He lived in terror of servants, concierges, plumbers. He could not make a decision, sign a contract of any sort; he did not know what he wanted.

Elena's energies rushed into these lacunas. Her mind became the more fecund. She bought the books and newspapers, incited activity, made decisions. Pierre permitted this. It suited his nonchalance. She gained in audacity.

She felt protective toward him. As soon as the sexual aggression was over, he reclined like a pasha and let her rule. He did not observe another Elena emerging, affirming new contours, habits, a new personality. Elena had discovered that women were drawn to her.

She was invited by Kay to meet Leila, a well-known nightclub singer, a woman of dubious sex. They went to Leila's house. She was lying in bed. The room was heavily charged with the perfume of narcissus, and Leila rested against the headboard in a languid, intoxicated way. Elena thought she was recovering from a night of drinking, but this was Leila's natural pose. And from this languid body came a man's voice. Then the violet eyes fixed themselves on Elena, appraising her with masculine deliberateness.

Leila's lover, Mary, entered the room then, with a rushing sound of wide silk skirts inflated by her quick steps. She threw herself at the foot of the bed and took Leila's hand. They looked at each other with so much desire that Elena lowered her eyes. Leila's face was sharp, Mary's vague; Leila's, drawn in heavy charcoal around the eyes as in the Egyptian frescos, Mary's, in pastels – pale eyes, sea-green eyelids and coral nails and lips; Leila's eyebrows natural, Mary's, a pencil line only. When they looked at each other, Leila's features seemed to dissolve, and Mary's to acquire some of Leila's definiteness. But her voice remained unreal, and her phrases unfinished, floating. Mary was uneasy in Elena's presence. Instead of expressing hostility or fear, she took the feminine attitude, as toward a man, and sought to charm her. She did not like the way Leila looked at Elena. She sat near Elena, folding her legs under her like a little girl, and turned her mouth up toward her as she talked, invitingly. But these childish mannerisms were the very ones Elena disliked in women. She turned toward Leila whose gestures were mature and simple.

Leila said, 'Let's go together to the studio. I'll get dressed.' As she leaped out of her bed she abandoned her languor. She was tall. She used apache French, like a boy, but with a royal audacity. No one could use it on her. She did not entertain at the nightclub; she ruled. She was a magnetic center for the world of women who considered themselves condemned by their vice. She whipped them into being proud of their deviations, not succumbing to bourgeois morality. She severely condemned suicides and disintegration. She wanted women who were proud of being Lesbians. She set the example. She wore men's clothes despite police regulations. She was never molested. She did it with grace and nonchalance. She rode horseback at the Bois in men's clothes. She was so elegant, so suave, so aristocratic, that people who did not know her bowed to her, almost unconsciously. She made other women hold up their heads. She was the one masculine woman men treated as a comrade. Whatever tragic spirit lay behind this polished surface went into her singing, with which she tore people's serenity to shreds, spreading anxiety and regrets and nostalgia everywhere.

In the taxi, sitting next to her, Elena felt not her strength but her secret wound. She ventured a gesture of tenderness. She took the royal hand and kept it. Leila did not let it lie there, but responded to the pressure with a nervous power. Already Elena knew what this power failed to obtain for her: fulfillment. Surely, the whimpering voice of Mary and her obvious little ruses could not satisfy Leila. Women were not as tolerant as men toward women who made themselves small and weak by calculation, thinking to inspire an active love. Leila must suffer more than a man, because of her lucidity about women, her incapacity to be deceived.

When they reached the studio, Elena smelled a curious odor of burnt cacao, of fresh truffle. They entered what seemed to be a smoke-filled Arabian mosque. It was a huge room surrounded by a gallery of alcoves furnished only with mats and little lamps. Everybody was wearing kimonos. Elena was handed one. And then she understood. This was an opium den: the lights veiled; people lying down, indifferent to newcomers; a great peace; no sustained conversations, but a sigh now and then. A few for whom opium awakened desire lay in the darkest corners, spoon-fashion, as if asleep. But in the silence, the voice of a woman began what seemed at first to be a song, and then turned out to be another sort of vocalizing, the vocalizing of the exotic bird finally caught in the mating season. Two young men held each other, whispering.

Elena heard at times the fall of pillows on the floor, the crushing of silks and cottons. The woman's vocalizing became clearer, firmer, rising in harmony with her pleasure, so even in its rhythm Elena accompanied it with a movement of her head, until it reached its height. Elena saw that this cadenza irritated Leila. She did not want to hear it. It was so explicit, so female, betraying women's soft cushion of love pierced by the male, uttering with each thrust a little cry of the ecstatic wound. No matter what women did to each other, they could never bring forth this rising cadenza, this vaginal song; only a sequence of stabbings, man's repeated assault, could produce this.

The three women fell on little mattresses, side by side. Mary wanted to lie close to Leila. Leila would not let her. The host offered them opium pipes. Elena refused one. She was sufficiently drugged by the veiled lamps, the smoky atmosphere, the exotic hangings, the doors, the muffled sounds of caresses. Her face was so entranced that Leila herself believed Elena was under the influence of some other drug. She did not realize that the pressure of Leila's hand in the taxi had plunged Elena into a state that was unlike anything Pierre had ever aroused in her.

Instead of reaching right to the center of her body, Leila's voice and touch had enveloped her in a voluptuous mantle of new sensations, something in suspense that did not seek fulfillment but prolongation. It was like this room, affecting one by its mysterious lights, its rich odors, its shadowy niches, its half-seen forms, its mysterious enjoyments. A dream. Opium could not have enlarged or dilated her senses any more than they were, could not have given her a greater sense of joy.

Her hand reached out to Leila's. Mary was smoking already with her eyes closed. Leila was lying back, with her eyes open, looking at Elena. She took Elena's hand, held it for a while, and then she slipped it under her kimono. She placed it over her breasts. Elena began caressing her. Leila had opened her tailored suit. She wore no blouse. But the rest of her body was sheathed in a tight skirt. Then Elena felt Leila's hand running delicately under her dress, seeking for an opening between the tops of her stockings and her underwear. Elena turned gently on her left side, so that she could place her head over Leila's breast and kiss it.

She was afraid Mary might open her eyes and get angry. Now and then she looked at her. Leila smiled. Then she turned over to whisper to Elena: 'We will meet sometime and be together. Do you want it? Will you come to my place tomorrow? Mary will not be there.'

Elena smiled, assented with a nod, stole one more kiss and lay back. But Leila did not withdraw her hand. She watched Mary and continued to caress Elena. Elena was dissolving under her fingers.

It seemed to Elena they had been lying there only a moment, but then she noticed the studio was growing colder and morning had come. She sprang up, surprised. The others seemed to be asleep. Even Leila had fallen back and slept now. Elena slipped on her coat and left. The early dawn revived her.

She wanted to talk to someone. She saw that she was quite near to Miguel's studio. Miguel was asleep with Donald. She woke him and sat at the foot of the bed. She talked. Miguel could barely understand her. He thought she was drunk.

'Why is my love for Pierre not strong enough to keep me from this?' she kept repeating. 'Why is it throwing me into other loves? And loves for a woman? Why?'

Miguel smiled. 'Why are you so afraid of a little detour? It's nothing. It will pass. Pierre's love has awakened your real nature. You're too full of love, you will love many people.'

'I don't want to, Miguel. I want to be whole.'

'That's not such a great infidelity, Elena. In another woman you're only seeking yourself.'

From Miguel's she went home, bathed and rested and went to Pierre. Pierre was in a tender mood. So tender he lulled her doubts and secret anguish, and she fell asleep in his arms.

Leila waited for her in vain. For two or three days Elena hid from thoughts of her, winning from Pierre greater proofs of love, seeking to be encircled, protected from wandering away from him.

He was quick to observe her distress. Almost by instinct, he held her back when she wanted to leave earlier, prevented her physically from going anywhere. Then with Kay, Elena met a sculptor, Jean. His face was soft, feminine, appealing. But he was a lover of women. Elena was on the defensive. He asked for her address. When he came to see her she talked volubly against intimacy.

He said, 'I would like something lovelier and warmer.'

She was frightened. She became even more impersonal. They were both uneasy. She thought: Now it is spoiled. He will not return. And she regretted it. There was an obscure attraction. She could not define it.

He wrote her a letter: 'When I left you, I felt newborn, cleansed of all falsities. How did you give birth to a new self without even wanting to? I will tell you what happened to me once. I stood on the corner of a street in London looking at the moon. I looked so persistently at it that it hypnotized me. I do not remember how I got home, hours and hours later. I always felt that during that time I had lost my soul to the moon. That is what you did to me, in that visit.'

As she read this she became vividly aware of his chanting voice, his charm. He sent other letters with pieces of rock crystal, with an Egyptian scarab. She left them unanswered.

She felt his attraction, but the night she spent with Leila had given her a strange fear. She had returned to Pierre that day feeling as if she were returning from a long trip and had been estranged from him. Each bond had to be renewed. It was this separateness she feared, the distance that it created between her deep love and herself.

Jean waited for her at the door of her house one day and caught her as she walked out, trembling, pale with excitement, unable to sleep. She was angry that he had the power to unnerve her.

By a coincidence, which he observed, they were both dressed in white. The summer enveloped them. His face was soft, and the emotional upheaval in his eyes enmeshed her. He had the laughter of a child, full of candor. She felt Pierre inside of her, clutching at her, holding her back. She closed her eyes so as not to see his. She thought she might be suffering merely from contagion, the contagion of his fervor.

They sat at a humble café table. The waitress spilled the vermouth. Annoyed, he demanded that the table be wiped, as if Elena were a princess.

Elena said, 'I feel a little like the moon who took possession of you for a moment and then returned your soul to you. You should not love me. One ought not to love the moon. If you come too near me, I will hurt you.'

But she saw in his eyes that she had already hurt him. He walked stubbornly beside her, almost to the very door of Pierre's apartment house.

She found him with a ravaged face. He had seen them in the street, had followed them from the little café. He had watched every gesture and expression that had passed between them. He said, 'There were quite a few emotional gestures between you.'

He was like a wild animal, his hair falling over his forehead, his eyes haggard. For an hour he was dark, beside himself with anger and doubt. She pleaded, pleaded with love, took his head and laid it on her breast, lulling him. Out of sheer exhaustion he fell asleep. She then slid out of the bed and stood by his window. The charm of the sculptor had faded. Everything faded beside the depth of Pierre's jealousy. She thought of Pierre's flesh, his flavor, the love they had, and at the same time she heard Jean's adolescent laughter, trusting, sensitive, and she saw the potent charm of Leila.

She was afraid. She was afraid because she was no longer securely tied to Pierre but to an unknown woman lying down, yielding, open, spreading.

Pierre awakened. He stretched out his arms and said, 'It is over now.'

Then she wept. She wanted to beg him to keep her imprisoned, to let no one lure her away. They kissed passionately. He answered her desire by locking her in his arms with such a force that her bones cracked. She laughed and said, 'You're suffocating me.' She lay dissolved, then, by a maternal feeling, a feeling that she wanted to protect him from pain; he, on the other hand, seemed to feel he could possess her once and for all. His jealousy incited him to a kind of fury. The sap rose in him with such vigor that he did not wait for her pleasure. And she did not want this pleasure. She felt herself as a mother receiving a child into herself, drawing him in to lull him, to protect him. She felt no sexual urge but the urge to open, to receive, to enfold only.

On days when she found Pierre weak, passive, uncertain, his body lax, eluding even the effort of dressing, of walking out into the street, then she felt herself incisive, active. She had strange feelings when they fell asleep together. In sleep he seemed vulnerable. She felt her strength aroused. She wanted then to enter him, like a man, take possession of him. She wanted to penetrate him with knifelike thrusts. She lay between sleep and wakefulness, identified with his virility, imagined herself becoming him and taking him as he took her.

And then, at other times, she fell back, became herself – sea and sand and moisture, and no embrace then seemed violent enough, brutal enough, bestial enough.

But if after Pierre's jealousy their lovemaking was more violent, at the same time the air was dense; their feelings were in tumult; there was hostility, confusion, pain. Elena did not know whether their love had grown a root or absorbed a poison that would hasten its decay.

Was there an obscure joy in this that she missed, as she missed so many morbid, masochistic tastes other people had for defeat, misery, poverty, humiliation, entanglements, failures? Pierre had said once, 'What I remember most are the great pains of my life. The pleasant moments I have forgotten.'

Then Kay came to see Elena, a newborn Kay, glittering. Her air of living among many lovers was finally a reality. She had come to tell Elena how she had balanced her life between her hasty lover and a woman. They sat on Elena's bed, smoking, talking.

Kay said, 'You know the woman. It's Leila.'

Elena could not help thinking: So Leila loves a little woman again. Will she never love an equal? Someone as strong as she? She was wounded with jealousy. She wanted to be in Kay's place being loved by Leila.

She asked, 'What is it like to be loved by Leila?'

'It's incredibly marvelous, Elena. Something incredible. In the first place, she always knows what one wants, what mood I'm in, what I desire. She is always accurate. She looks at me when we meet and she knows. To make love she takes so much time. She locks one up in some marvelous place – it must be a marvelous place first of all, she says. Once we were driven to use a hotel room, because Mary was staying in her apartment. The lamp was too strong. She covered it with her underwear. She makes love to the breasts first. We stay for hours merely kissing. She waits until we are drunk with kissing. She wants all our clothes removed, and then we lie glued together, rolling over each other, still kissing. She sits over me as if she were on horseback and then moves against me, rubbing. She does not let me come for a long time. Until it becomes excruciating. Such long, drawn-out lovemaking, Elena. It leaves you tingling, it leaves you wanting more.'

After a while she added, 'We talked about you. She wanted to know about your love life. I told her you were obsessed with Pierre.'

'What did she say?'

'She said she had never known Pierre to be anything but the lover of women like the prostitute Bijou.'

'Pierre loved Bijou?'

'Oh, for a few days.'

The image of Pierre making love to the celebrated Bijou effaced the image of Leila making love to Kay. It was a day of jealousies. Was love to become one long train of jealousies?

Every day Kay brought new details. Elena could not refuse to hear them. All through them, she hated Kay's femininity and she loved Leila's masculinity. She divined Leila's struggle to be fulfilled and her defeat. She saw Leila donning her man's silk shirt and silver cuff links. She wanted to ask Kay what her underwear was like. She wanted to see Leila dressing.

It seemed to Elena that, just as the passive homosexual male became a caricature of a woman for the active male homosexual, women who submitted to dominant Lesbian love became a caricature of women's pettiest qualities. Kay was showing this, exaggerating her whims – loving herself through Leila, really. Tormenting Leila, too, as she would not have dared torment a man. Feeling that the woman in Leila would be indulgent.

Elena was sure that Leila was suffering from the mediocrity of the women she could make love to. The relationship could never be magnificent enough, with its taint of infantilism. Kay would arrive, eating candy out of her pocket like a schoolgirl. She pouted. She hesitated at a restaurant before ordering, and then changed her order, to play the *cabotine*, the woman with irresistible caprices. Soon Elena began to elude her. She began to understand the tragedy behind all Leila's affairs. Leila had acquired a new sex by growing beyond man and woman. She thought of Leila as a mythic figure, enlarged, magnified. Leila haunted her.

Led by an obscure intuition, she decided to go to an English tearoom above a book shop on the Rue de Rivoli, where homosexuals and Lesbians liked to congregate. They sat in separate groups. Solitary middle-aged men looked for young boys; mature Lesbians were seeking young women. The light was dim, the tea fragrant, the cake properly decadent.

As Elena entered she saw Miguel and Donald sitting together and joined them. Donald was intent upon his whore role. He liked to show Miguel how he could attract men, how he could easily be paid for his favors. He was excited because a gray-haired Englishman of great distinction, a man who was known to pay sumptuously for his pleasures, stared at him. Donald spread his charms before him, giving oblique glances like the glances of a woman behind a veil. Miguel was half-angry. He said, 'If you only knew what this man requires of his boys, you would stop flirting with him.'

'What?' asked Donald, with a morbid curiosity.

'Do you really want me to tell you?'

'Yes. I want to know.'

'He only wants boys to lie under him while he crouches over their faces, and covers their face with – you can guess what.'

Donald made a grimace and looked at the gray-haired man.

He could hardly believe this, seeing the man's aristocratic bearing, the fineness of his features. Seeing how delicately he held his cigarette holder, the dreamy and romantic expression of his eyes. How could this man actually perform such an act? This ended Donald's provoking coquetries.

Then Leila came in, saw Elena and came to their table. She knew Miguel and Donald. She loved Donald's peacock travesties – the spreading of imaginary colors, plumes one did not possess; without the colored hair, colored eyelashes, colored nails, that women had. She laughed with Donald, admired Miguel's grace, then turned to Elena and plunged her dark eyes into Elena's very green ones.

'How is Pierre? Why don't you bring him to the studio some time? I go there every evening before I sing. You never have come to hear me sing. I am at the nightclub every night about eleven.'

Later she offered: 'Will you let me drive you where you are going?'

They left together and got into the back seat of Leila's black limousine. Leila leaned over Elena and covered her mouth with her own full lips in one interminable kiss in which Elena nearly lost consciousness. Their hats fell off as they threw their heads back against the seats. Leila engulfed her. Elena's mouth fell on Leila's throat, in the slit of her black dress, which was open between the breasts. She only had to push the silk away with her mouth to feel the beginning of the breasts.

'Are you going to elude me again?' asked Leila.

Elena pressed her fingers against the silk-covered hips, feeling the richness of the hips, the fullness of the thighs, caressing her. The tantalizing smoothness of the skin and the silk of the dress melted into one another. She felt the little prominence of the garter. She wanted to push open Leila's knees, right there. Leila gave an order to the chauffeur Elena did not hear. The car changed direction. 'This is an abduction,' said Leila, laughing deeply.

Hatless, hair flying, they entered her darkened apartment, where the blinds were drawn against the summer heat. Leila led Elena by the hand to her bedroom and they fell on the luxuriant bed together. Silk again, silk under the fingers, silk between the legs, silky shoulders, neck, hair. Lips of silk trembling under the fingers. It was like the night at the opium den; the caresses lengthened, the suspense was preciously sustained. Each time they approached the orgasm, either Leila or Elena, observing the quickening of the motion, took up the kissing again – a bath of lovemaking, such as one might have in an endless dream, the moisture creating little sounds of rain between the kisses. Leila's finger was firm, commanding, like a penis; her tongue, far-reaching, knowing so many nooks where it stirred the nerves.

Instead of having one sexual core, Elena's body seemed to have a million sexual openings, equally sensitized, every cell of the skin magnified with the sensibility of a mouth. The very flesh of her arm suddenly opened and contracted with the passage of Leila's tongue or fingers. She moaned, and Leila bit into the flesh, as if to arouse a greater moan. Her tongue between Elena's legs was like a stabbing, agile and sharp. When the orgasm came, it was so vibrant that it shook their bodies from head to foot.

Elena dreamed of Pierre and Bijou. The full-fleshed Bijou, the whore, the animal, the lioness; a luxuriant goddess of abundance, her flesh a bed of sensuality – every pore and curve of her. In the dream her hands were grasping, her flesh throbbed in a mountainous, heaving way, fermenting, saturated with moisture, folded into many voluptuous layers. Bijou was always prone, inert, awakening only for the moment of love. All the fluids of desire seeping along the silver shadows of her legs, around the violin-shaped hips, descending and ascending with a sound of wet silk around the hollows of her breasts.

Elena imagined her everywhere, in the tight skirt of the street-walker, always preying and waiting. Pierre had loved her obscene walk, her naïve glance, her drunken sullenness, her virginal voice. For a few nights he had loved that walking sex, that ambulant womb, open to all.

And now perhaps he loved her again.

Pierre showed Elena a photograph of his mother, the luxuriant mother. The resemblance to Bijou was startling in all but the eyes. Bijou's were circled with mauve. Pierre's mother had a healthier air. But the body –

Then Elena thought, I am lost. She did not believe Pierre's story that Bijou repulsed him now. She began to frequent the café where Bijou and Pierre had met, hoping for a discovery that would end her doubts. She discovered nothing, except that Bijou liked very young men, fresh-faced, fresh-lipped, fresh-blooded. That calmed her a little.

While Elena sought to meet Bijou and unmask the enemy, Leila was seeking to meet Elena, with ruses.

And the three women met, driven inside of the same café on a day of heavy rain: Leila, perfumed and dashing, carrying her head high, a silver fox stole undulating around her shoulders over her trim black suit; Elena, in a wine-colored velvet; and Bijou, in her streetwalker's costume, which she could never abandon, the tight-fitting black dress and high-heeled shoes. Leila smiled at Bijou, then recognized Elena. Shivering, the three sat down before apéritifs. What Elena had not expected was to be completely intoxicated with Bijou's voluptuous charm. On her right sat Leila, incisive, brilliant, and on her left, Bijou, like a bed of sensuality Elena wanted to fall into.

Leila observed her and suffered. Then she set about courting Bijou, which she could do so much better than Elena. Bijou had never known women like Leila, only the women who worked with her, who, when the men were not there, indulged with Bijou in orgies of kisses, to compensate for the brutality of the men – sitting and kissing themselves into a hypnotic state, that was all.

She was susceptible to Leila's subtle flattery, but at the same time she was spellbound with Elena. Elena was a complete novelty for her. Elena represented to men a type of woman who was the opposite of the whore, a woman who poetized and dramatized love, mixed it with emotion, a woman who seemed made of another substance, a woman one imagined created by a legend. Yes, Bijou knew men well enough to know this was also a woman they were incited to initiate to sensuality, whom they enjoyed seeing become enslaved by sensuality. The more legendary the woman, the greater the pleasure in desecrating, eroticizing her. Deep down, she was, under all the dreaminess, another courtesan, living also for the pleasure of man.

Bijou, who was the whore of whores, would have liked to exchange places with Elena. Whores always envy women who have the faculty of arousing desire and illusion as well as hunger. Bijou, the sex organ walking undisguised, would have liked to have the appearance of Elena. And Elena was thinking how she would have liked to change places with Bijou, for the many times when men grew tired of courting and wanted sex without it, bestial and direct. Elena pined to be raped anew each day, without regard for her feelings; Bijou pined to be idealized. Leila alone was satisfied to be born free of man's tyranny, to be free of man. But she did not realize that imitating man was not being free of him.

She paid her court suavely, flatteringly, to the whore of whores. As none of the three women abdicated, they finally walked out together. Leila invited Elena and Bijou to her apartment.

When they arrived, it was scented with burning incense. The only light came from illuminated glass globes filled with water and iridescent fish, corals and glass sea horses. This gave the room an undersea aspect, the appearance of a dream, a place where three diversely beautiful women exhaled such sensual auras that a man would have been overcome.

Bijou was afraid to move. Everything looked so fragile to her. She sat cross-legged like an Arab woman, smoking. Elena seemed to radiate light like the glass globes. Her eyes shone brilliant and feverish in the semidarkness. Leila emitted a mysterious charm for both women, an atmosphere of the unknown.

The three of them sat on the very low couch, on a heaving sea of pillows. The first one to move was Leila, who slid her jeweled hand under Bijou's skirts and gasped slightly with surprise at the unexpected touch of flesh where she had expected to find silky underwear. Bijou lay back and turned her mouth toward Elena, her strength tempted by the fragility of Elena, knowing for the first time what it was to feel like a man and to feel a woman's slightness bending under the weight of a mouth, the small head bent back by her heavy hands, the light hair flying about. Bijou's strong hands encircled the dainty neck with delight. She held the head like a cup between her hands to drink from the mouth long draughts of nectar breath, her tongue undulating.

Leila had a moment of jealousy. Each caress she gave to Bijou, Bijou transmitted to Elena – the very same caress. After Leila kissed Bijou's luxuriant mouth, Bijou took Elena's lips between hers. When Leila's hand slipped further under Bijou's dress, Bijou slid her hand under Elena's. Elena did not move, filling herself with languor. Then Leila slid to her knees and used both hands to stroke Bijou. When she pushed up Bijou's dress, Bijou threw her body back and closed her eyes to better feel the movements of the warm, incisive hands. Elena, seeing Bijou offered, dared to touch her voluptuous body and follow every contour of the rich curves – a bed of down, soft, firm flesh without bones, smelling of sandalwood and musk. Her own nipples hardened as she touched Bijou's breasts. When her hand passed around Bijou's buttocks, it met Leila's hand.

Then Leila began to undress, exposing a soft little black satin corselet, which held her stockings with tiny black garters. Her thighs, slender and white, gleamed, her sex lay in shadow. Elena loosened the garters to watch the polished legs emerging. Bijou threw her dress over her head and then leaned forward to finish pulling it off, exposing as she did so the fullness of her buttocks, the dimples at the bottom of the spine, the incurving back. Then Elena slid out of her dress. She was wearing black lace underwear that was slit open back and front, showing only the shadowy folds of her sexual secrets.

Under their feet was a big white fur. They fell on this, the three bodies in accord, moving against each other to feel breast against breast and belly against belly. They ceased to be three bodies. They became all mouths and fingers and tongues and senses. Their mouths sought another mouth, a nipple, a clitoris. They lay entangled, moving very slowly. They kissed until the kissing became a torture and the body grew restless. Their hands always found yielding flesh, an opening. The fur they lay on gave off an animal odor, which mingled with the odors of sex.

Elena sought the fuller body of Bijou. Leila was more aggressive. She had Bijou lying on her side, with one leg thrown over Leila's shoulder, and she was kissing Bijou between the legs. Now and then Bijou jerked backward, away from the stinging kisses and bites, the tongue that was as hard as a man's sex.

When she moved thus, her buttocks were thrown fully against Elena's face. With her hands Elena had been enjoying the shape of them, and now she inserted her finger into the tight little aperture. There she could feel every contraction caused by Leila's kisses, as if she were touching the wall against which Leila moved her tongue. Bijou, withdrawing from the tongue that searched her, moved into a finger which gave her joy. Her pleasure was expressed in melodious ripples of her voice, and now and then, like a savage being taunted, she bared her teeth and tried to bite the one who was tantalizing her.

When she was about to come and could no longer defend herself against her pleasure, Leila stopped kissing her, leaving Bijou halfway on the peak of an excruciating sensation, half-crazed. Elena had stopped at the same moment.

Uncontrollable now, like some magnificent maniac, Bijou threw herself over Elena's body, parted her legs, placed herself between them, glued her sex to Elena's, and moved, moved with desperation. Like a man now, she thumped against Elena, to feel the two sexes meeting, soldering. Then as she felt her pleasure coming she stopped herself, to prolong it, fell backward and opened her mouth to Leila's breast, to burning nipples that were seeking to be caressed.

Elena was now also in the frenzy before orgasm. She felt a hand under her, a hand she could rub against. She wanted to throw herself on this hand until it made her come, but she also wanted to prolong her pleasure. And she ceased moving. The hand pursued her. She stood up, and the hand again traveled toward her sex. Then she felt Bijou standing against her back, panting. She felt the pointed breasts, the brushing of Bijou's sexual hair against her buttocks. Bijou rubbed against her, and then slid up and down, slowly, knowing the friction would force Elena to turn so as to feel this on her breasts, sex and belly. Hands, hands everywhere at once. Leila's pointed nails buried in the softest part of Elena's shoulder, between her breast and underarm, hurting, a delicious pain, the tigress taking hold of her, mangling her.

Elena's body so burning hot that she feared one more touch would set off the explosion. Leila sensed this, and they separated.

All three of them fell on the couch. They ceased touching and looked at each other, admiring their disorder, and seeing the moisture glistening along their beautiful legs.

But they could not keep their hands away from each other, and now Elena and Leila together attacked Bijou, intent on drawing from her the ultimate sensation. Bijou was surrounded, enveloped, covered, licked, kissed, bitten, rolled again on the fur rug, tormented with a million hands and tongues. She was begging now to be satisfied, spread her legs, sought to satisfy herself by friction against the others' bodies. They would not let her. With tongues and fingers they pried into her, back and front, sometimes stopping to touch each other's tongue – Elena and Leila, mouth to mouth, tongues curled together, over Bijou's spread legs. Bijou raised herself to receive a kiss that would end her suspense. Elena and Leila, forgetting her, concentrated all their feelings in their tongues, flicking at each other. Bijou, impatient, madly aroused, began to stroke herself, then Leila and Elena pushed her hand away and fell upon her. Bijou's orgasm came like an exquisite torment. At each spasm she moved as if she were being stabbed. She almost cried to have it end.

Over her prone body, Elena and Leila took up their tongue-kissing again, hands drunkenly searching each other, penetrating everywhere, until Elena cried out. Leila's fingers had found her rhythm, and Elena clung to her, waiting for the pleasure to burst, while her own hands sought to give Leila the same pleasure. They tried to come in unison, but Elena came first, falling in a heap, detached from Leila's hand, struck down by the violence of her orgasm. Leila fell beside her, offering her sex to Elena's mouth. As Elena's pleasure grew fainter, rolling away, dying off, she gave Leila her tongue, flicking in the sex's mouth until Leila contracted and moaned. She bit into Leila's tender flesh. In the paroxysm of her pleasure, Leila did not feel the teeth buried there.

Elena now understood why some Spanish husbands refused to initiate their wives to all the possibilities of lovemaking – to avoid the risk of awakening in them an insatiable passion. Instead of being contented, calmed by Pierre's love, she had become more vulnerable. The more she desired Pierre, the greater her hunger for other loves. It seemed to her that she had little interest in the rooting of love, in its fixity. She wanted only the moment of passion from everyone.

She did not even want to see Leila again. She wanted to see the sculptor Jean because he was now in that state of fire that she loved. She wanted to be burnt. She thought to herself: I talk almost like a saint, to burn for love – for no mystic love, but for a ravaging sensual meeting. Pierre has awakened in me a woman I did not know, an insatiable woman.

Almost as if she had willed her desire to accomplish itself, she found Jean waiting at the door. He was, as usual, carrying some little offering in a package, which he held awkwardly. The way his body moved, the way his eyes trembled when she approached him, betrayed the strength of his desire. She was already possessed by his body, and he moved as if he were installed within her.

'You have never come to see me,' he said humbly. 'You have never seen my work.'

'Let's go now,' she answered, and with a light, dancing step, she walked at his side. They reached a curious, barren part of Paris, near one of the gates, a city of sheds turned into studios, side by side with workmen's homes. And there Jean lived with statues in place of furniture, massive statues. He himself was fluid, changeable, hypersensitive, and he had created a solidity and power with his trembling hands.

The sculptures were like monuments, five times life size, the women pregnant, the men indolent and sensual, with hands and feet like tree roots. One man and woman were so kneaded together that one could not detect the differences between their bodies. The contours were completely welded together. Bound by their genitals, they towered over Elena and Jean.

In the shadow of this statue, they moved toward each other, without a word, without a smile. Even their heads did not move. As they met, Jean pressed Elena against the statue. They did not kiss or touch each other with their hands. Only their torsos met, repeating in warm human flesh the welding of the bodies of the statue above them. He pressed his genitals against hers, with a low, entranced rhythm, as if he would thus enter her body.

He slid down, as if he were going to kneel at her feet, only to rise again, this time carrying her dress upward under his pressure, so that it ended in a swollen heap of material under her arms. And again he pressed against her, sometimes moving from left to right or right to left, sometimes in circles, sometimes pushing into her with compressed violence. She felt the bulk of his desire rubbing as if he were lighting a fire with two stones, drawing sparks each time he moved, and finally she slid downwards as if in a light-bodied dream. She fell in a heap, caught between his legs, and now he wanted to fix this position, to eternalize it, to nail down her body with the powerful thrust of his swollen virility. They moved again, she to offer the deepest recesses of her femininity, and he to bind them together. She contracted to feel his presence more, moving with a gasp of unbearable joy, as if she had touched the most vulnerable point of his being.

He closed his eyes to feel this elongation of his being into which all his blood had concentrated and which lay in the voluptuous darkness of her. He could no longer hold back and pushed out to invade her, to fill her womb to the brim with his blood, and as she received this, the little passageway where he moved closed tighter around him, swallowing the essences of his being within her.

The statue cast its shadow over their embrace, which did not dissolve. They lay as if turned to stone, feeling the very last drop of pleasure ebbing away. She was already thinking of Pierre. She knew she would not return to Jean. She thought: Tomorrow it would be less beautiful. She thought with an almost superstitious fear that if she stayed with Jean, then Pierre would sense the betrayal and punish her.

She expected to be punished. As she stood before Pierre's door she expected to find Bijou there on his bed, her legs wide apart. Why Bijou? Because Elena expected revenge for the betrayal of her love.

Her heart beat wildly as he opened the door. Pierre smiled innocently. But then, was not her smile innocent? To ascertain this, she looked at herself in the mirror. Had she expected the demon driving her to appear in her green eyes?

She observed the creases in her skirt, the specks of dust on her sandals. She felt that Pierre would know, if he made love to her, that it was Jean's essence which flowed together with her own moisture. She eluded his caresses and suggested they visit Balzac's house in Passy.

It was a soft rainy afternoon, with that gray Parisian melancholy that drove people indoors, that created an erotic atmosphere because it fell like a ceiling over the city, enclosing them all in a nerveless air, as in an alcove; and everywhere, some reminder of the erotic life – a shop, half-hidden, showing underwear and black garters and black boots; the Parisian woman's provocative walk; taxis carrying embracing lovers.

Balzac's house stood at the top of a hilly street in Passy, overlooking the Seine. First they had to ring at the door of an apartment house, then descend a flight of stairs that seemed to lead to a cellar but opened instead on a garden. Then they had to traverse the garden and ring at another door. This was the door of his house, concealed in the garden of the apartment house, a secret and mysterious house, so hidden and isolated in the heart of Paris.

The woman who opened the door was like a ghost from the past – faded face, faded hair and clothes, bloodless. Living with Balzac's manuscripts, pictures, engravings of the women he had loved, first editions, she was permeated with a vanished past, and all the blood had ebbed from her. Her very voice was distant, ghostly. She slept in this house filled with dead souvenirs. She had become equally dead to the present. It was as if each night she laid herself away in the tomb of Balzac, to sleep with him.

She guided them through the rooms, and then to the back of the house. She came to a trap door, slipped her long bony fingers through the ring and lifted it for Elena and Pierre to see. It opened on a little stairway.

This was the trap door Balzac had built so that the women who visited him could escape from the surveillance or suspicions of their husbands. He, too, used it to escape from his harassing creditors. The stairway led to a path and then to a gate that opened on an isolated street that in turn led to the Seine. One could escape before the person at the front door of the house had enough time to traverse the first room.

For Elena and Pierre, the effect of this trap door so evoked Balzac's love of life that it affected them like an aphrodisiac. Pierre whispered to her, 'I would like to take you on the floor, right here.'

The ghost woman did not hear these words, uttered with the directness of an apache, but she caught the glance which accompanied them. The mood of the visitors was not in harmony with the sacredness of the place, and she hurried them out.

The breath of death had whipped their senses. Pierre hailed a taxi. In the taxi he could not wait. He made Elena sit over him, with her back to him, the whole length of her body against his, concealing him completely. He raised her skirt.

Elena said, 'Not here, Pierre. Wait until we get home. People will see us. Please wait. Oh, Pierre, you're hurting me! Look, the policeman stared at us. And now we're stopped here, and people can see us from the sidewalk. Pierre, Pierre, stop it.'

But all the time that she feebly defended herself, and tried to slip off, she was conquered by pleasure. Her efforts to sit still made her even more keenly aware of Pierre's every movement. Now she feared that he might hurry his act, driven by the speed of the taxi and the fear that it would stop soon in front of the house and the taxi driver would turn his head toward them. And she wanted to enjoy Pierre, to reassert their bond, the harmony of their bodies. They were observed from the street. Yet she could not draw away, and he now had his arms around her. Then a violent jump of the taxi over a hole in the road threw them apart. It was too late to resume the embrace. The taxi had stopped. Pierre had just enough time to button himself. Elena felt they must look drunk, disheveled. The languor of her body made it difficult for her to move.

Pierre was filled with a perverse enjoyment of this interruption. He enjoyed feeling his bones half-melted in his body, the almost painful withdrawal of the blood. Elena shared his new whim, and later they lay on the bed caressing each other and talking. Then Elena told Pierre the story she had heard in the morning from a young French woman who sewed for her.

*

'Madeleine used to work for a big department store. She came from the poorest ragpicker's family in all Paris. Both her father and mother lived by picking garbage cans and selling the bits of tin, leather and paper they found. Madeleine was placed in the sumptuous bedroom furniture department, under the supervision of a suave, waxed, starched floorwalker. She had never slept on a bed, only on a pile of rags and newspapers in a shack. When people were not looking she felt the satin bedspreads, the mattresses, the feather pillows, as if they were ermine or chinchilla. She had a natural Parisian gift for appearing charmingly dressed on the money other women spent on stockings alone. She was attractive, with humorous eyes, curly black hair and well-rounded curves. She developed two passions, one to steal a few drops of perfume or cologne from the perfume department, another to wait until the store was closing so she could lie down on one of the softest beds and pretend she was to sleep there. She preferred the canopied ones. She felt more secure lying under the curtains. The floorwalker was usually in such a hurry to leave that she was left alone for a few minutes to indulge in this fantasy. She thought that while lying in such a bed her feminine charms were a million times enhanced, and she wished certain elegant men she had seen on the Champs Elysées could see her there and realize how well she would look in a beautiful bedroom.

'Her fantasy became more complex. She arranged to have a mirrored dressing table placed in front of the bed so she could admire herself lying down. Then one day when she had accomplished every step of the ceremony, she saw that the floorwalker had been watching her with amazement. As she was about to leap off the bed he stopped her.

'"Madame," he said (she had always been called Mademoiselle), "I am delighted to make your acquaintance. I hope you are pleased with the bed I made for you, according to your orders. Do you find it soft enough? Do you think Monsieur le Comte will like it?"

'"Monsieur le Comte is fortunately away for a week, and I will be able to enjoy my bed with someone else," she answered. Then she sat up and offered her hand to the man. "Now kiss it as you would kiss a lady's hand in a salon." Smiling, he did this with suave elegance. Then they heard a sound and they both vanished in different directions.

'Every day they stole five or ten minutes from the closing-hour rush. Pretending to put things in order, to dust, to rectify errors on the price tags, they planned the little scene. He added the most effective touch of all – a screen. Then lace-edged sheets from another department. Then he made up the bed and turned down the coverlet. After kissing her hands, they conversed. He called her Nana. As she did not know the book, he gave it to her. What concerned him now was the incongruous effect of her tight little black dress on the pastel bedspread. He would borrow a filmy negligée worn by a mannequin during the day and cover Madeleine with it. Even if salesmen or saleswomen passed by, they did not see the scene behind the screen.

'When Madeleine had enjoyed the hand-kissing, he deposited a kiss further up along her arm, in the nook within the elbow. There the skin was sensitive, and when she folded her arm, it seemed as if the kiss were enclosed and nurtured. Madeleine let it lie there like a preserved flower and then later, when she was alone, she opened her arm and kissed the same place as if to devour it more intimately. This kiss, deposited with such delicacy, was more potent than all the gross pinchings she had received in the street as tributes to her charms or the whispered obscenities of the workmen: *Viens que je te suce.*

'At first he sat at the foot of the bed, then he stretched himself alongside her to smoke a cigarette with all the ceremony of an opium dreamer. Alarming footsteps on the other side of the screen gave to their meeting the secrecy and dangers of a lovers' rendezvous. Then Madeleine would say, "I wish we could escape from the jealous surveillance of the Count. He is getting on my nerves." But her admirer was too wise to say, "Come with me to some humble little hotel." He knew this could not take place in some dingy room, in a brass bed with torn blankets and gray sheets. He placed a kiss in the warmest nook of her neck, under the curling hair, then on the tip of her ear, where Madeleine could not taste it later, where she could merely touch it with her fingers. Her ear burned all day after this kiss because he had begun to bite it.

'As soon as Madeleine lay down she was taken with languor,

which may have been due to her conception of aristocratic behavior, or to the kisses which now fell like necklaces around her throat and further down where the breasts began. She was no virgin, but the brutality of the attacks she had known, pushed against a wall in dark streets, thrown to the floor of a truck, or tumbled behind the ragpicker's shacks where people coupled without even troubling to see each other's faces, had never stirred her as much as this gradual and ceremonious courtship of her senses. He made love to her legs for three or four days. Made her wear furry bedroom slippers, slipped off her stockings and kissed her feet and held them as if he were possessing her whole body. By the time he was ready to lift her skirt he had inflamed the rest of her body so completely that she was ripe for the final possession.

'As the time was short and they were always expected to leave the shop with the others, he had to forgo the caresses when it came to taking her. And now she did not know which she liked best. If his caresses were too lingering he did not have time to take her. If he proceeded directly, she felt less enjoyment. Behind the screen now took place scenes enacted in the most lavish bedrooms, only more hurried, and each time the mannequin had to be dressed again, the bed straightened. Yet they never met outside of this moment. This was their dream for the day. He had contempt for the shabby adventures of his comrades in five-franc hotels. He acted as if he had visited the most courted prostitute in Paris, and was the *amant de coeur* of a woman kept by the richest men.'

'Was the dream ever destroyed?' Pierre asked.

'Yes. Do you remember the sit-down strike of the big department stores? The employees stayed in them for two weeks. During that time other couples discovered the softness of the best-quality beds, of the divans and couches and *chaises-longues*, and they discovered the variations that can be added to love positions when the beds are wide and low and rich materials tickle the skin. Madeleine's dream became public property and a vulgar caricature of the pleasures she had known. The uniqueness of her meeting with her lover came to an end. He called her Mademoiselle again, and she called him Monsieur. He even began to find fault with her salesmanship and she finally left the store.'

*

Elena took an old house in the country for the summer months, a house which needed painting. Miguel had promised to help her. They began in the attic, which was picturesque and complex, a series of small irregular rooms, rooms within rooms at times, added as afterthoughts.

Donald was there, too, but not interested in painting, he went off to explore the vast garden and the village and the forest surrounding the house. Elena and Miguel worked alone, covering themselves as well as the old walls with paint. Miguel held his brush as if he were painting a portrait, and stood off to survey his progress. Working together took them back into the moods of their youth.

To shock her, Miguel talked about his 'collection of asses', pretending that it was this particular aspect of beauty which held him enthralled, because Donald possessed it to the highest degree – the art of finding an ass that was not too globular, like most women's, not too flat, like most men's, but something between the two, something worth gripping.

Elena was laughing. She was thinking that when Pierre turned his back to her, he became like a woman for her, and she would have liked to rape him. She could well imagine Miguel's feelings when he lay against Donald's back.

'If the ass is sufficiently rounded, firm, and if the boy has not got an erection,' said Elena, 'then there is not so much difference from a woman. Do you still feel around for the difference?'

'Yes, of course. Think how distressing it would be to discover nothing there, and also to find too much of the mammary protrusions further up – breasts for milk, a thing to paralyze one's sexual appetite.'

'Some women have very small milk holders,' said Elena.

It was her turn to stand on the ladder to reach a cornice and the slanting corner of the roof. Raising her arm she brought her skirts up with her. She wore no stockings. Her legs were smooth and slender, without 'globular exaggerations', as Miguel said, paying her compliments now that their relationship was secure from any sexual hopes on her side.

Elena's desire to seduce a homosexual was a common error among women. Usually there was a point of female honor in this, a desire to test one's power against heavy odds, a feeling, perhaps, that all men were escaping from their rule and that they must be seduced again. Miguel suffered from these attempts every day. He was not effeminate. He held himself well, his gestures were manly. As soon as a woman began to display coquetry toward him, he was in a panic. He immediately foresaw the entire drama: the aggression of the woman, her interpretation of his passivity as mere timidity, her advances, his hatred of the moment when he would have to reject her. He could never do this with calm indifference. He was too tender and compassionate. He suffered at times more than the woman, whose vanity was all that mattered. He had such a familial relationship with women that he always felt as if he were wounding a mother, a sister, or Elena again, in her new transformations.

By now he knew what harm he had done to Elena in being the first one to instill in her a doubt of her ability to love or to be loved. Each time he brushed off an advance from a woman, he thought he was committing a minor crime, murdering a faith and confidence for good.

How nice it was to be with Elena, enjoying her feminine endowments without danger. Pierre was taking care of the sensual Elena. At the same time, how jealous Miguel was of Pierre just as he had been of his father when he was a child. His mother always sent him out of the room as soon as his father entered. The father was impatient for him to leave. He hated the way they locked themselves together for hours. As soon as his father left, his mother's love, embraces, kisses, returned to him.

When Elena said, 'I am going to see Pierre,' it was the same. Nothing could hold her back. No matter how much pleasure they had together, no matter how much tenderness she showered on Miguel, when it was time to be with Pierre, nothing could hold her back.

The mystery of Elena's masculinity charmed him, too. Whenever he was with her, he felt this vital, active, positive action of her nature. In her presence, he was galvanized from his laziness, his vagueness, his procrastinations. She was the catalyst.

He looked at her legs. Diana's legs, Diana the huntress, the boy-woman. Legs for running and leaping. He was taken with an overpowering curiosity to see the rest of her body. He moved nearer to the ladder. The stylized legs disappeared into the lace-edged panties. He wanted to see further.

She looked down at him and saw him standing and looking at her with dilated eyes.

'Elena, I would just like to see how you are made.'

She smiled at him.

'Will you let me look at you?'

'You are looking at me.'

He lifted the edge of her skirt outward and it opened like a summer umbrella over him, concealing his head from her. She began to step down the ladder but his hands stopped her. His hands had gripped the elastic belt of the panties and stretched them to slip them down. She remained midway on the ladder, one leg higher than the other, which prevented him from slipping the panties all the way down. He pulled the leg down toward him, so that he could slip off the panties altogether. His hands cupped her ass lovingly. Like a sculptor, he ascertained the exact contours of what he held, feeling the firmness, the roundness, as if it were merely a fragment of a statue he had unearthed, from which the rest of the body was missing. He disregarded the surrounding flesh, and curves. He caressed only the ass, and gradually brought it down nearer to his face, keeping Elena from turning around as she descended the ladder.

She abandoned herself to his whim, thinking it was to be an orgy of the eyes and hands only. When she reached the bottom rung, he had one hand on each round promontory and was kneading them as if they were breasts, bringing the caress back to where it had begun, hypnotically.

Now Elena faced him, leaning against the ladder. She sensed that he was trying to take her. At first he touched where the opening was too small for him and where it hurt her. She cried out. Then he moved forward and found the real female opening, found he could slip in this way, and she was amazed to find him so strong, remaining inside of her and moving about. But although he moved vigorously, he did not accelerate his movements to reach a climax. Was he becoming more and more aware that he was inside of a woman and not a boy? Slowly he withdrew, left her thus half-taken, hid his face away from her so that she would not see his disillusion.

She kissed him, to prove to him that this did not cloud their relationship, that she understood.

Sometimes in the street or in a café, Elena was hypnotized by the *souteneur* face of a man, by a big workman with knee-deep boots, by a brutal, criminal head. She felt a sensual tremor of fear, an obscure attraction. The female in her was fascinated. For a second she felt as if she were a whore who expected a stab in the back for some infidelity. She felt anxiety. She was trapped. She forgot that she was free. A dark fungus layer was awakened, a subterranean primitivism, a desire to feel the brutality of man, the force which could break her open and sack her. To be violated was a need of woman, a secret, erotic desire. She had to shake herself from the domination of these images.

She remembered that what she had first loved in Pierre was the dangerous light in his eyes, the eyes of a man who was without guilt and scruples, who took what he wanted, enjoyed, who was unconscious of risks and consequences.

What had become of this unruly, self-willed savage she had met on that mountain road one dazzling morning? He was now domesticated. He lived for lovemaking. Elena smiled at this. That was a quality one rarely found in a man. But he was still a man of nature. At times she said to him, 'Where is your horse? You always look as if you had left your horse at the door and were soon to start on a gallop again.'

He slept naked. He hated pyjamas, kimonos, bedroom slippers. He threw his cigarettes on the floor. He washed in ice-cold water like a pioneer. He laughed at comfort. He chose the hardest chair. Once, his body was so hot and dusty and the water he used so ice-cold, that evaporation took place and smoke issued from his pores. He held his steaming hands toward her, and she said, 'You are the god of fire.'

He could not submit to time. He did not know how much could or could not be done in an hour. Half of his being was forever asleep, coiled in the maternal love she gave him, coiled in reverie, in laziness, talking about the voyages he was going to make, the books he was going to write.

He was pure, too, at strange moments. He had the reserve of the cat. Although he slept naked, he would not walk about naked.

Pierre touched all the regions of understanding with intuition. But he did not live there, he did not sleep and eat in those superior regions as she did. Often he quarreled, warred, drank, with a company of ordinary friends, spent evenings with ignorant people. She could not do this. She liked the exceptional, the extraordinary. This separated them. She would have liked to be like him, near to everyone, anyone, but she could not. It saddened her. Often, when they went out together, she left him.

Their first serious quarrel was about time. Pierre would tele-phone and say, 'Come to my apartment about eight.' She had her own key. She would go in and pick up a book. He would arrive at nine. Or he would call her when she was already there waiting and say, 'I will be right over,' and come two hours later. One evening when she had waited too long a time (and the waiting was all the more painful because she imagined him making love to someone else), he arrived and found her gone. Then it was his turn to rage. But it did not change his habits. Another time she locked him out. She stood behind the door listening to him. She was already hoping he would not go away. She deeply regretted their night being spoiled. But she waited. He rang the bell again, so gently. If he had rung the bell angrily she might have remained unmoved, but he rang gently and guiltily, and she opened the door. She was still angry. He desired her. She resisted him. He was stirred by her resistance. And she was saddened by the spectacle of his desire.

She had a feeling that Pierre sought this scene. The more aroused he became, the greater her aloofness. She closed herself sexually. But honey seeped through the closed lips, and Pierre was in ecstacy. He became more passionate, forcing her knees open with his strong legs, pouring himself into her with impetus, coming with tremendous intensity.

Whereas at other times if she had not felt pleasure she would have feined it so as not to hurt him, this time she deliberately made no pretense. When Pierre's passion was satisfied he asked her, 'Did you come?' 'No,' she said. And he was hurt. He felt the full cruelty of her holding back. He said, 'I love you more than you love me.' Yet he knew how much she loved him, and he was baffled.

Afterwards she lay with her eyes wide open, thinking that his lateness was innocent. He had already fallen asleep like a child, with his fists closed, his hair in her mouth. He was still asleep when she left. In the street, such a wave of tenderness washed over her that she had to return to the apartment. She threw herself over him, saying, 'I had to come back, I had to come back.'

'I wanted you to come back,' he said. He touched her. She was so wet, so wet. Sliding in and out of her he said, 'I like to see how I hurt you there, how I stab you there, in the little wound.' Then he pounded into her, to draw from her the spasm she had withheld.

When she left him she was joyous. Could love become a fire that did not burn, like the fire of the Hindu religious men; was she learning to walk magically over hot coals?

The Basque and Bijou

It was a rainy night, the streets like mirrors, reflecting everything. The Basque had thirty francs in his pocket and he was feeling rich. People were telling him that in his naïve, crude way he was a great painter. They did not realize he copied from postcards. They had given him thirty francs for the last painting. He was in a euphoric mood and wanted to celebrate. He was looking for one of those little red lights that spelled pleasure.

A maternal woman opened the door, but a maternal woman whose cold eyes traveled almost immediately to the man's shoes, for she judged from them how much he could afford to pay for his pleasure. Then for her own satisfaction, her eyes rested for a while on the trouser buttons. Faces did not interest her. Her life was spent exclusively in dealings with this region of man's anatomy. Her big eyes, still bright, had a piercing way of looking into the trousers as if they could gauge the size and weight of the man's possessions. It was a professional look. She liked to pair people off with more acumen than other mothers of prostitution. She would suggest certain conjunctions. She was as expert as a glove fitter. Even through the trousers, she could measure the client, and set about getting him the perfect glove, a neat fit. It gave no pleasure if there was too much room, and no pleasure if the glove was too tight. Maman thought people today did not know enough about the importance of a fit. She would have liked to spread this knowledge she possessed, but men and women were growing more careless, they were less exacting than she. If a man today found himself floating in too large a glove, moving about as in an empty apartment, he made the best of it. He let his member flap around like a flag and come out without the real clutching embrace which warmed his entrails. Or he slipped it in with saliva, pushing as if he were trying to slip under a closed door, pinched in the narrow surroundings and shrinking even more just to stay there. And if the girl happened to laugh heartily with pleasure or with the pretense of pleasure, he was immediately ousted, for there was no expansion allowed for the swelling of laughter. People were losing their knowledge of good conjunctions.

It was only after Maman had stared at the Basque's trousers that she recognized him and smiled. The Basque, it is true, shared this passion for nuances with Maman, and she knew he was not easily satisfied. He had a capricious member. Faced with a letter-box vagina, it rebelled. Faced with an astringent tube, it withdrew. He was a connoisseur, a gourmet, of women's jewel boxes. He liked them velvet-lined and cozy, affectionate and clinging. Maman gave him a more lingering look than she gave other customers. She liked the Basque, and it was not for his short-nosed, classical profile, his almond-shaped eyes, his glossy black hair, his gliding smooth walk, his nonchalant gestures. It was not for his red scarf and his cap sitting at a roguish angle on his head. It was not for his seductive ways with women. It was for his royal *pendentif*, the noble bulk of it, the sensitive and untiring responsiveness of it, its friendliness, its cordiality, its expansiveness. She had never seen such a one. He would lay it on the table sometimes as if he were depositing a bag of money, rap with it as if calling for attention. He took it out naturally, as other men take off their coats when they are warm. He gave the impression that it was not at ease shut in, confined, that it was to be aired, to be admired.

Maman indulged herself continuously in her habit of looking at men's possessions. When men came out of the *urinoirs*, finishing their buttoning, she had the luck to catch the last flash of some golden member, or some dark-brown one, or some fine-pointed one, which she preferred. On the boulevards she was often rewarded with the sight of carelessly buttoned trousers, and her eyes, which were gifted with keen vision, could penetrate the shaded opening. Better still if she caught a tramp unburdening himself against a tenement wall, holding his member pensively in his hand, as though it were his very last silver piece.

One might think that Maman was deprived of the more intimate possession of such pleasure, but it was not so. The clients of her house found her appetizing, and they knew her virtues and advantages over the other women. Maman could produce a truly delectable juice for the feasts of love, which most of the women had to manufacture artificially. Maman could give a man the full illusion of a tender meal, something very soft under the teeth and wet enough to satisfy anyone's thirst.

Among themselves they often talked about the delicate sauces in which Maman knew how to wrap her shell-pink morsels, the drumlike tightness of her offerings. One could trap this round shell, once, twice, it was enough. Maman's delectable flavoring would appear, something her girls could rarely produce, a honey that smelled of seashell and that made the passage into the female alcove between her thighs a delight to the male visitor.

The Basque liked it there. It was emollient, saturating, warm and grateful – a feast. For Maman it was a holiday, and she gave her maximum.

The Basque knew she did not need long preparation. All day Maman had nourished herself with the expeditions of her eyes, which never traveled above or below the middle of a man's body. They were always on a level with the trouser opening. She appraised the wrinkled ones, too hastily closed after a quick séance. The finely pressed ones, not yet crushed. The stains, oh, the stains of love! Strange stains, which she could detect as if she carried a magnifying glass. There, where the trousers had not been pulled down sufficiently, or where, in its gesticulations, a penis had returned to its natural place at the wrong moment, there lay a jeweled stain, for it had tiny glittering specks in it, like some mineral that had melted; and a sugary quality which stiffened the clothes. A beautiful stain, the stain of desire, either sprayed there like a perfume by the fountain of a man, or glued there by too fervent and clinging a woman. Maman would have liked to begin where an act had already taken place. She was sensitive to contagion. This little stain stirred her between the legs as she walked. A fallen button made her feel the man at her mercy. At times, in great crowds, she had the courage to reach out and touch. Her hand moved like a thief's, with an incredible agility. She never fumbled or touched the wrong place, but went straight to the place below the belt where soft rolling prominences lay, and sometimes, unexpectedly, an insolent baton.

In subways, on dark rainy nights, on crowded boulevards or in dance halls, Maman delighted in appraising and calling to arms. How many times her call was answered and arms were extended to her passing hand! She would have liked an army standing aligned like this, presenting the only arms that could conquer her. In her daydreams she saw this army. She was the general, marching by, decorating the long ones, the beautiful ones, pausing before each man she admired. Oh, to be Catherine the Great and reward the spectacle with a kiss from her avid mouth, a kiss, just on the tip, merely to draw that first tear of pleasure!

Maman's greatest adventure had been the parade of the Scots soldiers one spring morning. While drinking at a bar, she had heard a conversation about the Scotsmen.

A man said, 'They take them young and train them to walk that way. It's a special walk. Difficult, very difficult. There is a *coup de fesse*, a swing which makes the hips and the sporran swing just right. If the sporran does not swing, it's a failure. The step is more intricate than a ballet dancer's.'

Maman was thinking: Each time the sporran swings, and the skirt swings, why, the other hangings must swing too. And her old heart was moved. Swing. Swing. All at the same time. There was an ideal army. She would have liked to follow such an army, in any capacity. One, two, three. She was already moved enough by the swing of the pendants when the man at the bar added: 'And do you know, they wear nothing underneath.'

They wore nothing underneath! These sturdy men, such upright, lusty men! Heads high, strong naked legs and skirts – why, it made them as vulnerable as a woman. Big lusty men, tempting as a woman and naked underneath. Maman wanted to be turned into a cobblestone, to be stepped on, but to be allowed to look under the short skirt at the hidden 'sporran' swinging with each step. Maman felt congested. The bar was too hot. She needed air.

She watched for the parade. Each step taken by the Scotsmen was like a step taken into her very own body, she vibrated so. One, two, three. A dance over her abdomen, savage and even, the fur sporran swinging like pubic hair. Maman was as warm as a day in July. She could think of nothing else but of elbowing her way to the front of the crowd and then slipping on her knees and simulating a faint. But all she saw were vanishing legs under pleated plaid skirts. Later, lying against the policeman's knee, she rolled her eyes upward as if she were going to have an attack. If the parade would only turn and walk over her!

Thus Maman's sap never withered. It was properly nourished. At night her flesh was as tender as if it had been simmering slowly over a delicate fire all day.

Her eyes would pass from the clients to the women who worked for her. Their faces did not attract her attention either, but only their figures from the waist down. She made them turn before her, gave them a little slap to feel the firmness of the flesh, before they donned their chemises.

She knew Melie, who rolled herself around a man like a ribbon and gave him a feeling that several women were fondling him. She knew the lazy one, who pretended to be asleep and gave the timid men audacities no one else could, letting them touch her, manipulate her, explore her as if there were no danger in doing so. Her big body concealed her secrets well in rich folds, yet her laziness permitted them to be exposed by prying fingers.

Maman knew the slender, fiery one who attacked men and made them feel victims of circumstance. She was a great favorite among the guilty men. They permitted themselves to be raped. Their conscience was at ease. They could have said to their wives: She threw herself on me and forced herself on me, and the like. They would lie back and she would sit on them, as upon a horse, spurring them to inevitable gestures by her pressure and galloping over the rigid virility, or trotting softly, or taking long strides. She pressed powerful knees against the flanks of her subdued victims, and like a noble rider, raised herself elegantly and fell back, with all her weight concentrated on the middle of the body, while her hand occasionally slapped the man to increase his speed and his convulsions, so that she could feel a greater animal vigor between her legs. How she rode this animal under her, with spurring legs and great pushes from her raised body until the animal began to foam, and then incited him more with cries and slaps, to gallop faster and faster.

Maman knew the smoldering charms of Viviane from the south. Her flesh was of hot embers, contagious, and even the coolest flesh would warm at her touch. She knew suspense, leisure. She liked first of all to sit on the bidet for the ceremony of washing herself. Legs spread over the little seat, she had bulging buttocks, two enormous dimples at the base of her spine, two golden-brown hips, wide and firm like the back of a circus horse. As she sat, the curves were swollen. If the man tired of seeing her from the back, he could face her and watch her throw water over her pubic hair and between her legs, watch her carefully spread the lips as she soaped. White foam covered her now, then water again, and the lips emerged glistening pink. At times she examined the lips calmly. If too many men had passed by that day, she saw that they were slightly swollen. The Basque liked to watch her then. She dried herself more gently so as not to increase the irritation.

The Basque came on such a day and divined he could benefit from the irritation. Other days Viviane was lethargic, heavy and indifferent. She laid her body down as in some classical painting, in such a manner as to accentuate the tremendous rise and fall of her curves. She lay on her side with her head resting on her arm, her flesh, of copper-colored tones, distended at times as if it were laboring under the erotic swelling of a caress from some invisible hand. Thus she offered herself, sumptuous and almost impossible to arouse. Most men did not try. She turned her mouth away from them with contempt, offering her body all the more, but with detachment. They could stretch open her legs and stare as long as they wanted. They could not draw any sap from her. But once a man was inside of her, she behaved as if he were pouring hot lava into her, and her contortions were more violent than those of women taking pleasure because they were dramatized to simulate the real. She twisted herself like a python, jerked herself in all directions as if she were being burnt or beaten. Powerful muscles gave to her motions a strength which stirred the most bestial desires. Men fought to arrest the contortions, to calm the orgiastic dance she did around them, as if she were pinned to something that was torturing her. Then suddenly, at her own caprice, she would lie still. And this, perversely in the middle of their rising fury, cooled them so that the fulfillment was delayed. She became a mass of quiet flesh. She took to gentle sucking then, as if she were sucking a thumb before falling asleep. Then her lethargy irritated them. They sought to arouse her again, touching her everywhere, kissing her. She submitted, unmoved.

The Basque bided his time. He watched Viviane's ceremonious ablutions. Today she was swollen from many assaults. No matter how small a sum was placed for her on the table, she had never been known to stop a man from satisfying himself.

The big, rich lips, too much rubbed, were slightly distended, and a slight fever burned her. The Basque was very gentle. He deposited his little gift on the table. He undressed. He promised her a balm, a cotton, a veritable padding. These delicacies put her off her guard. The Basque handled her as if he were a woman. Only a little touch there, to smooth, to quieten the fever. Her skin was as dark as a gypsy's, very smooth and clean, and even powdered. His fingers were sensitive. He touched her only by accident, brushing by, and laid his sex on her belly like a toy, merely for her to admire. It answered when spoken to. Her belly vibrated to its weight, heaving slightly to feel it there. As he showed no impatience to move it where it would be sheltered, enclosed, she permitted herself the luxury of expanding, abandoning herself.

The gluttony of other men, their egotism, their eagerness to satisfy themselves without appreciation of her, made her hostile. But the Basque was gallant. He compared her skin to satin, her hair to moss, her odor to the scent of precious woods. Then he placed his sex at the opening and said tenderly, 'Does it hurt? I won't push it in if it hurts.'

Such delicacy moved Viviane. She said, 'It hurts just a little, but try.'

He advanced only half an inch at a time. 'Does it hurt?' He offered to take it out. Then Viviane had to press him: 'Just the tip. Try again.'

So the tip slipped in an inch or so, then rested. This gave Viviane plenty of time in which to feel its presence, time that other men did not give her. Between each tiny advance into her, she had leisure to feel how pleasant its presence was between the soft walls of flesh, how well it fitted, neither too tight nor too loose. Again he waited, then advanced a little more. Viviane had time to feel how good it was to be filled, how well suited the female crevice was to hold and to keep. The pleasure of having something to hold there, exchanging warmth, mingling the two moistures. He moved again. The suspense. The awareness of the emptiness when he withdrew – her flesh withered almost immediately. She closed her eyes. His gradual entrance threw radiations all around it, invisible currents warning the deeper regions of her womb that some explosion was coming, something made to fit in the soft-walled tunnel and to be devoured by its hungry depths, where restless nerves lay waiting. Her flesh yielded more and more. He entered further.

'Does it hurt?' He took it out. She was disappointed and did not want to confess how she withered inside without his expanding presence.

She was forced to beg, 'Slip it in again.' It was sweet. Then he placed it halfway in, where she could feel and yet not clutch at it, where she could not truly hold it. He acted as if he would leave it halfway there for good. She wanted to move toward it and engulf it but she restrained herself. She wanted to scream. The flesh he did not touch was burning at his nearness. At the back of the womb there lay flesh that demanded to be penetrated. It curved inwards, opened to suck. The flesh walls moved like sea anemones, seeking by suction to draw his sex in, but it was only near enough to send currents of excruciating pleasure. He moved again, watching her face. Then he saw her mouth open. She wanted to raise her body now, to take his sex in wholly, but she waited. By this slow teasing he had her on the edge of hysteria. She opened her mouth as if to reveal the openness of her womb, its hunger, and only then did he plunge to the very bottom and felt her contractions.

This is how the Basque found Bijou.

One day when he arrived at the house he was met by a melted Maman who told him that Viviane was busy. Then she offered to console him, almost as if he were a deceived husband. The Basque said that he would wait. Maman continued her teasing and caresses. Then the Basque said, 'May I look in?'

Every room was arranged so that amateurs could watch through a secret aperture. Now and then the Basque liked to see how Viviane behaved with her visitors. So Maman took him to the partition, where she hid him behind a curtain and let him look.

There were four people in the room: a foreign man and woman, dressed with discreet elegance, watching two women on the large bed. Viviane, the heavy, dark-skinned one, lay sprawled on the bed. On her hands and knees over her was a magnificent woman with ivory-colored skin, green eyes and long, thick, curly hair. Her breasts pointed high, her waist tapered to extreme slenderness and spread again for a rich display of hips. She was shaped as if she had been molded in a corset. Her body had a firm, marble smoothness. There was nothing flabby or loose in her, but a hidden strength, like the strength of a puma, an extravagance and vehemence in her gestures as in those of Spanish women. This was Bijou.

The two women were beautifully matched, without timorousness or sentimentality. Women of action, who both carried an ironic smile and a corrupt expression.

The Basque could not tell whether they were pretending or actually enjoying themselves, so perfect were their gestures. The foreigners must have asked to see a man and woman together, and this was Maman's compromise. Bijou had tied on a rubber penis, which possessed the advantage of never wilting. So no matter what she did, this penis protruded from her female bush of hair as if nailed there by a perpetual erection.

Crouching, Bijou was sliding this fake virility not inside but between Viviane's legs, as if she were churning milk, and Viviane was contracting her legs as if she were being tantalized by a real man. But Bijou had only begun to tease her. She seemed intent on making Viviane feel the penis only from the outside. She handled it like a door knocker, knocking gently against Viviane's belly and loins, then gently teasing the hair, then the tip of the clitoris. At the last, Viviane jumped a little, and so Bijou repeated it, and Viviane jumped again. The foreign woman then leaned over as if she were nearsighted, to catch the secret of this sensitivity. Viviane rolled with impatience and offered Bijou her sex.

Behind the curtain, the Basque was smiling at Viviane's excellent performance. The man and woman were fascinated. They stood right next to the bed, with dilated eyes. Bijou said to them, 'Do you want to see how we make love when we feel lazy?'

'Turn over,' she commanded Viviane. Viviane turned on her right side. Bijou laid herself against her, entangling their feet. Viviane closed her eyes. Then, with her two hands Bijou made room for her entrance, spreading the dark-brown flesh of Viviane's buttocks so she could slip the penis in, and she began to push. Viviane did not move. She let her push, thump. Then unexpectedly she gave a jerk like that of a horse kicking. Bijou, as if to punish her, withdrew. But the Basque saw the rubber penis glistening now, almost like a real one, still triumphantly erect.

Bijou began teasing again. She touched Viviane's mouth with the tip of the penis, her ears, her neck, she rested it between her breasts. Viviane pressed her breasts together to hold it. She moved to join Bijou's body, to rub herself against her, but Bijou was evasive now that Viviane was becoming a little wild. The man, bending over them, began to grow restless. He wanted to fall on the women. His companion would not let him, though her face was flushed.

The Basque suddenly opened the door. He bowed and said, 'You wanted a man and here I am.' He threw off his clothes. Viviane looked at him gratefully. The Basque realized she was in heat. Two virilities would satisfy her more than that teasing, elusive one. He threw himself between the women. Everywhere the foreign man and woman looked something was happening that enthralled them. A hand was opening someone's buttocks and slipping in an inquisitive finger. A mouth was closing upon a leaping, charging penis. Another mouth was enclosing a nipple. Faces were covered by breasts or buried in pubic hair. Legs were closing over a burrowing hand. A glistening wet penis would appear and plunge again into flesh. The ivory skin and the gypsy skin were tangled with the man's muscular body.

Then a strange thing happened. Bijou lay full length under the Basque. Viviane was abandoned for a moment. The Basque was crouching over this woman who bloomed under him like some hothouse flower, odorous, moist, with erotic eyes and wet lips, a full-blown woman, ripe and voluptuous; yet her rubber penis stood erect between them, and the Basque was overtaken with an odd feeling. The penis touched his own and defended the opening of the woman like a lance. He commanded almost angrily, 'Take it off.' She slid her hands under her back, unfastened the belt and pulled the rubber penis off. Then he threw himself on her, and she, still holding the penis, held it over the buttocks of the man who was now buried inside of her. When he raised himself to thump into her again, she pushed the rubber penis inside of his buttocks. He leaped like a wild animal and attacked her only more furiously. Each time he raised himself, he found himself attacked from behind. He felt the breasts of the woman crushed beneath him, rolling under his chest, her ivory-skinned belly heaving under his, her hips against his, her moist vagina engulfing him; and each time she plunged the penis into him, he felt not only his turmoil but hers as well. He thought the doubled sensation would drive him mad. Viviane lay there watching them, panting. The foreign man and woman, still clothed, had fallen over her and were rubbing against her frantically, too confused in wild sensations to seek an opening.

The Basque was sliding back and forth. The bed rocked as they rolled, clutching and folding, all curves filled, the machine of Bijou's voluptuous body yielding honey. Ripples extended from the roots of their hair to the tips of their toes. Their toes sought each other and intertwined. Their tongues projected like pistils. Bijou's cries now mounted in endless spirals, ah, ah, ah, ah, widening, expanding, becoming more savage. The Basque answered every cry with only a deeper plunge. They were oblivious to the twisted bodies near them; he must now possess her to annihilation – Bijou, this whore, with a thousand tentacles on his body, lying first under him and then over him and seeming to be everywhere inside of him, her fingers everywhere, her breasts in his mouth.

She cried as if he had murdered her. She lay back. The Basque stood up, drunk, burning. His lance still erect, red, inflamed. The disordered clothes of the foreign woman lured him. He could not see her face, which was hidden under her raised skirts. The man was lying over Viviane, belaboring her. The woman was lying over both of them, her legs kicking in the air. The Basque pulled her down by the legs to take her. But she screamed and stood up.

She said, 'I only wanted to look.' She arranged her clothes. The man abandoned Viviane. Disheveled as they were, they bowed ceremoniously and hurriedly left.

Bijou was sitting up, laughing, her tilted eyes long and narrow. The Basque said, 'We gave them a good spectacle. Now you get dressed and follow me. I'm going to take you home. I'm going to paint you. I'll pay Maman whatever she wants.'

And he took her home to live with him.

If Bijou thought that the Basque had taken her home to have her all to himself, she was soon to be disillusioned. The Basque used her as a model almost continuously, but in the evenings he always had his artist friends for dinner, and Bijou was then the cook. After dinner he would make her lie on the bed in the studio while he talked with his friends. He merely kept her at his side and fondled her. His friends could not help watching them. His hand would mechanically circle over her ripe breasts. Bijou would not move. She would fall into a languid pose. The Basque would touch the material of her dress as if it were her skin. Her dresses always molded her body tightly. His hand would appraise and pat and caress, then circle over her belly, then suddenly tickle her to make her squirm. He would open her dress, take out one breast and say to his friends, 'Did you ever see such a breast? Look!' They looked. One was smoking, one was sketching Bijou, the other talking; but they looked. Against the black dress the breast, so perfect in its contours, had the color of old ivory marble. The Basque pinched the nipples, which reddened.

Then he would close the dress again. He would feel along the legs until he touched the prominence of the garters. 'Isn't it too tight for you? Let's see. Has it left a mark?' He would lift the skirt and carefully remove the garter. As Bijou lifted her leg to him the men could see the smooth gleaming lines of her thighs above the stocking. Then she covered herself again and the Basque would continue to fondle her. Bijou's eyes would blur as if she were drunk. But because she was now like the Basque's wife and in the company of the Basque's friends, each time he exposed her she fought to cover herself again, hiding away each new secret in the black folds of her dress.

She stretched her legs. She kicked off her shoes. The erotic light that shone from her eyes, a light that her heavy eyelashes could not shade sufficiently, traversed the bodies of the men like fire.

On nights like this she knew the Basque was not intent on giving her pleasure but on torturing her. He would not be satisfied until the faces of his friends were altered, decomposed. He would pull the zipper on the side of her dress and slip in his hand. 'You are not wearing panties today, Bijou.' They could see his hand under the dress, caressing the belly and descending toward the legs. Then he would stop and withdraw his hand. They watched his hand coming out of the black dress and closing the zipper again.

Once he asked one of the painters for his warm pipe. The man handed it to him. He slipped the pipe up Bijou's skirt and laid it against her sex. 'It's warm,' he said. 'Warm and smooth.' Bijou moved away from the pipe because she did not want them to know that all the Basque's fondlings had wetted her. But the pipe came out revealing this, as if it had been dipped in peach juice. The Basque handed it back to its owner, who was thus given a little of Bijou's sexual odor. Bijou was afraid of what the Basque would invent next. She tightened her legs. The Basque was smoking. The three friends sat around the bed, talking disconnectedly as if the gestures which were taking place had nothing to do with their conversation.

One of them was talking about the woman painter who was filling the galleries with giant flowers in rainbow colors. 'They're not flowers,' said the pipe smoker, 'they're vulvas. Anyone can see that. It is an obsession with her. She paints a vulva the size of a full-grown woman. At first it looks like petals, the heart of a flower, then one sees the two uneven lips, the fine center line, the wavelike edge of the lips when they are spread open. What kind of a woman can she be, always exhibiting this giant vulva, suggestively vanishing into a tunnel-like repetition, growing from a large one to a smaller, the shadow of it, as if one were actually entering into it. It makes you feel as though you were standing before those sea plants which open only to suck in whatever food they can catch, open with the same wavering edges.'

At this moment the Basque had an idea. He asked Bijou to

bring the shaving brush and razor. Bijou obeyed. She was glad for a chance to move about and shake off the erotic lethargy his hands had woven around her. His mind was on something else now. He took the brush and soap from her and began to mix a lather. He placed a new blade in the razor. Then he said to her, 'Lie on the bed.'

'What are you going to do?' she said. 'I have no hairs on my legs.'

'I know you haven't. Show them.' She extended them. They were indeed so smooth that they looked as if they had been polished. They shone like some pale precious wood, highly burnished, not a hair showing, no veins, no roughness, no scars, no defects. The three men bent over her legs. As she shook them, the Basque caught them against his trousers. Then he raised her skirt while she fought to bring it down.

'What are you going to do?' she asked again.

He raised her skirt and exposed such a luxuriant tuft of curled hair that the three men whistled. She kept her legs tightly closed, her feet against the Basque's trousers, where he suddenly felt a swarming sensation, like a hundred ants traveling over his sex.

He asked the three men to hold her. Bijou squirmed at first and then realized it was less dangerous to lie still, for he was carefully shaving her pubic hair, beginning at the edges, where it lay sparse and shining on her velvety belly. The belly came down in a soft curve there. The Basque lathered, then shaved gently, wiping off the hair and soap with a towel. With her legs tightly closed the men could not see anything but the hair, but as the Basque shaved on and reached the center of the triangle, he exposed a mount, a smooth promontory. The feeling of the cold blade there agitated Bijou. She was half-angry, half-stirred, intent on not showing her sex, but the shaving revealed where the smoothness descended into a fine incurving line. It revealed the bud of the opening, the soft folded flesh that enclosed the clitoris, the tip of the more intensely colored lips. She wanted now to move away but she was afraid of being hurt by the blade. The three men held her and bent over her to watch. They thought the Basque would stop there. But he ordered her to part her legs. She shook her feet against him, which only excited him more. He said again, 'Part your legs.

There are some more hairs down there.' She was forced to open them, and he gently began to shave off the hairs, sparse again, delicately curled, on each side of the vulva.

And now everything was exposed – the long vertically placed mouth, a second mouth, which opened not like the mouth of the face, but which opened only if she chose to push out a little. But Bijou would not push, and they could see just the two lips, closed, barring the way.

The Basque said, 'Now she looks like the paintings by that woman, doesn't she?'

But in the paintings, the vulva was open, the lips parted, showing the paler inner layer like the inside of the lips of the mouth. This, Bijou would not show. Once shaved, she had closed her legs again.

The Basque said, 'I will make you open there.'

He had rinsed the soap off the brush. Now he brushed the vulva lips, up and down, gently. At first, Bijou contracted herself even more. The men's heads leaned closer. The Basque, holding her legs against his erection, meticulously brushed the vulva and the tip of the clitoris. Then the men saw that Bijou could no longer contract her buttocks and sex, that as the brush moved, her buttocks rolled a little forward, the lips of the vulva parted, at first imperceptibly. The nakedness exposed every nuance of her motion. Now the lips parted and exposed a second aura, of a paler shade, then a third, and now Bijou was pushing, pushing as if she would open. Her belly moved in accord, swelling and falling. The Basque leaned more firmly against her writhing legs.

'Stop,' begged Bijou, 'stop.' The men could see the moisture oozing from her. Then the Basque stopped, not wanting to give her pleasure, reserving that for himself later.

Bijou was eager to make a distinction between her life in the whorehouse and her life as the companion and model of an artist. The Basque was intent on making only one little distinction, merely in the matter of actual possession. But he liked to expose her and delight his visitors with the sight of her. He made them assist at her bath. They liked to watch how her breasts floated in the water, how the swelling of her belly could make the water heave, how she raised herself to pass soap between her legs. They liked to dry her wet body. But if any of them tried to see Bijou privately, and possess her, then the Basque became a demon and a man to fear.

In revenge for these games, Bijou felt she had a right to go where she wanted. The Basque maintained her in a highly eroticized condition and did not always trouble to satisfy her. Her infidelities started then, but they were done so elusively that the Basque could never catch her. Bijou collected her lovers at the Grande Chaumière, where she posed for the drawing class. On winter days she did not undress quickly and surreptitiously as the other models did, next to the stove near the model's stand, in view of everybody. Bijou had an art for this.

First she loosened her wild hair, shook it like a mane. Then she unbuttoned her coat. Her hands were slow and caressing. She did not handle herself objectively, but like a woman ascertaining with her hands the exact condition of her body, patting it in gratitude for its perfections. Her perennial black dress clung to her body like a second skin and was filled with mysterious openings. One gesture opened the shoulders and let the dress fall over her breasts but no further. At this point she decided to look at her face mirror and examine her eyelashes. Then she opened the zipper which exposed the ribs, the beginning of the breasts, the beginning of the belly's curve. All the students were watching her from behind their easels. Even the women rested their eyes on the luxuriant parts of Bijou's body, which burst from the dress dazzlingly. The flawless skin, the soft contours, the firm flesh fascinated them all. Bijou had a way of shaking herself, as if to loosen her muscles, as the cat does before he leaps. This shake, which ran through her body, gave the breasts an air of being handled with violence. Then she took the dress lightly at the hem and lifted it slowly over her shoulders. When it reached her shoulders, she was always stuck for a moment. Something caught with her long hair. No one helped her. They were all petrified. The body which emerged, hairless, now absolutely naked, as she stood with her legs apart to keep her balance, startled them by the sensuality in every curve, by its richness and femininity. The wide black garters were placed high. She wore black stockings, and, if it was a rainy day, high leather boots, men's boots. As she struggled with the boots, she was at the mercy of anyone who approached her. The students were sorely tempted. One might pretend to help her, but as he approached her she would kick him, sensing his real intention. She continued to struggle with the entangled dress, shaking herself as if in a spasm of love. Finally, she freed herself, after the students had satisfied their eyes. She freed her rich breasts and tangled hair. Sometimes she was asked to keep her boots on, the heavy boots from which expanded, like a flower, the ivory-colored female body. Then a wind of desire would sweep the entire class.

Once on the stand she became a model, and the students remembered they were artists. If she saw one that she liked, she rested her eyes on him. This was the only time she had to make engagements, for the Basque would be coming to fetch her at the end of the afternoon. The student knew what her look meant: She would accept a drink with him in the café nearby. The initiated knew, too, that this café had two floors. The upper one was occupied by card players in the evening, but was absolutely deserted in the afternoon. Only lovers knew this. The student and Bijou would go there, climb the flight of stairs with the sign marked *lavabos*, and find themselves in a semi-dark room of mirrors and tables and chairs.

Bijou ordered the waiter to bring them a drink, then she lay back on the leather banquette and relaxed. The young student she had selected was trembling. Emanating from her body was a heat he had never felt before. He fell on her mouth, his fresh skin and beautiful teeth luring her to open fully to his kiss and respond with her tongue. They tussled on the long narrow bench, and he began to feel as much of her body as he could, fearing that at any time she would say, 'Stop, someone might come up the stairs.'

The mirrors reflected their tussling, the disorder of her dress and her hair. The student's hands were supple and audacious. He slipped under the table and raised her skirt. Then she did say, 'Stop, someone might come upstairs.' He replied, 'Let them. They won't see me.' It is true they could not see him there under the table. She sat forward, resting her face on her cupped hands, as if she were dreaming, and let the young student kneel and bury his head under her skirt.

She became languid and abandoned herself to his kisses and caresses. Where she had felt the Basque's shaving brush, she now felt the young man's tongue. She fell forward, overwhelmed with pleasure. Then they heard steps, and the student quickly raised himself and sat next to her. To cover his confusion he kissed her. The waiter found them embracing and left hurriedly after accomplishing his errand. Now Bijou's hands were burrowing into the young student's clothes. He was kissing her so furiously that she fell on her side on the bench and he over her. He whispered, 'Come to my room. Please come to my room. It isn't far.'

'I can't,' said Bijou. 'The Basque is coming for me soon.' Then each took the other's hand and placed it where it could give the greatest pleasure. Sitting there in front of the drinks as if they were conversing together, they caressed each other. The mirrors revealed them as if they were about to sob, their features constricted, their lips trembling, their eyes batting. From their faces one could follow the movement of their hands. At times the young student looked as if he were being wounded and were gasping for air. Another couple came upstairs while their hands were still at work, and they had to kiss again, like romantic lovers.

The young student, unable to conceal the condition he was in, went off somewhere to calm himself. Bijou returned to the class, her body on fire. When the Basque came for her at closing hour, she was calm again.

Bijou had heard of a clairvoyant and went to consult him. He was a big colored man from West Africa. All the women of her quarter went to him. The waiting room was full. In front of her hung a huge black silk Chinese curtain embroidered with gold. The man appeared from behind it. Except for his everyday suit, he looked like some magician. He gave Bijou a heavy stare with his lustrous eyes, then vanished behind the curtain with the last of the women who had arrived before her. The séance lasted half an hour. Then the man lifted the black curtain and politely accompanied the woman to the front door.

It was Bijou's turn. He let her pass under the curtain and she found herself in an almost dark room, very small, hung with

Chinese curtains and illuminated only by a crystal ball with a light under it. This shone on the clairvoyant's face and hands and left everything else in darkness. His eyes were hypnotic.

Bijou decided to resist being hypnotized and to remain fully aware of what was taking place. He told her to lie on the couch, and to be very quiet for a moment while he, sitting at her side, concentrated his attention on her. He closed his own eyes, so Bijou decided to close hers. For fully one minute he remained in this abstracted state, and then he laid his hand on her forehead. It was a warm, dry hand, heavy and electric.

Then his voice said, as in a dream, 'You are married to a man who makes you suffer.'

'Yes,' said Bijou, thinking of the Basque who exposed her to his friends.

'He has peculiar habits.'

'Yes,' said Bijou, amazed. Her eyes closed, she envisioned the scenes so clearly. It seemed that the clairvoyant could see them too.

He added, 'You are unhappy, and you compensate by being very unfaithful.'

'Yes,' said Bijou again.

Then she opened her eyes and she saw the Negro looking at her intently, and she closed them again.

He rested his hand on her shoulder.

'Go to sleep,' he said.

She was calmed by his words, in which she detected a shade of pity. But she could not sleep. Her body was keyed up. She knew how the breath changed in sleep, and the movements of the breasts. So she pretended to fall asleep. All the time she felt the hand on her shoulder, and its warmth penetrated right through her clothes. He began to caress her shoulder. He did this so quietly that she was afraid she would fall asleep, but she did not want to lose the pleasant sensation that was running down her spine at the round touch of his hand. She relaxed completely.

He touched her throat and waited. He wanted to be sure that she was asleep. He touched her breasts. Bijou did not stir.

Cautiously, deftly, he caressed her belly, and with a pressure of the finger pushed the black silk of her dress so as to outline the shape of her legs and the space between the legs. When he made this valley clear, he continued to caress the legs. He had not yet touched her legs beyond the dress. Then he noiselessly left his chair, went to the foot of the couch and kneeled down. In this position, Bijou knew, he could look up her dress and see that she wore nothing underneath. He looked for a long while.

Then she felt him lifting the hem of the skirt slightly to be able to see more. Bijou had stretched herself out with her legs slightly parted. She was melting under his touch and his eyes. How wonderful it was to be looked at while apparently asleep, to feel that the man was entirely free. She felt the silk being lifted, felt her legs exposed to the air. He was staring at them.

With one hand he caressed them softly, slowly, enjoying them to the full, feeling the smooth lines, the long silk passage leading up under the dress. Bijou found it difficult to lie absolutely still. She wanted to part her legs a little more. How slowly his hand traveled. She could feel how he followed the contours of the legs, lingering over the curves, how his hand stopped at the knee, then continued. He stopped just before touching the sex. He must have been watching her face to see if she was deeply hypnotized. With two fingers he began to feel her sex, knead it.

When he felt the honey that had been quietly flowing, he slipped his head under the skirt, hid himself between her legs and began to kiss her. His tongue was long and agile, penetrating. She had to restrain herself from moving toward his voracious mouth.

The little lamp gave so dim a light that she risked opening her eyes halfway. He had withdrawn his head from her skirt and was slowly taking off his clothes. He stood near her, magnificent, tall, like some African king, his eyes glowing, his teeth bared, his mouth wet.

Not to move, not to move, so as to permit him to do all he wanted. What would a man do with a hypnotized woman whom he did not need to fear or please in any way?

Naked, he towered over her, and then surrounding her with his two arms, he carefully turned her over. Now Bijou lay offering her sumptuous buttocks. He raised her dress and spread the two mounts. He paused, so as to feast his eyes. His fingers were firm and warm, as they parted her flesh. He leaned over and began to kiss the fissure. Then he slipped his hands around her body and raised her toward him, so that he could penetrate her from behind. At first he found only the opening of the ass, which was too small and tight to enter, then he found the larger opening. He swung in and out of her for a moment and then stopped.

Once again he turned her over, so he could watch himself taking her from the front. His hands sought her breasts under the dress and crushed them with violent caresses. His sex was large and filled her completely. He introduced it with such violence that Bijou thought she would have an orgasm and betray herself. She wanted to take her pleasure without his knowing it. He stirred her so much by his beating sexual rhythm that once, as he slipped out to fondle her, she felt the orgasm coming.

Her whole desire was bent on feeling it again. He now tried to push his sex into her half-opened mouth. She refrained from responding and only opened her mouth a little more. To keep her hands from touching him, to keep herself from moving, was a great effort. But she wanted to feel again that strange pleasure of a stolen orgasm, as he was feeling the pleasure of these stolen caresses.

Her passivity was driving him into a frenzy. He had touched her body everywhere, had penetrated her in every way he could. Now he sat over her belly and pushed his sex between her two breasts, tightening them around himself, and moving. She could feel his hairs brushing against her.

Then Bijou lost control. She opened her mouth and her eyes at the same time. The man grunted with delight, pressed her mouth with his, and rubbed his whole body against her. Bijou's tongue was beating against his mouth, while he bit her lips.

He suddenly stopped and said, 'Will you do something for me?'
She nodded.

'I will lie on the floor and you come and crouch over me, and let me look under your dress.'

He stretched himself on the floor. She crouched over his face and held her dress so that it fell and covered his head. With his two hands he held her buttocks like a fruit and passed his tongue between the mounts over and over again. Now he also stroked her clitoris, which made Bijou move forward and backward. His tongue felt every response, every contraction. As she crouched over him, she saw his erect penis vibrate with each gasp of pleasure he uttered.

There was a knock on the door. Bijou rose quickly, startled, with her lips still wet from the kisses and her hair undone.

The clairvoyant answered quietly however, 'I am not ready yet.' And then turned and smiled at her.

She smiled back. He dressed himself quickly. Soon everything was outwardly in order. They agreed to meet again. Bijou wanted to bring her friends Leila and Elena. Would he like it? He begged her to do this. He said, 'Most of the women who come here do not tempt me. They are not beautiful. But you – come whenever you want to. I'll dance for you.'

His dance for the three women took place one evening when all the clients were gone. He stripped himself, showing his gleaming golden-brown body. To his waist he tied a fake penis modeled like his own and the same color.

He said, 'This is a dance from my own country. We do this for the women on feast days.' In the dimly lit room, where the light shone like a small fire over his skin, he began to move his belly, making the penis wave in a most suggestive way. He jerked his body as if he were entering a woman and simulated the spasms of a man caught in the varied tonalities of an orgasm. One, two, three. The final spasm was wild, like that of a man giving up his life in the act of sex.

The three women watched. At first only the fake penis dominated, but then the real one, in the heat of the dance, began to compete in length and weight. Now they both moved in rhythm with his gestures. He closed his eyes as though he had no need of the women. The effect on Bijou was powerful. She took her dress off. She began to dance around him temptingly. But he merely touched her now and then with the tip of his sex, wherever he encountered her, and continued to turn and jerk his body in space like a savage dancing against an invisible body.

The teasing affected Elena, too, and she slipped her dress off and kneeled near them, just to be in the orbit of their sexual dance. She suddenly wanted to be taken until she bled, by this big, strong, firm penis dangled in front of her, as he performed a male *danse du ventre*, with its tantalizing motions.

Now Leila, who did not desire men, became caught up by the moods of the two women and tried to embrace Bijou, but Bijou would not have it. She was fascinated with the two penises.

Leila tried to kiss Elena also. Then she rubbed her nipples against both women, trying to entice them. She pressed herself against Bijou to profit from her excitement, but Bijou continued to concentrate on the male organs dangled before her. Her mouth was open, and she, too, was dreaming of being taken by a double-sexed monster who could satisfy her two centers of response at once.

When the African dropped, exhausted from the dance, Elena and Bijou leaped on him simultaneously. Bijou quickly inserted one penis in her vagina and one in her rectum and then she twisted over his belly wildly and continuously until she fell satisfied, with a long cry of pleasure. Elena pushed her away, and assumed the same position. But seeing the African was tired, she did not move, waiting for him to recuperate his strength.

His penis remained erect inside her, and while she waited she began to contract herself, very slowly and gently, fearing to have the orgasm too quickly and bring her pleasure to an end. After a moment he gripped her buttocks and raised her so that she could follow the rapid pulse of his blood. He bent and molded and pushed and pulled her to suit his rhythm until he cried out, and then she moved in a circle around the swollen penis until he came.

Next he made Leila crouch over his face as he had done earlier with Bijou and hid his face between her legs.

Although Leila had never desired a man, she became aware of a sensation never experienced before as the African's tongue caressed her. She wanted to be taken from behind. She moved from her position and asked him to introduce the fake penis. She was on her hands and knees now, and he did as she asked.

Elena and Bijou watched her with amazement, exposing her buttocks with evident excitement, and the African scratched and bit as he moved the fake penis inside of her. Pain and pleasure mixed in her, for the penis was large, but she remained on her hands and knees, with the African soldered to her, and she moved convulsively until she found her pleasure.

Bijou went often to see the African. One day they lay together on his couch and he buried his face under her arms; he inhaled her odor, then instead of kissing her, he began to smell her all over like an animal – first under her arms, then in her hair, then between her legs. As he did this he became excited, but he would not take her.

He said, 'You know, Bijou, I would love you more if you did not bathe so often. I love the smell of your body, but it is faint. It vanishes with so much washing. That is why I rarely desire white women. I like the strong female smell. Please wash a little less.'

To please him, Bijou washed herself less often; he especially loved the odor between her legs when she had not washed, the wonderful seashell odor of sperm and semen. Then he asked her to keep her underwear for him. To wear it a few days and then to bring it to him.

First she brought him a nightgown she had worn often, a fine black one with lace edges. With Bijou lying beside him, the African covered his face with the nightgown and inhaled its odors; he lay back ecstatic and silent. Bijou saw that under his trousers his desire was bulging. She gently leaned over and began to open one button, then another, then the third. She spread open the trousers and searched for his sex, which was pointing downward, caught beneath his tight underwear. Again she had to unfasten buttons.

At last she saw the flash of the penis, so brown and smooth. She inserted her hand softly, as if she were about to steal it. The African, with his head covered by the nightgown, did not look at her. She pulled the penis slowly upward, unbending it from its cramped position, and freed it. Up it went, straight and smooth and hard. But she had barely touched it with her mouth when the African pulled it away from her. Now he took the nightgown, all crumpled and frothy, laid it on the bed, and threw himself over it full length, burying his sex into it, and began to move up and down against it, as if it were Bijou lying there.

She watched, fascinated by the way he pushed himself over the nightgown and ignored her. His motions excited her. He was in such a frenzy that he was perspiring, and an intoxicating animal smell came from his whole body. She fell over him. He carried her weight on his back, unheeding, and continued to move against the nightgown.

She saw him hastening his movements. Then he stopped himself. He turned and began undressing her very gently. Bijou thought that now he had lost interest in the nightgown and would make love to her. He took her stockings off, leaving her garters on her naked flesh. Next he lifted off the dress, which was still warm from the contact with her body. To please him Bijou was wearing black panties. These he slowly pulled down, and stopped halfway to look at the emerging ivory flesh, part of her ass, the beginning of the dimpled valley. There, he kissed her, slipping his tongue along the delicious crevice, as he continued to pull off the panties. He left no part unkissed as he drew them along her thighs, and the silk felt like another hand on her flesh.

As she raised one leg to free herself from the panties, he could see fully into her sex. He kissed her there, and then she raised her other leg and rested them both on his shoulders.

He held the panties in his hand and continued to kiss her, leaving her moist and panting. Then he turned away and buried his face in the panties, in the nightgown, wrapped the stockings around his penis, laid the black silk dress over his belly. The clothes seemed to have on him the same effect as a hand. He was convulsed with excitement.

Bijou again tried to touch his penis with her mouth, her hands, but he repulsed her. She lay naked and hungry at his side, watching his pleasure. It was tantalizing and cruel. She tried to kiss the rest of his body, but he did not respond.

He continued to caress and kiss and smell the clothes until his body began to tremble. He lay back, his penis shaking in the air, with nothing to encircle it, hold it. He shook with pleasure from head to foot, biting into the panties, chewing on them, all the time his erect penis near Bijou's mouth, yet inaccessible to her. Finally the penis shuddered violently, and as the white foam appeared at the tip of it, Bijou threw herself on it to gather the last spurts.

One afternoon when Bijou and the African were together, and Bijou had found it impossible to attract his desire to her own body, she said in exasperation, 'Look, I am getting an over-developed vulva from your constant kissing and biting there: you pull at the lips as if they were nipples. They are growing longer.'

He took the lips between his thumb and forefinger, and examined them. He spread them open like the petals of a flower, and said, 'One could pierce them and hang an earring on them, as we do in Africa. I want to do that to you.'

He continued to play with the vulva. It grew stiff under his touch, and he saw white moisture appear at the edge of it, like the delicate foam of some small wave. He was aroused. He touched it with the tip of his penis. But he did not enter. He was obsessed with the idea of piercing the lips as if they were ear lobes and hanging on them a small gold earring, as he had seen done to the women of his country.

Bijou did not believe he was in earnest. She was enjoying his attentiveness. But then he rose and went to fetch a needle. Bijou fought him off and fled.

Now she was without a lover. The Basque continued to tease her, arousing great desires for revenge. She was only happy when she was deceiving him.

She walked the streets and frequented the cafés with a feeling of hunger and curiosity; she wanted something new, something she had not yet experienced. She sat at cafés and refused invitations.

One evening she walked down the stairway to the quays and the river. This part of the city was lighted only dimly by the street lamps overhead. The noise of the traffic barely reached it.

The moored barges were without lights, their occupants asleep at this time of the night. She came to a very low stone wall and stopped to watch the river. She leaned over, fascinated by the lights reflected on the water. Then she heard the most extraordinary voice speaking in her ear, a voice that immediately enchanted her.

It said, 'I beg you not to move. I will not hurt you. But stay where you are.'

The voice was so deep, rich, refined, that she obeyed and merely turned her head. She found a tall, handsome, well-dressed man standing behind her. He was smiling in the dim light, with a friendly, disarming, gallant expression.

Then, he too leaned over the wall and said, 'Finding you here, this way, has been one of the obsessions of my life. You don't know how beautiful you look, with your breasts crushed against the wall, your dress so short behind you. What beautiful legs you have.'

'But you must have a lot of friends,' said Bijou, smiling.

'None that I have ever wanted as much as I want you. Only I beg you, don't move.'

Bijou was intrigued. The stranger's voice fascinated her and kept her in a trance at his side. She felt his hand gently passing over her leg, and under her dress.

As he stroked her, he said, 'One day I watched two dogs playing. The one dog was busy eating a bone she had found, and the other took advantage of the situation to approach her from behind. I was fourteen. I felt the wildest excitement from watching them. It was the first sexual scene I witnessed, and I discovered the first sexual excitement in myself. From then on, only a woman leaning over as you are can arouse my desire.'

His hand continued to stroke her. He pressed a little against her and, seeing her pliant, began to move behind her so as to cover her with his body. Bijou was suddenly afraid and sought to escape from his embrace. But the man was powerful. She was already under him, and all he had to do was bend her body over even more. He forced her head and shoulders down on the wall and raised her skirt.

Bijou was again without underclothes. The man gasped. He began to murmur words of desire that soothed her, but at the same time he held her down, entirely at his mercy. She felt him against her back, but he was not taking her. He was merely pressing against her as tightly as he could. She felt the strength of his two legs, and she heard his voice enveloping her, but that was all. Then she felt something soft and warm against her, something that did not penetrate her. In a moment she was covered with warm sperm. The man abandoned her and ran away.

Leila took Bijou horseback riding in the Bois. Leila looked very beautiful on horseback, slim, masculine and haughty. Bijou looked more luxuriant but less poised.

Riding in the Bois was a lovely experience. They passed elegant people, then rode through long stretches of isolated, wooded paths. Every now and then they came across a café, where one could rest and eat.

It was spring. Bijou had taken several riding lessons and was now on her own for the first time. They rode slowly, talking all the while. Then Leila set off at a gallop and Bijou followed. After they had galloped for a time, they slowed down. Their faces were flushed.

Bijou felt a pleasurable irritation between her legs and a warmth over her buttocks. She wondered if Leila felt the same. After another half an hour of riding, her excitation was growing. Her eyes were brilliant, her lips moist. Leila looked at her with admiration.

'Horseback riding becomes you,' she said.

Her hand held a whip with regal assurance. Her gloves fitted her long fingers tightly. She wore a man's shirt and cuff links. Her riding habit showed the shapeliness of her waist and breast and buttocks. Bijou filled her clothes more abundantly. Her breasts were high and pointed provocatively upward. Her hair hung loose in the wind.

But oh, the warmth across her buttocks and between the legs – feeling as if she had been rubbed with alcohol, or with wine, and slightly patted by an experienced masseuse. Each time she rose and fell in the saddle she felt a delicious tingling. Leila liked to ride behind her and watch her figure as it moved on the horse. Not fully trained, Bijou leaned forward in the saddle and showed her buttocks, round and tight in the jodhpurs, and her shapely legs.

The horses were hot and beginning to lather. A strong odor came from them and seeped into the two women's clothes. Leila's body seemed to grow lighter. She held her whip nervously. They galloped again, side by side now, with their mouths half-open and the wind on their faces. As her legs gripped the flanks of her horse, Bijou remembered how she had once ridden on the stomach of the Basque. And then she stood up, her feet on his chest and her genitals directly in the line of his vision, and he had maintained her in this position to feast his eyes. Another time he had been on his hands and knees on the floor, and she had ridden on his back and had tried to hurt him with the pressure of her knees on his flanks. Laughing nervously, he had urged her on. Her knees were as strong as those of a man riding a horse, and the Basque had felt such excitement that he had crawled like this all around the room with his penis stretched out.

Now and then Leila's horse raised his tail in the speed of the gallop, and then swatted himself vigorously, exposing glossy hairs in the sun. When they reached the deepest part of the forest, the women stopped and dismounted. They walked their horses to a mossy corner and sat down to rest. They smoked; Leila had kept her riding whip in her hand.

Bijou said, 'My buttocks are burning hot from the riding.'

'Let me see,' said Leila. 'For this first time we should not have ridden so much. Let me see how you look.'

Bijou unfastened her belt slowly, unbuttoned the trousers, and pulled them down a little, turning over for Leila to see.

Leila pulled her over her knees and said, 'Let me see.' She finished pulling down the trousers to uncover the buttocks completely. She touched Bijou.

'Does it hurt?' she asked.

'It does not hurt. It's just warm, as if it had been toasted.'

Leila's hand cupped the round buttocks. 'Poor little things,' she said. 'Does it hurt here?' Her hand went deeper into the trousers, deeper between the legs.

'It's warm and burning there,' said Bijou.

'Take the trousers off so it will cool,' said Leila, pulling them down a little further and keeping Bijou over her knees, exposed to the air.

'What beautiful skin you have, Bijou. It catches the light and shines. Let the air cool you off there.'

She continued to stroke Bijou's skin between the legs as if she were a kitten. Whenever the trousers threatened to cover all this again, she pulled them back out of the way.

'It still burns,' said Bijou, not moving.

'If it continues to burn then we should try something else,' said Leila.

'Do whatever you want to me,' said Bijou.

Leila lifted up her riding whip and let it fall, not too hard at first.

Bijou said, 'That makes me warmer still.'

'I want you warmer, Bijou, I want you hot down there, as warm as you can stand it.'

Bijou did not move. Leila used the whip again, leaving a red mark this time.

Bijou said, 'It is so warm, Leila.'

'I want you to burn down there,' said Leila, 'until you cannot burn any more, cannot bear any more. Then I'll kiss it.'

She struck again, and Bijou did not move. She struck a little harder.

Bijou said, 'It's so hot there, Leila, kiss it.'

Leila leaned over and gave her one long kiss where the buttocks valleyed into the sexual parts. Then she struck Bijou again. And again. Bijou contracted her buttocks as if they hurt, but she felt a burning pleasure.

'Strike hard,' she said to Leila.

Leila obeyed. Then she said, 'Do you want to do it to me?'

'Yes,' said Bijou, rising, but she did not pull up her trousers. She sat on the cool moss, took Leila over her knees, unbuttoned her trousers, and began whipping her gently at first, then harder, until Leila contracted and expanded at each blow. Her buttocks were red and burning hot now.

She said, 'Let's take off our clothes and get on the horses together.'

They took off their clothes and both mounted one of the horses. The saddle was warm. They fitted snugly against each other: Leila, behind, put her arms around Bijou's breasts and kissed her shoulder. They rode a little way in this position, each movement of the horse rubbing the saddle against their genitals. Leila was biting Bijou's shoulder and Bijou would turn now and then and bite Leila's nipple. They returned to their moss bed and put on their clothes.

Before Bijou had finished pulling on her trousers, Leila stopped her to kiss her clitoris; but what Bijou felt was her burning buttocks, and she begged Leila to put an end to her irritation.

Leila caressed her buttocks and then used the whip again, used it hard, and Bijou contracted under the blows. Leila spread the buttocks with one hand so that the whip would fall between the buttocks, there in the sensitive opening, and Bijou cried out. Leila struck her there again and again until Bijou was convulsed.

Then Bijou turned and struck Leila hard, angry that she was so aroused and yet unsatisfied, burning and unable to put an end to the sensation. Each time she struck she felt herself palpitating between the legs, as if she were taking Leila, penetrating her. After they were both whipped to redness and fury they fell on each other with hands and tongues until they reached the full effulgence of their pleasure.

It was planned that they would all go together for a picnic: Elena, her lover Pierre, Bijou and the Basque, Leila, and the African.

They set out for a spot outside of Paris. They ate at a restaurant on the Seine. Then, leaving the car in the shade, they set out on foot into the forest. At first they walked in a group, then Elena fell behind with the African. She suddenly decided to climb a tree. The African laughed at her, thinking she could not do it.

But Elena knew how. Very deftly, she put one foot on the first low branch and climbed. The African stood at the foot of the tree and watched her. As he looked up he could see under her skirt. She wore shell-pink underwear, tight-fitting and short, so that most of her legs and thighs showed as she climbed. The African stood there laughing and teasing her, as he began to get an erection.

Elena was sitting quite far up. The African could not reach her, because he was too heavy and big to step on the first branch. All he could do was to sit there and watch her and feel his erection becoming stronger.

He asked, 'What gift will you make me today?'

'This,' said Elena, and threw down some chestnuts.

She sat on a branch swinging her legs.

Then Bijou and the Basque returned to look for her. Bijou, a little jealous when she saw the two men looking up at Elena, threw herself on the grass and said, 'Something has crawled into my clothes. I'm frightened.'

The two men approached her. She pointed first to her back, and the Basque slipped his hand down her dress. Then she said she felt it along the front, and the African slipped his hand inside of her dress and began to search below the breasts. All at once Bijou felt that something really was crawling along her belly, and this time she began to shake herself and roll herself over the grass.

The two men tried to help her. They lifted her skirt and began to search. She wore satin underclothing that covered her completely. She unhooked one side of her panties for the Basque, who, in everyone's eyes, had more right to search her secret places. This excited the African. He turned Bijou over rather roughly and began slapping her body, saying, 'This will kill it, whatever it is.' The Basque was also feeling Bijou all over.

'You'll have to undress,' he said finally. 'There is nothing else to do.'

They both helped her to undress, as she lay on the grass. Elena was watching from the tree and feeling warm and tingling, wishing it were being done to her. When Bijou was undressed she searched between her legs, and through the pubic hair, and finding nothing, began to put on her underwear. But the African did not want to see her completely dressed. He picked up some harmless little insect and laid it on Bijou's body. It crawled along her legs, and Bijou began to roll and try to shake it off, not wanting to touch it with her fingers.

'Take it off, take it off!' she cried, rolling her beautiful body on the grass, and offering whatever part the insect was traveling over. But neither man wanted to rescue her. The Basque took a branch and began slapping at the insect. The African took another branch. The blows were not painful, merely tickling and stinging a little.

Then the African remembered Elena and returned to the tree.

'Come down,' he said, 'I will help you. You can put your foot on my shoulder.'

'I won't come down,' said Elena.

The African pleaded. She began to climb down, and when she was about to reach the lowest branch the African gripped her leg and placed it over his shoulder. She slipped then, and fell with her legs around his neck, her sex against his face. The African inhaled her odor in ecstasy and held her in the strong grip of his arms.

Through the dress he could smell and feel her sex, and he maintained her there, as he bit into the clothes and held her legs. She struggled to escape, kicking him and hitting his back.

Then her lover appeared, furious, his hair wild, at seeing her caught like this. In vain she tried to explain that the African had caught her because she had slipped on her way down. He remained angry, with desire for revenge. When he saw the pair on the grass he tried to join them. But the Basque would not let anyone touch Bijou. He continued to hit her with the branches.

As she lay there a big dog appeared through the trees and came up to her. He began to sniff at her, with evident pleasure. Bijou screamed and struggled to raise herself. But the enormous dog had planted himself over her and was trying to insert his nose between her legs.

Then the Basque, a cruel expression in his eyes, made a signal to Elena's lover. Pierre understood. They held Bijou's arms and legs still and let the dog sniff his way to the place he wanted to smell. He began to lick the satin chemise with delight, in the very place a man would have liked to lick it.

The Basque unfastened her underwear and let the dog continue to lick her carefully and neatly. His tongue was rough, much rougher than a man's, and long and strong. He licked and licked with much vigor, and the three men were watching now.

Elena and Leila also felt as if they were being licked by the dog. They were restless. They all watched, wondering if Bijou was feeling any pleasure.

At first she was terrified and struggled violently. Then she grew weary of moving uselessly and hurting her wrists and ankles, held so strongly by the men. The dog was beautiful, with a big tousled head, a clean tongue.

The sun fell on Bijou's pubic hair, which looked like brocade. Her sex was glistening wet, but no one knew whether it was from the dog's tongue or her pleasure. When her resistance began to die down, the Basque got jealous, kicked off the dog and freed her.

There came a time when the Basque tired of Bijou and abandoned her. Bijou was so accustomed to his fantasies and cruel games, particularly the way he always managed to have her bound and helpless while all kinds of things were done to her, that for months she could not enjoy her newfound liberty or have a relationship with any other man. She could not enjoy women either.

She tried to pose but did not like exposing her body any longer, or being watched and desired by the students. She wandered off by herself all day, once again walking the streets.

The Basque, on the other hand, returned to the pursuit of his former obsession.

Born into a well-to-do family, he was seventeen when his family took a French governess for his younger sister. This woman was short, plump, and always coquettishly dressed. She wore little patent leather boots and sheer black stockings. Her foot was small and extremely arched and pointed.

The Basque was a handsome boy and the French governess took notice of him. They and the younger sister would go on walks together. Under the eyes of the sister very little could take place between them, except long searching glances. The governess had a small mole at the corner of her mouth. The Basque was fascinated with it. One day he complimented her on it.

She answered: 'I have another where you would never imagine one to be, and where you will never see it.'

The boy tried to imagine where the other mole was placed. He tried to picture the French governess naked. Where was the mole? He had seen only pictures of naked women. He had a postcard showing a dancer with a short feathery skirt. When he breathed on it, the skirt raised itself and the woman stood exposed. One of her legs was in the air, like a ballet dancer's, and the Basque could see how she was made.

As soon as he got home that day he took out this postcard and breathed on it. He imagined he was seeing the body of the governess, her plump, full breast. Then with a pencil he drew a tiny mole between the legs. By then he was thoroughly aroused and wanted to see the governess naked at all cost. But in the midst of the Basque's large family, they had to be cautious. There was always someone on the stairs, someone in every room.

The next day during their walk she gave him a handkerchief. He went to his room, threw himself on the bed and covered his mouth with the handkerchief. He could smell the odor of her body on it. She had been holding it in her hand on a hot day and it had received some of her perspiration. The odor was so vivid and affected him so much that for the second time he knew what it was to feel a turmoil between his legs. He saw that he had an erection, which until now had happened only in dreams.

The next day she gave him something wrapped up in paper. He slipped it in his pocket and after their walk went straight to his room, where he opened the package. It contained flesh-tinted panties, with lace edging. She had worn them. They, too, smelled of her body. The boy buried his face in them and experienced the wildest pleasure. He imagined himself taking the panties off her body. The feeling was so vivid that he had an erection. He began to touch himself as he continued to kiss the panties. Then he rubbed his penis with them. The touch of the silk entranced him. It seemed to him that he was touching her flesh, perhaps the very place where he imagined she had the little mole. Suddenly he had an ejaculation, his first, in a spasm of joy that sent him rolling over the bed.

The next day she gave him another package. It contained a brassière. He repeated the ceremony. He wondered what else she could give him that would stir him to such pleasure.

This time it was a big package. His sister's curiosity was aroused.

'It's only books,' said the governess, 'nothing of any interest to you.'

The Basque hurried to his room. He found that she had given him a small black corset with lace edges, and this carried the imprint of her body. The lace was worn from all the times she had pulled at it. The Basque was stirred again. This time he took his clothes off and slipped the corset on himself. He pulled at the lacing as he had seen his mother do. He felt compressed and it hurt him, but he delighted in the pain. He imagined the governess was holding him and tightening her arms around him to the point of suffocating him. As he loosened the lace he imagined himself freeing her body so he could see her naked. Again he grew feverish, and all kinds of images haunted him – the governess's waist, her hips, her thighs.

At night he concealed all her clothes in his bed with him, and fell asleep on them, burying his sex in them as if it were into her body. He dreamed of her. The tip of his penis was constantly wet. In the morning there were rings under his eyes.

She gave him a pair of her stockings. Then she gave him a pair of her black patent leather boots. He placed the boots on his bed. He lay naked now among all her belongings, struggling to create her presence, yearning for her. The shoes looked so alive. They made it appear that she had entered the room and was walking on his bed. He stood them up between his legs to look at them. It seemed as if she were going to walk on his body with her dainty pointed feet, crush him. The thought aroused him. He began to tremble. He drew the boots nearer to his body. Then he brought one near enough to touch the tip of his penis. It aroused him so violently he had an ejaculation all over the shiny leather.

But this had become a form of torture. He began to write the governess letters, begging her to come to his room at night. She read them with pleasure, right in his presence, her dark eyes glittering, but she would not risk her position.

Then one day she was called home by the illness of her father. The boy never saw her again. He was left with a devouring hunger for her, and her clothes haunted him.

One day he made a package of all the clothing and went to a house of prostitution. He found a woman who was physically similar to the governess. He made her dress in the governess's clothes. He watched her lace up the corset, which lifted up her breasts and set off her buttocks; watched her button the brassière and slip on the panties. Then he asked her to put on the stockings and the boots.

His excitement was tremendous. He rubbed himself against the woman. He stretched himself at her feet and begged her to touch him with the tip of her boot. She touched his chest first of all, then his belly, then the tip of his penis. This caused him to leap with ardor, and he imagined it was the governess who was touching him.

He kissed the underclothing and tried to possess the girl, but as soon as she opened her legs to him, his desire died, for where was the little mole?

Pierre

When he was a youth, Pierre wandered off toward the quays very early one morning. He had been walking along the river for some time when he was arrested by the sight of a man trying to pull up a nude body from the river to the deck of one of the barges. The body was caught on the anchor chain. Pierre rushed to the man's help. Together they managed to get the body on the deck.

Then the man turned to Pierre and said, 'You wait while I get the police,' and he ran off. The sun was just beginning to rise, and it touched the naked body with a roseate glow. Pierre saw it was not only a woman, but a very beautiful woman. Her long hair clung to her shoulders and full, round breasts. Her smooth golden skin glistened. He had never seen a more beautiful body, washed clear by the water, with lovely soft contours exposed.

He watched her with fascination. The sun was drying her. He touched her. She was still warm and must have died but a short while before. He felt for her heart. It was not beating. Her breast seemed to cling to his hand.

He shivered, then leaned over and kissed the breast. It was elastic and soft under his lips, like a live breast. He felt a sudden violent sexual urge. He continued to kiss the woman. He parted her lips. As he did so, a little water came out from between them, which seemed to him like her very own saliva. He had the feeling that if he kissed her long enough she would come to life. The heat of his lips was passing into hers. He kissed her mouth, her nipples, her neck, her belly, and then his mouth descended to the wet curled pubic hair. It was like kissing her under water.

She lay stretched out, with her legs slightly parted, her arms straight along her sides. The sun was turning her skin to gold, and her wet hair looked like seaweed.

How he loved the way her body lay, exposed and defenseless. How he loved her closed eyes and slightly opened mouth. Her body had the taste of dew, of wet flowers, of wet leaves, of early morning grass. Her skin was like satin under his fingers. He loved her passivity and silence.

He felt himself burning, tense. Finally he fell on her, and as he began to penetrate her, water flowed from between her legs, as if he were making love to a naiad. His movements caused her body to undulate. He continued to thrust himself into her, expecting at any moment to feel her response, but her body merely moved in rhythm with his.

Now he was afraid the man and the police would arrive. He tried to hurry and satisfy himself, but he couldn't. He had never taken so long. The coolness and wetness of the womb, her passivity, his enjoyment so prolonged – yet he could not come.

He moved desperately, to rid himself of his torment, to inject his warm liquid into her cold body. Oh, how he wanted to come at this moment, while kissing her breasts, and he frantically urged his sex within her, but still he could not come. He would be found there by the man and the policeman, lying over the body of the dead woman.

Finally he lifted her body from the waist, bringing her up against his penis and pushing violently into her. Now he heard shouts all around, and at that moment he felt himself exploding inside of her. He withdrew, dropped the body, and ran away.

This woman haunted him for days. He could not take a shower without remembering the feel of the wet skin and seeing how she shone in the dawn. Never again would he see so beautiful a body. He could not hear rain without remembering how the water came out between her legs and out of her mouth, and how soft and smooth she was.

He felt he had to escape from the city. After a few days, he found himself in a fishing village, and stumbled on a row of cheaply built artists' studios. He rented one. He could hear everything through the walls. In the middle of the row of studios, next to Pierre's, was a community water closet. When he lay trying to sleep, he suddenly caught a faint streak of light between the wall boards. He applied his eye to a crack and saw, standing before the water closet, with one hand resting on the wall, a boy of about fifteen.

He had taken down his pants halfway and opened his shirt,

bowing his curled head over his labor. In his right hand, he was thoughtfully fingering his young sex. Now and then he pressed it hard and a convulsion shook his body. In the dim light, with his curly hair and young pale body, he looked quite like an angel, except for the fact that he was holding his sex in his right hand.

He dropped his other hand from the wall where it had been resting and took hold of his balls very firmly, while he continued to maul, press and squeeze his penis. It did not get very hard. He was experiencing pleasure, but he could not reach a climax. He was disappointed. He had tried every motion of finger and hand. Now he held his limp penis wistfully. He weighed it, puzzled over it and then covered it within his pants, buttoned his shirt and left the place.

Pierre was wide awake now. The memory of the drowned woman haunted him again, mingled now with the picture of the young boy playing with himself. He was lying there, tossing, when a light again appeared from the water closet. Pierre could not keep from looking. Sitting there was a woman of about fifty, enormous, solid, with a heavy face and gluttonous mouth and eyes.

She had only sat for a moment when someone tried the door. Instead of sending him away, she opened it. And there appeared the boy who had been there earlier. He was amazed that the door had opened. The old woman did not move from the seat but drew him in with a smile and closed the door.

'What a lovely boy you are,' she said. 'Surely you must have a little friend already, no? Surely you must already have had a little pleasure with women?'

'No,' said the boy timidly.

She talked to him easily, as if they had met in the street. He had been taken by surprise and stared at her. All he could see was her full-lipped mouth smiling and her insinuating eyes.

'Never had any pleasure at all, my boy, you can't tell me that?'

'No,' said the boy.

'Don't you know how?' asked the woman. 'Haven't your friends in school told you how?'

'Yes,' said the boy, 'I have seen them do it, with their right hand they do it. I tried, but nothing happened.'

The woman laughed. 'But there is another way. Never learned

another way, really? No one told you anything? You mean you only know how to do it with your own hand? Why, there's another way that always works.'

The boy eyed her with suspicion. But her smile was wide, generous, reassuring.

The caresses he had given himself must have left a certain disturbance in him, because he made a step toward the woman.

'What's the way you know?' he said with curiosity.

She laughed.

'You really want to know, eh? And what happens if you enjoy it? If you really enjoy it, will you promise to come and see me again?'

'I promise,' said the boy.

'Well, then, climb on my lap, this way, just kneel on me, don't be afraid, now.'

The middle of his body was just at the same level as her big mouth. She deftly unbuttoned his pants and took out the small penis. The boy watched her with amazement as she took it into her mouth.

Then, as her tongue began to move and the small penis grew larger, the boy was taken with such pleasure that he fell forward over her shoulder and let her mouth take in his whole penis and touch the pubic hair. What he felt was so much more stimulating than when he had tried to manipulate himself. All that Pierre could see now was the big full-lipped mouth working on the delicate penis, now and then letting it halfway out of the cavern, and then swallowing it altogether until nothing showed but the hair around it.

The old woman was gluttonous but patient. The boy was exhausted with pleasure, almost swooning over her head, and the blood was coming to her face. Still she vigorously chewed and licked, until the boy began to tremble. She had to put both her arms around him or he might have shaken himself out of her mouth. He began to utter moaning sounds like some cooing bird. She went at him more feverishly, and then it happened. The boy almost fell asleep on her shoulder from exhaustion, and she had to unclasp him gently with her big hands. He smiled wanly and ran out.

*

While he lay there Pierre remembered a woman he had known who was already fifty when he was only seventeen. She was a friend of his mother's. She was eccentric and willful and still dressed in fashions of ten years earlier, which meant wearing an endless number of petticoats, tight corsets, long and heavily laced panties, and full-skirted dresses that were cut very low over her breasts so Pierre could see the little valley between them, a black shadowy line vanishing inside the lace and frills.

She was a handsome woman, with luxuriant reddish hair and a fine down over her skin. Her ears were small and delicate, her hands plump. Her mouth was particularly attractive – very red, naturally so, with great fullness and width, and with small, even teeth, which she always showed, as if she were about to bite into something.

She came to visit his mother one very rainy day when the servants were out. She shook her filmy umbrella, took off her important hat, and unloosened her veil. As she stood there, her long dress all wet, she began to sneeze. Pierre's mother was already in bed with the grippe. She called out from her room, 'Darling, do take off your clothes if they are wet, and Pierre will dry them for you before the fire. There is a screen in the parlor. You can undress there and Pierre will give you a kimono of mine.'

Pierre hustled about with evident eagerness. He got the kimono from his mother and he opened the screen. In the parlor there was a beautiful fire burning brightly in the fireplace. The room was warm and smelled of narcissus, which filled every vase, of the wood fire, of the visitor's sandalwood perfume.

From behind the screen she handed her dress to Pierre. It was still warm and scented from her body. He held it in his arms and smelled it, intoxicated, before laying it over a chair before the fire. Then she handed him a large, very full petticoat, the hem extremely wet and covered with mud. He sniffed at this with pleasure before placing it, too, before the fire.

Meanwhile she talked and smiled and laughed unconcernedly, not noticing his excitement. She threw him another petticoat, a lighter one, warm and musky. Then, with a shy laugh, she threw him her long, lace-edged panties. Suddenly Pierre realized that they were not wet, that this was unnecessary, that she had thrown them at him because she wanted to and that now she stood nearly naked behind the screen, knowing he was aware of her body.

As she looked at him over the top of the screen, he could see her full, rounded shoulders, soft and gleaming, like cushions. She laughed and called out to him, 'Give me the kimono now.'

'Aren't your stockings wet, too?' said Pierre.

'Yes, indeed they are. I am taking them off.' She leaned down. He could imagine her snapping loose the garters and unrolling the stockings. He wondered what her legs looked like, her feet. He could contain himself no longer and gave the screen a pull.

It fell down before her and exposed her in the pose he had pictured. She was leaning down and unrolling her black stockings. Her whole body had the golden color and delicate texture of her face. It was long-waisted, full-breasted, ample, but firm.

She was unaffected by the fall of the screen. She said, 'Now look what I have done taking my stockings off. Hand me the kimono.' He approached, staring at her – the first naked woman he had seen, so much like paintings he had studied in the museum.

She was smiling. Then she covered herself as if nothing had happened and went to the fire, extending her hand to the heat. Pierre was completely unnerved. His body was burning, yet he did not quite know what to do about it.

She was careless about holding the kimono around her, intent on warming herself. Pierre sat at her feet and stared at her smiling, open face. Her eyes seemed to invite him. He moved closer to her, still kneeling. Suddenly she opened the kimono, took his head between her hands, placed it on her sex for his mouth to feel. The tendrils of pubic hair touched his lips and maddened him. At that very moment his mother's voice came from the far-off bedroom. 'Pierre! Pierre!'

He straightened himself. His mother's friend closed her kimono. They were left trembling, burning, unsatisfied. The friend went to his mother's room, sat at the foot of her bed and chatted with her. Pierre sat with them, nervously waiting until the woman was ready to get dressed again. The afternoon seemed endless. Then, finally, she rose and said she must dress. But Pierre's mother detained him. She wanted something to drink. She wanted the curtains drawn. She kept him occupied until the friend was dressed. Had she guessed what might have been happening in the parlor? Pierre was left with the touch of her hair and rosy skin on his lips, nothing else.

When the friend left, his mother talked to him in the half-dark room.

'Poor Mary Ann,' she said. 'Did you know, a terrible thing happened to her when she was young. It was when the Prussians invaded Alsace-Lorraine. She was raped by soldiers. And now she will not let a man near her.'

The image of Mary Ann being violated inflamed Pierre. He could barely conceal his disturbance. Mary Ann had trusted his youth and innocence. She had lost her fear of men with him. He was like a child to her. So she had permitted his young, tender face between her legs.

That night he dreamed of soldiers tearing her clothes, spreading her legs, and he awakened with a violent desire for her. How could he see her now? Would she ever let him do more to her than kiss her sex gently as he had done? Was she closed forever?

He wrote her a letter. He was amazed when he received an answer. She asked him to come and see her. Wearing a loose robe, she greeted him in a dimly lighted room. His first movement was to kneel before her. She smiled indulgently. 'How gentle you are,' she said. Then she pointed to a wide divan in the corner and stretched herself on it. He stretched himself beside her. He felt timid and could not move.

Then he felt her hand deftly inserting itself under his belt, slipping inside his pants, sliding along, close to the belly, arousing every bit of flesh she touched, gliding, descending.

The hand stopped at his pubic hair, played with it, moved around the penis without touching it. It began to stir. He thought if she touched his penis it would kill him with pleasure. His mouth opened with the suspense.

Her hand continued to move slowly, slowly around and over his pubic hair. A finger sought the tiny rivulet between the hair and the sex where the skin was smooth, sought every sensitive part of the young man, slid along under his penis, pressed his balls.

Finally her hand closed around his throbbing penis. And it was a shock of such intense pleasure that he sighed. His own hand went out, blindly fumbling through her clothes. He, too, wanted to touch the core of her sensations. He, too, wanted to glide along and enter into her secret places. He fumbled with her clothes. He found an opening. He touched her pubic hair and the rivulet between the leg and the mount of Venus, felt the tender flesh, found moisture and dipped his finger into it.

Then in a frenzy he tried to push his penis into her. He saw all the soldiers charging into her. The blood rushed to his head. She thrust him away and would not let him take her. She whispered in his ear, 'Only with the hands,' and then lay open to him while continuing to caress him inside his pants.

When he again turned over to push his wild sex against her she pushed him away, angrily this time. Her hand aroused him, and he could not lie still.

She said, 'I will make you come this way. Enjoy yourself.' He lay back quietly enjoying the caresses. But as soon as he closed his eyes he saw the soldiers bending over her naked body, he saw her legs forced apart, the opening dripping from the attacks, and what he felt resembled the furious panting desire of the soldiers.

Mary Ann suddenly closed her robe and stood up. She had grown completely cold now. She sent him away, and he was never allowed to see her again.

At forty Pierre was still a very handsome man, whose successes with women, and the long and now broken liaison with Elena, had given the local people much to talk about in the small country place where he had settled. He was now married to a very delicate and charming woman, but two years after their marriage her health had grown poor and she was a semi-invalid. Pierre had loved her ardently, and his passion at first seemed to revive her but slowly had become a danger to her weak heart. Finally her doctor advised against all lovemaking, and poor Sylvia entered into a long period of chastity. Pierre, too, was suddenly deprived of his sexual life.

Sylvia was naturally forbidden to have children, and so she and Pierre finally decided to adopt two from the village orphanage. It was a great day for Sylvia, and she dressed lavishly for the occasion. It was a great day for the orphanage, too, because all the children knew that Pierre and his wife had a beautiful house, a big estate, and that they were reputed to be kind.

It was Sylvia who chose the children – John, a delicate fair-haired boy, and Martha, a dark and vivid girl, both about sixteen years of age. The two had been inseparable in the orphanage, as close as a brother and sister.

They were taken to the big, lovely house, where each was given a room overlooking the wide park. Pierre and Sylvia gave them all their care and tenderness and guidance. In addition, John watched over Martha.

At times Pierre observed them with envy of their youth and comradeship. John was fond of wrestling with Martha. For a long time she was the stronger. But one day while Pierre watched them, it was John who pinned Martha down to the ground and managed to sit on her chest and cry out his triumph. Pierre then noticed that the victory, following a heated mingling of their two bodies, did not displease Martha. There is the woman beginning to form herself already, he thought. She wants the man to be stronger.

But if the woman was appearing timidly now in the young girl, she obtained no gallant treatment from John. He seemed intent on treating her only as a playmate, even as a boy. He never complimented her, never noticed the way she dressed or her coquetries. In fact, he went out of his way to be harsh with her when she threatened to be tender, and to call attention to her defects. He treated her without sentimentality. And poor Martha was perplexed and hurt but refused to show it. Pierre was the only one aware of this wounded femininity in Martha.

He was lonely on the big estate. He had the care of the farm adjoining it, of other properties owned by Sylvia throughout the country, but it was not enough. He had no companion. John dominated Martha so completely that she would pay no attention to him. At the same time, with the experienced eye of the older man, he could see very well that Martha was in need of another kind of relationship.

One day when he found Martha crying and alone in the park,

he ventured to say tenderly, 'What is the matter, Martha? You can always confide to a father what you can't confide to a playmate.'

She looked up at him, for the first time aware of his gentleness and sympathy. She confessed that John had said she was ugly and awkward and too animal.

'What a stupid boy,' said Pierre, 'that is absolutely untrue. He says that because he is too much of a girl and can't appreciate your type of healthy and vigorous beauty. He is a sissy, really, and you are wonderfully strong and beautiful in a way he cannot understand.'

Martha looked at him with gratitude.

Henceforth it was Pierre who greeted her every morning with some charming phrase – 'That blue color suits your skin so well' or 'That is a very becoming way of wearing your hair.'

He surprised her with gifts of perfume and scarves and other little vanities. Sylvia never left her bedroom now, and only occasionally sat in a chair in the garden on exceptional, sunny days. John was becoming absorbed in scientific studies and had been giving less attention to Martha.

Pierre had a car in which he did all the errands for the supervision of the farm. He had always gone alone. Now he began to take Martha with him.

She was seventeen, beautifully formed by a healthy life, with a clear skin and brilliant black hair. Her eyes were fiery and ardent and rested lingeringly upon the slender body of John – too often, thought Pierre as he watched her. Obviously she was in love with John, but John did not notice it. Pierre felt a pang of jealousy. He looked at himself in the mirror and compared himself with John. The comparison was rather in his favor, for if John was a handsome youth, at the same time there was a coldness in his appearance, whereas Pierre's green eyes were still compelling to women, and his body exuded great warmth and charm.

Subtly he began his courtship of Martha, with compliments and attentiveness, becoming her confidant in all matters, until she even confessed her attraction to John, but added, 'He is absolutely inhuman.'

One day John insulted her openly in Pierre's presence. She had been dancing and running, and looked exuberant and alive.

Suddenly John looked at her reproachfully and said, 'What an animal you are. You will never sublimate your energy.'

Sublimation! So that was what he wanted. He wanted to take Martha into his world of studies and theories and researches, to deny the flame in her. Martha looked at him angrily.

Nature was working in favor of Pierre's humanness. The summer made Martha languid, the summer undressed her. Wearing fewer clothes, she was becoming more and more aware of her own body. The breeze seemed to touch her skin like a hand. At night she tossed in bed with a restlessness she could not understand. Her hair was unbraided, and she felt as if a hand had loosened it around her throat and were touching it.

Pierre was quick to sense what was happening to her. He made no advances. When he helped her out of the car his hand rested on her fresh bare arm. Or when she was sad and talking about John's indifference, he would caress her hair. But his eyes rested on her and knew every bit of her body, whatever he could divine through the dress. He knew how fine the down was over her skin, how free of hair her legs were, how firm her young breasts were. Her hair, wild and thick, often brushed against his face when she leaned over to study the farm reports with him. Her breath often mingled with his. Once he let his hand stray around her waist, paternally. She did not move away. Somehow his gestures answered deeply her need of warmth. She thought that she was yielding to an enveloping, paternal warmth, and gradually it was she who sought to stand near him when they were together, it was she who put his arm around her when they were driving, it was she who rested her head on his shoulder late afternoons on their way home.

They returned from these supervising trips always glowing with a secret understanding, which John observed. It made him even more sullen. But now Martha was in open rebellion against him. The more reserved and severe he became with her, the more she wanted to assert the fire in her, her love of life and movement. She flung herself into the comradeship with Pierre.

About an hour's drive away, there was an abandoned farm they had once rented out. It had fallen into disuse, and now Pierre decided he wanted to have it repaired for the day John married.

Before calling in the workmen, he and Martha went together to look it over and see what needed to be done.

It was a very big one-story house. A mass of ivy had almost completely smothered it, covering the windows with a natural curtain, darkening the interior. Pierre and Martha opened a window. They found much dust, the furniture musty and a few rooms ruined where the rain had come in. But one room was nearly intact. It was the master bedroom. A big, somber bed, many draperies, mirrors and a worn carpet gave it, in the semi-darkness, a certain grandeur. Over the bed a heavy velvet cover had been thrown.

Pierre, looking around with the eye of an architect, sat on the edge of the bed. Martha stood near him. The summer warmth came into the room in waves, stirring their blood. Again Martha felt this invisible hand caressing her. It did not seem strange to her that a real hand should suddenly be slipping among her clothes, with the same gentleness and softness as the summer wind, touching her skin. It seemed natural and pleasant; she closed her eyes.

Pierre drew her body toward him and stretched her on the bed. She kept her eyes closed. This seemed merely like the continuation of a dream. Lying alone for many summer nights, she had been expecting this hand, and it was doing all that she had expected. It was stealing softly through her clothes, stripping her of them as if they were a light skin to be peeled, setting free the real, warm skin. The hand moved all over her, to places she had not even known it would go, to secret places, which were throbbing.

Then suddenly she opened her eyes. She saw the face of Pierre right over her face preparing to kiss her. She sat up brusquely. While her eyes were closed she had imagined it was John who was stealing thus into her flesh. But when she saw Pierre's face, she was disappointed. She escaped from him. They returned home silent, but not angry. Martha was like a drugged person. She could not rid herself of the sensation of Pierre's hand on her body. Pierre was tender, and seemed to understand her resistance. They found John rigid and sullen.

Martha was unable to sleep. Every time she dozed off she began to feel the hand again, to await its movements, as it came up her leg and worked its way to the secret place where she had felt a throbbing, an expectancy. She got up and stood by the window. Her whole body was crying out for this hand to touch her again. It was worse than hunger or thirst, this yearning of the flesh.

The next day she rose pale and determined. As soon as lunch was over, she turned to Pierre and said, 'We have to see about that farm today?' He assented. They drove off. It was a relief. The wind struck her face and she was free now. She watched his right hand on the wheel of the car – a beautiful hand, youthful, supple, and tender. Suddenly she leaned over and pressed her lips on it. Pierre smiled at her with such a gratitude and joy that it made her heart leap to see it.

Together they walked through the tangled garden, up the moss-covered path, into the green dark room with its curtains of ivy. Straight to the large bed they walked, and it was Martha who stretched herself on it.

'Your hands,' she murmured, 'oh, your hands, Pierre. I felt them all night.'

How suavely, how gently his hands began to search her body, as if he were searching for the place where her sensations were gathered and did not know whether it was around her breasts, or under her breasts, along her hips or in the valley between the hips. He waited for her flesh to respond, perceiving by the slightest tremor that his hand had touched the place she wanted to be touched. Her dresses, sheets, nightgowns, the water of her bath, the wind, the heat, everything had conspired to sensitize her skin until this hand fulfilled the caresses they all had given her, adding warmth and the power to penetrate the secret places everywhere.

But as soon as Pierre leaned over too close to her face to take a kiss, then the image of John interfered. She closed her eyes, and Pierre felt her body also closing against him. So with wisdom, he pursued his caresses no further.

When they returned home that day, Martha was filled with a kind of drunkenness that made her behave recklessly. The house was so arranged that Pierre and Sylvia's apartment was connected to Martha's room, and hers in turn communicated with the bathroom used by John. When the children were younger all the doors were left open. Now Pierre's wife preferred to lock her bedroom door, and the one between Martha and Pierre was also locked. On this day Martha took a bath. Lying quietly in the water she could hear John's movements in his room. Her body was in a great fever from Pierre's caresses, but she still desired John. She wanted to make one more attempt to awaken John's desire, to force him into the open, so she would know whether or not there was any hope of his loving her.

Once bathed, she wrapped herself in a long white kimono, with her long thick black hair hanging loose. Instead of returning to her own room she entered John's. He was startled by the sight of her. She explained her presence by saying, 'I am terribly anxious, John, I need your advice. I'm leaving this house soon.'

'Leaving?'

'Yes,' said Martha. 'It is time I leave. I must learn to become independent. I want to go to Paris.'

'But you are so needed here.'

'Needed?'

'You are my father's companion,' he said bitterly.

Could it be that he was jealous? Martha waited breathlessly for him to say more. Then she added, 'I should be meeting people and trying to get married. I cannot be a burden forever.'

'Married?'

Then he saw Martha as a woman for the first time. He had always considered her a child. What he saw was a voluptuous body, clearly outlined in the kimono, moist hair, a fevered face, a soft mouth. She waited. The expectancy in her was so intense that her hands fell to her sides, and the kimono opened and revealed her completely naked body.

Then John saw that she wanted him, that she was offering herself, but instead of being stirred, he recoiled. 'Martha! Oh, Martha!' he said. 'What an animal you are, you are truly the daughter of a whore. Yes, in the orphanage everybody said it, that you were the daughter of a whore.'

Martha's blood rushed to her face. 'And you,' she said, 'you are impotent, a monk, you're like a woman, you're not a man. Your father is a man.'

And she rushed out of his room.

Now the image of John ceased to torment her. She wanted to

efface it from her body and her blood. It was she who waited that night for everyone to fall asleep so she could unlock the door to Pierre's room, and it was she who came to his bed, silently offering her now cool and abandoned body to him.

Pierre knew that she was free of John, that she was his now, by the way she came into his bed. What joy to feel the soft youthful body sliding against his body. Summer nights he slept naked. Martha had dropped her kimono and was naked too. Immediately his desire sprang up and she felt the hardness of it against her belly.

Her diffuse feelings were now concentrated in only one part of her body. She found herself making gestures she had never learned, found her hand surrounding his penis, found herself gluing her body to his, found her mouth yielding to the many kinds of kisses Pierre could give. She gave herself in a frenzy, and Pierre was aroused to his greatest feats.

Every night was an orgy. Her body became supple and knowing. The tie between them was so strong that it was difficult for them to pretend otherwise during the day. If she looked at him, it was as if he had touched her between the legs. Sometimes in the dark hall they embraced. He pressed her against the wall. At the entrance there was a big dark closet full of coats and snow shoes. No one ever entered there in the summer. Martha hid there and Pierre came in. Lying over the coats, in the small space, enclosed, secret, they abandoned themselves.

Pierre had been without sexual life for years, and Martha was meant for this and only came to life at these moments. She received him always with her mouth open and already wet between the legs. His desire rose in him before he saw her, at the mere idea of her waiting in this dark closet. They acted like animals in a struggle, about to devour each other. If his body won and he pinned her down under him, then he took her with such a force that he seemed to be stabbing her with his sex, over and over again, until she fell back exhausted. They were in marvelous harmony, their excitement rising together. She had a way of climbing over him like an agile animal. She would rub herself against his erect penis, against his pubic hair, with such frenzy that he panted. This dark closet became an animal den.

They sometimes drove to the abandoned farmhouse and spent the afternoon there. They became so saturated with lovemaking that if Pierre kissed Martha's eyelids she could feel it between her legs. Their bodies were charged with desire, and they could not exhaust it.

John seemed a pale image. They did not notice that he was observing them. The change in Pierre was apparent. His face glowed, his eyes looked ardent, his body became younger. And the change in her: Voluptuousness was inscribed all over her body. Every move she made was sensual – serving coffee, reaching for a book, playing chess, playing the piano, she did everything caressingly. Her body became fuller and her breasts tauter under her clothes.

John could not sit between them. Even when they did not look at each other or speak to each other, he could feel a powerful current between them.

One day when they had driven to the abandoned farm, John, instead of continuing his studies, felt a wave of laziness and the desire to be out-of-doors. He got on his bicycle and began to ride aimlessly, not thinking of them but perhaps half-consciously remembering the rumor in the orphanage that Martha had been abandoned by a well-known prostitute. All his life, it seemed to him that, while he loved Martha, he also feared her. He felt that she was an animal, that she could enjoy people as she enjoyed food, that her point of view about people was completely opposed to his. She would say, 'He is beautiful,' or 'She is charming.' He would say, 'He is interesting,' or 'She has character.'

Martha had expressed sensuality even as a little girl, in wrestling with him, in caressing him. She liked to play hide-and-seek, and if he could not find her she would give away her hiding place so he would catch her, gripping her dress. Once they were playing together and had built a small tent. They found themselves huddled together, very close. Then he saw Martha's face. She had closed her eyes to enjoy the warmth of their bodies together, and John had felt a tremendous fear. Why fear? All through his life he was haunted by this recoil from sensuality. He could not explain it to himself. But there it was. He had seriously thought of becoming a monk.

Now, without thinking of his destination, he had reached the old farmhouse. He had not seen it for a long time. He walked softly over the moss and overgrown grass. Out of curiosity he entered it and began to explore. So he came quietly upon the bedroom where Pierre and Martha were. The door was open. He stopped, transfixed by the sight. It was as if his greatest fear had come alive. Pierre was lying back, eyes half-closed, and Martha, completely naked, was behaving like a demon, climbing over him, in a frenzy of hunger for his body.

John stood paralyzed with the shock of the scene, and yet took it all in. Martha, smooth, voluptuous, was not only kissing Pierre's sex, but crouching over his mouth, and then throwing herself against his body and rubbing her breasts against his, and he lay back, entranced, hypnotized by her caresses.

After a moment John rushed off without being heard. He had seen the very worst of the infernal vices, confirming his fear that it was Martha who was the erotic one, and he believed that his adopted father was merely yielding to her passion. The more he sought to erase this scene from his mind, the more it penetrated into his whole being, stark, indelible, haunting.

When they returned he looked at their faces and was amazed at how different people could look in daily life from the way they looked while they made love. The changes were obscene. Martha's face now seemed closed, whereas before it was crying out her enjoyment, through her eyes, hair, mouth, tongue. And Pierre, the serious Pierre, a short time ago was not a father but a rather youthful body stretched on a bed, abandoned to the furious lust of an unleashed woman.

John felt he could no longer stay at home without betraying his discovery to his sick mother, to everyone. When he declared his intention of leaving to join the army, Martha gave him a quick stabbing glance of surprise. Until now she thought John was merely puritanical. But she also believed that he loved her and that sooner or later he would succumb to her. She wanted them both. Pierre was a lover such as women dream of. John, she could have educated, even against his nature. And now he was going. Something remained unfinished between them, as if the warmth created during their games together had been interrupted and had been intended to continue into their adult lives.

That night she tried to reach through to him again. She went to his room. He received her with such revulsion that she demanded an explanation, drove him to confess, and then he blurted out the scene he had witnessed. He could not believe that she loved Pierre. He believed it was the animal in her. And when she saw his reaction, she sensed she would never be able to possess him now.

She stopped herself at the door and said to him, 'John, you are convinced that I am animal. Well, I can easily prove to you that I am not. I have told you that I love you. I will prove it to you. I will not only break with Pierre, but I will come every night to you and stay with you and we will sleep like children, together, and I will prove to you how chaste I can be, how free of desire.'

John's eyes opened wide. He was deeply tempted. The thought of Martha and his father making love was intolerable to him. He explained it on moral grounds. He did not recognize that he was jealous. He did not see how much he would have liked to be in Pierre's place, with all of Pierre's experience of women. He did not ask himself why he repudiated Martha's love. But why was he so removed from the natural hungers of other men and women?

He assented to Martha's offer. With cunning, Martha did not break with Pierre in such a way as to alarm him, but merely told him she thought John was suspicious and she wanted to calm all his doubts before he left for the army.

As John waited for Martha's visit the next night, he tried to remember all he could of his sexual feelings. His first impressions were linked with Martha – he and Martha in the orphanage, protecting each other, inseparable. His love for her then was ardent and spontaneous. He delighted in touching her. Then one day when Martha was eleven, a woman came to see her. John caught a glimpse of her waiting in the parlor. He had never seen anyone like her. She wore tight clothes that outlined her full, voluptuous figure. Her hair was red-gold, waved, her lips so thickly painted that they fascinated the boy. He stared at her. Then he saw her receiving Martha and embracing her. It was then he was told this was Martha's mother, who had abandoned her as a child, and then later acknowledged her but was

not able to keep her because she was the favorite prostitute of
the town.

After that, if Martha's face glowed with excitement or became
flushed, if her hair shone, if she wore a tight dress, if she made the
slightest coquettish gesture, then John would feel a great disturbance, anger. It seemed to him that he could see her mother in
her, that her body was provocative, that she was lustful. He
would question her. He wanted to know what she thought, what
she dreamed, her most secret desires. She answered him naïvely.
What she liked best in the world was John. What gave her the
greatest pleasure was to be touched by him.

'What do you feel then?' asked John.

'Contentment, a pleasure I cannot explain.'

John was convinced it was not from him she derived these half-
innocent pleasures, but from any man. He imagined that Martha's
mother felt the same with all the men who touched her.

Because he turned away from Martha and starved her of the
affection she needed, he had lost her. But this he could not see.
Now he felt a great pleasure in dominating her. He would show
her what chastity was, what love, love without sensuality, could
be between human beings.

Martha came at midnight, noiselessly. She wore a long white
nightgown, and over this her kimono. Her long thick black hair
fell over her shoulders. Her eyes shone unnaturally. She was quiet
and gentle, as if she were a sister. Her usual vivaciousness was
controlled and subdued. In this mood she did not frighten John.
She seemed like another Martha.

The bed was very wide and low. John turned out the light.
Martha slipped into it and rested her body without touching
John. He was trembling. This reminded him of the orphanage
where, in order to be able to talk to her a little longer, he escaped
from the boys' dormitory and went and talked with her through
her window. She wore a white nightgown then and her hair was
braided. He said this to her and asked her if she would let him
braid her hair again. He wanted to see her as a little girl again.
She let him. In the dark his hands touched her rich hair and
braided it. Then they both pretended to fall asleep.

But John was tormented by images. He saw Martha naked, and

then he saw her mother in the tight dress that revealed every curve, and then again he saw Martha crouching like an animal over Pierre's face. The blood beat in his temples, and he wanted to stretch out his hand. He did. Martha took hold of it and laid it over her heart, over her left breast. Through the clothes he could feel her heart beating. And in this way they finally slept. In the morning they awakened together. John found he had come near to Martha and slept with his body against hers, spoon-fashion. He awakened wanting her, feeling her warmth. In anger he leaped out of bed and pretended he had to dress quickly.

And so passed the first night. Martha kept herself gentle and subdued. John was tormented with desire. But his pride and fear were greater.

He now knew what it was he feared. He was afraid he might be impotent. He was afraid that his father, known as a Don Juan, was more potent and more knowing. He was afraid to be awkward. He was afraid that once he aroused the volcanic fires in Martha, he could not satisfy them. A less fiery woman might not have frightened him as much. He had been so eager to control his own nature and sexual flow. He had succeeded perhaps too well. He was doubtful of his power now.

With feminine intuition, Martha must have guessed all this. Every night she came more quietly, she was more gentle, more humble. They fell asleep together innocently. She did not betray the heat she felt between her legs as he lay near her. She actually slept. He remained awake sometimes, with the haunting sexual images of her naked body.

Once or twice in the middle of the night he awakened, and he drew his body close and breathlessly fondled her. Her body was limp and warm in sleep. He dared to lift her nightgown by the hem, to raise it high over her breasts and pass his hand over her body to feel the outline of it. She did not awaken. This gave him courage. He did nothing more than stroke her, softly feeling the curves of her body with care, every line of it, until he knew just where the skin grew softer, where the fullest flesh lay, where the valleys were, where the pubic hair began.

What he did not know was that Martha was half awake and enjoying his caresses, but never moving for fear of frightening him. Once she was so warmed with the searching of his hands that she almost reached an orgasm. And once he dared to place his erect desire against her buttocks, but no more.

Each night he dared a little more, surprised that he did not waken her. His desire was constant, and Martha was kept in such a state of erotic fever that she marveled at her own power of deception. John became bolder. He had learned to slip his sex between her legs and to rub very gently without penetrating her. The pleasure was so great he then began to understand all the lovers of the world.

Tantalized by so many nights of repression, John one night forgot his precautions and took the half-sleeping Martha like a thief, and was amazed to hear little sounds of pleasure coming from her throat at his thrusts.

He did not go into the army. And Martha kept her two lovers satisfied, Pierre during the day and John at night.

Manuel

Manuel had developed a peculiar form of enjoyment that caused his family to repudiate him, and he lived like a Bohemian in Montparnasse. When not obsessed with his erotic exigencies, he was an astrologer, an extraordinary cook, a great conversationalist and an excellent café companion. But not one of these occupations could divert his mind from his obsession. Sooner or later Manuel had to open his pants and exhibit his rather formidable member.

The more people there were, the better. The more refined the party, the better. If he got among the painters and models, he waited until everybody was a little drunk and gay, and then he undressed himself completely. His ascetic face, dreamy and poetic eyes and lean monklike body were so much in dissonance with his behavior that it startled everyone. If they turned away from him, he had no pleasure. If they looked at him for any time at all, then he would fall into a trance, his face would become ecstatic, and soon he would be rolling on the floor in a crisis of orgasm.

Women tended to run away from him. He had to beg them to stay and resorted to all kinds of tricks. He would pose as a model and look for work in women's studios. But the condition he got into as he stood there under the eyes of the female students made the men throw him out into the street.

If he were invited to a party, he would first try to get one of the women alone somewhere in an empty room or on a balcony. Then he would take down his pants. If the woman was interested he would fall into ecstasy. If not, he would run after her, with his erection, and come back to the party and stand there, hoping to create curiosity. He was not a beautiful sight but a highly incongruous one. Since the penis did not seem to belong to the austere religious face and body, it acquired a greater prominence – as it were, an apartness.

He finally found the wife of a poor literary agent who was dying of starvation and overwork, with whom he reached the following arrangement. He would come in the morning and do all her housework for her, wash her dishes, sweep her studio, run errands, on condition that when all this was over he could exhibit himself. In this case he demanded all her attention. He wanted her to watch him unfasten his belt, unbutton his pants, pull them down. He wore no underwear. He would take out his penis and shake it like a person weighing a thing of value. She had to stand near him and watch every gesture. She had to look at his penis as she would look at food she liked.

This woman developed the art of satisfying him completely. She would become absorbed in the penis, saying, 'It's a beautiful penis you have there, the biggest I have seen in Montparnasse. It's so smooth and hard. It's beautiful.'

As she said these words, Manuel continued to shake his penis like a pot of gold under her eyes, and saliva came to his mouth. He admired it himself. As they both bent over it to admire it his pleasure would become so keen that he would close his eyes and be taken with a bodily trembling from head to foot, still holding his penis and shaking it under her face. Then the trembling would turn into undulation and he would fall on the floor and roll himself into a ball as he came, sometimes all over his own face.

Often he stood at dark corners of the streets, naked under an overcoat, and if a woman passed he opened his coat and shook his penis at her. But this was dangerous and the police punished such behavior rather severely. Oftener still he liked to get into an empty compartment of a train, unbutton two of the buttons, and sit back as if he were drunk or asleep, his penis showing a little through the opening. People would come in at other stations. If he were in luck it might be a woman who would sit across from him and stare at him. As he looked drunk, usually no one tried to wake him. Sometimes one of the men would rouse him angrily and tell him to button himself. Women did not protest. If a woman came in with little schoolgirls, then he was in paradise. He would have an erection, and finally the situation would become so intolerable, the woman and her little girls would leave the compartment.

One day Manuel found his twin in this form of enjoyment. He had taken his seat in a compartment, alone, and was pretending to fall asleep when a woman came in and sat opposite him. She was a rather mature prostitute as he could see from the heavily painted eyes, the thickly powdered face, the rings under her eyes, the over-curled hair, the worn-down shoes, the coquettish dress and hat.

Through half-closed eyes he observed her. She took a glance at his partly opened pants and then looked again. She too sat back and appeared to fall asleep, with her legs wide apart. When the train started she raised her skirt completely. She was naked underneath. She stretched open her legs and exposed herself while looking at Manuel's penis, which was hardening and showing through the pants and which finally protruded completely. They sat in front of each other, staring. Manuel was afraid the woman would move and try to get hold of his penis, which was not what he wanted at all. But no, she was addicted to the same passive pleasures. She knew he was looking at her sex, under the very black and bushy hair, and finally they opened their eyes and smiled at each other. He was entering his ecstatic state, but he had time to notice that she was in a state of pleasure herself. He could see the shining moisture appearing at the mouth of the sex. She moved almost imperceptibly to and fro, as if rocking herself to sleep. His body began to tremble with voluptuous pleasure. She then masturbated in front of him, smiling all the time.

Manuel married this woman, who never tried to possess him in the way of other women.

Linda

Linda stood in front of her mirror examining herself critically in full daylight. Now past thirty, she was becoming concerned with her age, although nothing about her betrayed any lessening of her beauty. She was slender, youthful in appearance. She could well deceive everyone but herself. In her own eyes her flesh was losing some of its firmness, some of that marble smoothness that she had admired so often in her own mirror.

She was no less loved. If anything she was more loved than ever, because now she attracted all the young men who sense that it is from such a woman that they will really learn the secrets of lovemaking, and who feel no attraction to the young girls of their age who are backward, innocent, inexperienced, and still possessed by their families.

Linda's husband, a handsome man of forty, had loved her with the fervor of a lover for many years. He closed his eyes to her young admirers. He believed that she did not take them seriously, that her interest was due to her childlessness and the need to pour her protective feelings over people who were beginning to live. He himself was reputed to be a seducer of women of all classes and character.

She remembered that on her wedding night André had been an adoring lover, worshiping each part of her body separately, as if she were a work of art, touching her and marveling, commenting on her ears, her feet, her neck, her hair, her nose, her cheeks, and her thighs, as he fondled them. His words and voice, his touch, opened her flesh like a flower to the heat and light.

He trained her to be a sexually perfect instrument, to vibrate to every form of caress. One time he taught her to put the rest of her body to sleep, as it were, and to concentrate all her erotic feelings in her mouth. Then she was like a woman half-drugged, lying there, her body quiet and languid, and her mouth, her lips, became another sex organ.

André had a particular passion for her mouth. In the street he looked at women's mouths. To him the mouth was indicative of the sex. A tightness of a lip, thinness, augured nothing rich or voluptuous. A full mouth promised an open, generous sex. A moist mouth tantalized him. A mouth that opened out, a mouth that was parted as if ready for a kiss, he would follow doggedly in the street until he could possess the woman and prove again his conviction of the revelatory powers of the mouth.

Linda's mouth had seduced him from the first. It had a perverse, half-dolorous expression. There was something about the way she moved it, a passionate unfolding of the lips, promising a person who would lash around the beloved like a storm. When he first saw Linda, he was taken into her through this mouth, as if he were already making love to her. And so it was on their wedding night. He was obsessed with her mouth. It was on her mouth that he threw himself, kissing it until it burned, until the tongue was worn out, until the lips were swollen; and then, when he had fully aroused her mouth, it was thus that he took her, crouching over her, his strong lips pressed against her breasts.

He never treated her as a wife. He wooed her over and over again, with presents, flowers, new pleasures. He took her to dinner at the *cabinets particuliers* of Paris, to the big restaurants, where all the waiters thought she was his mistress.

He chose the most exciting food and wine for her. He made her drunk with his caressing words. He made love to her mouth. He made her say that she wanted him. Then he would ask: 'And how do you want me? What part of you wants me tonight?'

Sometimes she answered, 'My mouth wants you, I want to feel you in my mouth, way down in my mouth.' Other times she answered, 'I am moist between the legs.'

This is how they talked across restaurant tables, in the small private dining rooms created especially for lovers. How discreet the waiters, knowing when not to return. Music would come from an invisible source. There would be a divan. When the meal was served, and André had pressed Linda's knees between his and stolen kisses, he would take her on the divan, with her clothes on, like lovers who do not have time to undress.

He would escort her to the opera and to the theaters famed for their dark boxes, and make love to her while they watched a spectacle. He would make love to her in taxis, in a barge anchored in front of Notre Dame that rented cabins to lovers. Everywhere but at home, on the marital bed. He would drive her to little far-off villages and stay at romantic inns with her. He would take a room for them in the luxurious houses of prostitution he had known. Then he would treat her like a prostitute. He would make her submit to his whims, ask to be whipped, ask her to crawl on her hands and knees and not to kiss him but to pass her tongue all over him like an animal.

These practices had aroused her sensuality to such a degree that she was frightened. She was afraid of the day when André would cease to be sufficient for her. Her sensuality was, she knew, vigorous; his was the last burst of a man who had spent himself on a life of excess and now gave her the flower of it.

A day came when André had to leave her for ten days for a trip. Linda was restless and feverish. A friend telephoned her, André's friend, the painter of the day in Paris, the favorite of all women. He said to her, 'Are you bored with yourself, Linda? Would you care to join us in a very special kind of party? Do you have a mask?'

Linda knew exactly what he meant. She and André had often laughed at Jacques's parties in the Bois. It was his favorite form of amusement: on a summer night, to gather society people wearing masks, drive to the Bois with bottles of champagne, find a clearing in the wooded section and disport themselves.

She was tempted. She had never participated in one. That, André had not wanted to do. He said playfully that the question of the masks might confuse him and that he did not want to make love to the wrong woman.

Linda accepted the invitation. She put on one of her new evening dresses, a heavy satin dress which outlined her body like a wet glove. She wore no underwear, no jewelry that could identify her. She changed her hair style, from a page-boy frame around her face to a pompadour style, which revealed the shape of her face and neck. Then she tied the black mask on her face, pinning the elastic to her hair for greater security.

At the last minute she decided to change the color of her hair and had it washed and tinted blue-black instead of pale blond. Then she put it up again and found herself so altered that it startled her.

About eighty people had been asked to meet at the big studio of the fashionable painter. It was dimly lit so as to preserve the guests' identities better. When they were all there, they were whisked to the waiting automobiles. The chauffeurs knew where to go. In the deepest part of the woods there was a beautiful clearing covered with moss. There they sat, having sent the chauffeurs away, and began to drink champagne. Many of the caresses had already begun in the crowded automobiles. The masks gave people a liberty that turned the most refined ones into hungry animals. Hands ran under the sumptuous evening dress to touch what they wanted to touch, knees intertwined, breaths came quicker.

Linda was pursued by two men. The first of them did all he could to arouse her by kissing her mouth and breasts, while the other, with more success, caressed her legs under her long dress, until she revealed by a shudder that she was aroused. Then he wanted to carry her off into the darkness.

The first man protested but was too drunk to compete. She was carried away from the group to where the trees made dark shadows and lowered onto the moss. From nearby there were cries of resistance, there were grunts, there was a woman shrieking, 'Do it, do it, I can't wait any more, do it, do it to me!'

The orgy was in full bloom. Women caressed one another. Two men would set about teasing a woman into a frenzy and then stop merely to enjoy the sight of her, with her dress half-undone, a shoulder strap fallen, a breast uncovered, while she tried to satisfy herself by pressing obscenely against the men, rubbing against them, begging, lifting her dress.

Linda was astonished by the bestiality of her aggressor. She, who had known only the voluptuous caresses of her husband, found herself now in the grip of something infinitely more powerful, a desire so violent it seemed devouring.

His hands gripped her like claws, he lifted her sex to meet his penis as if he did not care if he broke her bones in doing so. He used *coups de belier*, truly like a horn entering her, a goring that did not hurt but which made her want to retaliate with the same fury. After he had satisfied himself once with a wildness and violence that stunned her, he whispered, 'Now I want you to satisfy yourself, fully, do you hear me? As you never did before.' He held his erect penis like a primitive wooden symbol, held it out for her to use as she wished.

He incited her to unleash her most violent appetite on him. She was hardly aware of biting into his flesh. He panted in her ears, 'Go on, go on, I know you women, you never really let yourself take a man as you want to.'

From some depths of her body that she had never known, there came a savage fever that would not spend itself, that could not have enough of his mouth, his tongue, his penis inside of her, a fever that was not content with an orgasm. She felt his teeth buried in her shoulder, as her teeth bit into his neck, and then she fell backward and lost consciousness.

When she awakened, she was lying on an iron bed in a shabby room. A man was asleep beside her. She was naked, and he too, but half-covered by the sheet. She recognized the body which had crushed her the night before in the Bois. It was the body of an athlete, big, brown, muscular. The head was handsome, strong, with wild hair. As she looked at him admiringly, he opened his eyes and smiled.

'I could not let you go back with the others, I might never have seen you again,' he said.

'How did you get me here?'

'I stole you.'

'Where are we?'

'In a very poor hotel, where I live.'

'Then you're not . . .'

'I'm not a friend of the others, if that is what you mean. I am simply a workman. One night, bicycling back from my work, I saw one of your *partouzes*. I got undressed and joined it. The women seemed to enjoy me. I was not discovered. When I had made love to them, I stole away. Last night I was passing by again and I heard the voices. I found you being kissed by that man, and I carried you off. Now I have brought you here. It may make trouble for you, but I could not give you up. You're a real woman, the others are feeble compared to you. You've got fire.'

'I have to leave,' said Linda.

'But I want your promise that you will come back.'

He sat up and looked at her. His physical beauty gave him a grandeur, and she vibrated at his nearness. He began to kiss her and she felt languid again. She put her hand on his hard penis. The joys of the night before were still running through her body. She let him take her again almost as if to make sure that she had not dreamed. No, this man who could make his penis burn through her whole body and kiss her as if it were to be the last kiss, this man was real.

And so Linda returned to him. It was the place where she felt most alive. But after a year she lost him. He fell in love with another woman and married her. Linda had become so accustomed to him that now everyone else seemed too delicate, too refined, too pale, feeble. Among the men she knew, there was none with that savage strength and fervor of her lost lover. She searched for him again and again, in small bars, in the lost places of Paris. She met prizefighters, circus stars, athletes. With each she tried to find the same embraces. But they failed to arouse her.

When Linda lost the workman because he wanted to have a woman of his own, a woman to come home to, a woman who would take care of him, she confided in her hairdresser. The Parisian hairdresser plays a vital role in the life of a French-woman. He not only dresses her hair, about which she is particularly fastidious, but he is an arbiter of fashion. He is her best critic and confessor in matters of love. The two hours that it takes to get one's hair washed, curled and dried is ample time for confidences. The seclusion of the little cabinet protects secrets.

When Linda had first arrived in Paris from the little town in the South of France where she was born and she and her husband had met, she was only twenty years old. She was badly dressed, shy, innocent. She had luxuriant hair which she did not know how to arrange. She used no make-up. Walking down the Rue Saint-Honoré admiring the shop windows, she became fully aware of her deficiences. She became aware of what the famous Parisian chic meant, that fastidiousness of detail which made of any woman a work of art. Its purpose was to heighten her physical attributes. It was created largely by the skill of the dressmakers.

What no other country was ever able to imitate was the erotic quality of French clothes, the art of letting the body express all its charms through clothes.

In France they know the erotic value of heavy black satin, giving the shimmering quality of a wet naked body. They know how to delineate the contours of the breast, how to make the folds of the dress follow the movements of the body. They know the mystery of veils, of lace over the skin, of provocative underwear, of a dress daringly slit.

The contour of a shoe, the sleekness of a glove, these give the Parisian woman a trimness, an audacity, that far surpasses the seductiveness of other women. Centuries of coquetry have produced a kind of perfection that is apparent not only in the rich women but in the little shop girls. And the hairdresser is the priest of this cult for perfection. He tutors the women who come from the provinces. He refines vulgar women; he brightens pale women; he gives them all new personalities.

Linda was fortunate enough to fall into the hands of Michel, whose salon was near the Champs Elysées. Michel was a man of forty, slender, elegant and rather feminine. He spoke suavely, had beautiful salon manners, kissed her hand like an aristocrat, kept his little mustache pointed and glazed. His talk was bright and alive. He was a philosopher and a creator of women. When Linda came in, he cocked his head like a painter who is about to begin a work of art.

After a few months Linda emerged a polished product. Michel became, besides, her confessor and director. He had not always been a hairdresser of well-to-do women. He did not mind telling that he had begun in a very poor quarter where his father was a hairdresser. There the women's hair was spoiled by hunger, by cheap soaps, carelessness, rough handling.

'Dry as a wig,' he said. 'Too much cheap perfume. There was one young girl – I have never forgotten her. She worked for a dressmaker. She had a passion for perfume but could not afford any. I used to keep the last of the toilet water bottles for her. Whenever I gave a woman a perfume rinse, I saw to it that a little was left in the bottle. And when Gisele came I liked to pour it down between her breasts. She was so delighted that she did not notice how I enjoyed it. I would take the collar of her dress between my thumb and forefinger, pull it out a little, and drop the perfume down, stealing a glance at her young breasts. She had a voluptuous way of moving afterward, of closing her eyes and taking in the smell and reveling in it. She would cry out sometimes, "Oh, Michel, you've wet me too much this time." And she would rub her dress against her breasts to dry herself.

'Then once I could not resist her any more. I dropped the perfume down her neck, and when she threw her head back and closed her eyes, my hand slipped right to her breasts. Well, Gisele never came back.

'But that was only the beginning of my career as a perfumer of women. I began to take the task seriously. I kept perfume in an atomizer and enjoyed spraying it on the breasts of my clients. They never refused that. Then I learned to give them a little brushing after they were ready. That's a very enjoyable task, dusting the coat of a well-formed woman.

'And some women's hair puts me in a state which I cannot describe to you. It might offend you. But there are women whose hair smells so intimate, like musk, that it makes a man – well, I cannot always keep myself under control. You know how helpless women are when they are lying back to have their hair washed, or when they are under the dryer, or having a permanent.'

Michel would look a client over and say, 'You could easily get fifteen thousand francs a month,' which meant an apartment on the Champs Elysées, a car, fine clothes, and a friend who would be generous. Or she might become a woman of the first category, the mistress of a senator or of the writer or actor of the day.

When he helped a woman reach the position due her, he maintained her secret. He never talked about anybody's life except in disguised terms. He knew a woman married for ten years to the president of a big American corporation. She still had her prostitute's card and was well known to the police and to the hospitals where the prostitutes went for weekly examinations. Even today, she could not become altogether accustomed to her new position and at times forgot that she had the money in her pocket to tip the men who waited on her during her Clipper trip across the ocean. Instead of a tip she handed out a little card with her address.

It was Michel who counseled Linda never to be jealous, that she must remember there were more women in the world than men, especially in France, and that a woman must be generous with her husband – think how many women would be left without a knowledge of love. He said this seriously. He thought of jealousy as a sort of miserliness. The only truly generous women were the prostitutes, actresses, who did not withhold their bodies. To his mind, the meanest type of woman was the American gold digger who knew how to extract money from men without giving herself, which Michel thought a sign of bad character.

He thought that every woman should at one time or another be a whore. He thought that all women, deep down, wished to be a whore once in their lives and that it was good for them. It was the best way to retain a sense of being a female.

When Linda lost her workman, therefore, it was natural for her to consult Michel. He advised her to take up prostitution. That way, he said, she would have the satisfaction of proving to herself that she was desirable entirely apart from the question of love, and she might find a man who would treat her with the necessary violence. In her own world she was too worshiped, adored, spoiled, to know her true value as a female, to be treated with the brutality that she liked.

Linda realized that this would be the best way to discover whether she was aging, losing her potency and charms. So she took the address Michel gave her, got into a taxi and was taken to a place on the Avenue du Bois, a private house with a grandiose appearance of seclusion and aristocracy. There she was received without questions.

'*De bonne famille*?' That was all they wanted to ascertain. This was a house which specialized in women *de bonne famille*. Immediately the caretaker would telephone a client: 'We have a newcomer, a woman of most exquisite refinement.'

Linda was shown into a spacious boudoir with ivory furniture, brocade draperies. She had taken off her hat and veil and was standing before the large gold-framed mirror arranging her hair, when the door opened.

The man who came in was almost grotesque in appearance. He was short and stout, with a head too big for his body, features like an overgrown child's, too soft and hazy and tender for his age and bulk. He walked very swiftly toward her and kissed her hand ceremoniously. He said, 'My dear, how wonderful it is that you were able to escape from your home and husband.'

Linda was about to protest when she became aware of the man's desire to pretend. Immediately she fell into the role but trembled within herself at the thought of yielding to this man. Already her eyes were turning towards the door, and she wondered if she could make her escape. He caught her glance and said very quickly, 'You need not be afraid. What I ask of you is nothing to be frightened about. I am grateful to you for risking your reputation to meet me here, for leaving your husband for me. I ask very little, this presence of yours here makes me very happy. I have never seen a woman more beautiful than you are, and more aristocratic. I love your perfume, and your dress, your taste in jewelry. Do let me see your feet. What beautiful shoes. How elegant they are, and what a delicate ankle you have. Ah, it is not very often that so beautiful a woman comes to see me. I have not been lucky with women.'

Now it seemed to her that he looked more and more like a child, everything about him, the awkwardness of his gestures, the softness of his hands. When he lit a cigarette and smoked, she felt that this must be his first cigarette, because of the awkward way he handled it and the curiosity with which he watched the smoke.

'I cannot stay very long,' she said, impelled by the need to escape. This was not at all what she had expected.

'I will not keep you very long. Will you let me see your handkerchief?'

She offered him a delicate, perfumed handkerchief. He smelled it with an air of extreme pleasure.

Then he said, 'I have no intention of taking you as you expect me to. I am not interested in possessing you as other men do. All I ask of you is that you pass this handkerchief between your legs and then give it to me, that is all.'

She realized that this would be so much easier than what she had feared. She did it willingly. He watched her as she leaned over, raised her skirt, unfastened the lace pants and passed the handkerchief slowly between her legs. He leaned over then and put his hand over the handkerchief merely to increase the pressure and so that she would pass it again.

He was trembling from head to foot. His eyes were dilated. Linda realized that he was in a state of great excitement. When he took the handkerchief away he looked at it as if it were a woman, a precious jewel.

He was too absorbed to talk. He walked over to the bed, laid the handkerchief on the bedspread and then threw himself on it, unbuttoning his trousers as he fell. He pushed and rubbed. After a moment he sat up on the bed, wrapped his penis with the handkerchief and then continued jerking, finally reaching an orgasm which made him cry out with joy. He had completely forgotten Linda. He was in a state of ecstasy. The handkerchief was wet from his ejaculation. He lay back panting.

Linda left him. As she walked through the hallways of the house she met the woman who had received her. The woman was amazed that she should want to leave so soon. 'I gave you one of our most refined clients,' she said, 'a harmless creature.'

It was after this episode that Linda sat in the Bois one day watching the parade of spring costumes on a Sunday morning. She was drinking in the colors and elegance and perfumes when she became conscious of a particular perfume near her. She turned her head. To her right sat a handsome man of about forty, elegantly dressed, with his glossy black hair carefully combed back. Was it from his hair that this perfume came? It reminded Linda of her voyage to Fez, of the great beauty of the Arab men there. It had a potent effect on her. She looked at the man. He turned and smiled at her, a brilliant white smile of big strong teeth with two smaller milk teeth, slightly crooked, which gave him a roguish air.

Linda said, 'You use a perfume which I smelled in Fez.'

'That's right,' said the man, 'I was in Fez. I bought this at the market there. I have a passion for perfumes. But since I found this one I have never used any other.'

'It smells like some precious wood,' said Linda. 'Men should smell like precious wood. I have always dreamed of finally reaching a country in South America where there are whole forests of precious woods which exude marvelous odors. Once I was in love with patchouli, a very ancient perfume. People no longer use it. It came from India. The Indian shawls of our grandmothers were always saturated with patchouli. I like to walk along the docks, too, and smell spices in the warehouses. Do you do that?'

'I do. I follow women sometimes, just because of their perfume, their smell.'

'I wanted to stay in Fez and marry an Arab.'

'Why didn't you?'

'Because I fell in love with an Arab once. I visited him several times. He was the handsomest man I had ever seen. He had a dark skin and enormous jet eyes, an expression of such emotion and fervor that it swept me off my feet. He had a thundering voice and the softest manner. Whenever he talked to anyone, he would stand, even in the street, holding their two hands, tenderly, as if he wanted to touch all human beings with the same great softness and tenderness. I was completely seduced, but . . .'

'What happened?'

'One day, when it was extremely hot, we sat drinking mint tea in his garden and he took off his turban. His head was completely shaved. It is the tradition of the Arabs. It seems that all their heads are completely shaved. That somehow cured me of my infatuation.'

The stranger laughed.

With perfect synchronization, they got up and started to walk together. Linda was as much affected by the perfume, which came from the man's hair, as she would have been by a glass of wine. Her legs felt unsteady, her head foggy. Her breasts swelled and fell with the deep breaths she took. The stranger watched the heaving of her breasts as if he were watching the sea unfolding at his feet.

At the edge of the Bois he stopped. 'I live right up there,' he said, pointing with his cane to an apartment with many balconies. 'Would you care to come in and have an apéritif with me on my terrace?'

Linda accepted. It seemed to her that, were she deprived of the perfume which enchanted her, she would suffocate.

They sat on his terrace, quietly drinking. Linda leaned back languidly. The stranger continued to watch her breasts. Then he closed his eyes. Neither of them made a movement. Both had fallen into a dream.

He was the first to move. As he kissed her Linda was carried back to Fez, to the garden of the tall Arab. She remembered her sensations of that day, the desire to be enfolded in the white cape of the Arab, the desire for his potent voice and his burning eyes. The smile of the stranger was brilliant, like the smile of the Arab. The stranger *was* the Arab, the Arab with thick black hair, perfumed like the city of Fez. Two men were making love to her. She kept her eyes closed. The Arab was undressing her. The Arab was touching her with fiery hands. Waves of perfume dilated her body, opened it, prepared her to yield. Her nerves were set for a climax, tense, responsive.

She half opened her eyes and saw the dazzling teeth about to bite into her flesh. And then his sex touched her and entered her. It was like something electrically charged, each thrust sending currents throughout her body.

He parted her legs as if he wanted to break them apart. His hair fell on her face. Smelling it, she felt the orgasm coming and called out to him to increase his thrusts so that they could come together. At the moment of the orgasm he cried out in a tiger's roar, a tremendous sound of joy, ecstasy and furious enjoyment such as she had never heard. It was as she had imagined the Arab would cry, like some jungle animal, satisfied with his prey, who roars with pleasure. She opened her eyes. Her face was covered with his black hair. She took it into her mouth.

Their bodies were completely tangled. Her panties had been so hurriedly pulled down that they had fallen the length of her legs and lay around her ankles, and he had somehow inserted his foot into one half of the panties. They looked at their legs bound together by this bit of black chiffon, and they laughed.

She returned many times to this apartment. Her desire would begin long before each meeting, as she dressed for him. At all hours of the day his perfume would issue from some mysterious source and haunt her. Sometimes as she was about to cross a street, she would remember his scent so vividly that the turmoil between her legs would make her stand there, helpless, dilated. Something of it clung to her body and disturbed her at night when she was sleeping alone. She had never been so easily aroused. She had always needed time and caresses, but for the Arab, as she called him to herself, it seemed as if she were always erotically prepared, so much so that she was aroused long before he touched her, and what she feared was that she would come at the very first touch of his finger on her sex.

That happened once. She arrived at his apartment moist and trembling. The lips of her sex were as stiff as if they had been caressed, her nipples hard, her whole body quivering, and as he kissed her he felt her turmoil and slipped his hand directly to her sex. The sensation was so acute that she came.

And then one day, about two months after their liaison, she went to him and when he took her in his arms she felt no desire. He did not seem to be the same man. As he stood in front of her she coldly observed his elegance and his ordinariness. He looked like any elegant Frenchman one could see walking down the Champs Elysées, or at opening nights, or at the races.

But what had changed him in her eyes? Why did she not feel this great intoxication she felt ordinarily in his presence? There was something so usual now about him. So like any other man. So unlike the Arab. His smile seemed less brilliant, his voice less colorful. Suddenly she fell into his arms and tried to smell his hair. She cried out, 'Your perfume, you have no perfume on!'

'It's finished,' said the Arab Frenchman. 'And I cannot get any like it. But why should that upset you so?'

Linda tried to recapture the mood he threw her into. She felt her body cold. She pretended. She closed her eyes and she began to imagine. She was in Fez again, sitting in a garden. The Arab was sitting at her side, on a low, soft couch. He had thrown her back on the couch and kissed her while the little water fountain sang in her ears, and the familiar perfume burned in an incense holder at her side. But, no. The fantasy was broken. There was no incense. The place smelled like a French apartment. The man at her side was a stranger. He was deprived of his magic that made her desire him. She never went to see him again.

Although Linda had not relished the adventure of the hand-kerchief, after a few months of not moving from her own sphere she became restless again.

She was haunted by memories, by stories she heard, by the feeling that everywhere around her men and women were enjoying sensual pleasure. She feared that now that she had ceased to enjoy her husband, her body was dying.

She remembered being sexually awakened by an accident at a very early age. Her mother had bought her panties that were too small for her and very tight between the legs. They had irritated her skin, and at night while falling asleep she had scratched herself. As she fell asleep, the scratching became softer and then she became aware that it was a pleasurable sensation. She continued to caress her skin and found that as her fingers came nearer the little place in the center, the pleasure increased. Under her fingers she felt a part which seemed to harden at her touch, and there found an even greater sensibility.

A few days later she was sent to confession. The priest sat at his chair and she was made to kneel at his feet. He was a Dominican and wore a long cord with a tassel which fell at his right side. As Linda leaned against his knees, she felt this tassel against her. The priest had a big warm voice which enveloped her, and he leaned down to talk to her. When she had finished with the ordinary sins – anger, lies and so on – she paused. Observing her hesitation, he began to whisper in a much lower tone, 'Do you ever have impure dreams?'

'What dreams, Father?' she asked.

The hard tassel that she felt just at the sensitive place between her legs affected her like her fingers' caresses of the nights before. She tried to move closer to it. She wanted to hear the voice of the priest, warm and suggestive, asking about the impure dreams. He said, 'Do you ever have dreams of being kissed, or of kissing someone?'

'No, Father.'

Now she felt that the tassel was infinitely more affecting than her fingers because, in some mysterious way or other, it was part of the priest's warm voice and his words, like 'kisses'. She pressed against him harder and looked at him.

He felt that she had something to confess, and asked, 'Do you ever caress yourself?'

'Caress myself how?'

The priest was about to dismiss the question, thinking his intuition had been an error, but the expression of her face confirmed his doubts.

'Do you ever touch yourself with your hands?'

It was at this moment that Linda wanted so much to be able to make one movement of friction and once again reach that extreme, overwhelming pleasure she had discovered a few nights ago. But she was afraid the priest would become aware and repulse her and she would lose the sensation completely. She was determined to hold his attention, and began, 'Father, it is true, I have something very terrible to confess. I scratched myself one night and then I caressed myself, and –'

'My child, my child,' said the priest, 'you must stop this immediately. It is impure. It will ruin your life.'

'Why is it impure?' asked Linda, pressing against the tassel. Her excitement was rising. The priest leaned over so close that his lips almost touched her forehead. She was dizzy. He said, 'Those are the caresses that only your husband can give you. If you do it and abuse them, you will grow weak, and no one will love you. How often have you done it?'

'For three nights, Father. I have had dreams too.'

'What sort of dreams?'

'I have had dreams of someone touching me there.'

Every word she said increased her excitement, and with a pretense of guilt and shame she threw herself against the priest's knees and bowed her head as if she would cry, but it was because the touch of the tassel had brought on the orgasm and she was shaking. The priest, thinking it was guilt and shame, took her in his arms, raised her from her kneeling position and comforted her.

Marcel

Marcel came to the houseboat, his blue eyes full of surprise and wonder, full of reflections like the river. Hungry eyes, avid, naked. Over the innocent, absorbing glance fell savage eyebrows, wild like a bushman's. The wildness was attenuated by the luminous brow and the silkiness of the hair. The skin was fragile too, the nose and mouth vulnerable, transparent, but again the peasant hands, like the eyebrows, asserted his strength.

In his talk it was the madness that predominated, his compulsion to analyze. Everything which befell him, everything which came into his hands, every hour of the day, was constantly commented upon, ripped apart. He could not kiss, desire, possess, enjoy, without immediate examination. He planned his moves beforehand with the help of astrology; he often met with the marvelous; he had a gift for evoking it. But no sooner had the marvelous befallen him than he grasped it with the violence of a man who was not sure of having seen it, lived it; and who longed to make it real.

I liked his pregnable self, sensitive and porous, just before he talked, when he seemed a very soft animal, or a very sensual one, when his malady was not perceptible. He seemed then without wounds, walking about with a heavy bag full of discoveries, notes, programs, new books, new talismans, new perfumes, photographs. He seemed then to be floating like the houseboat without moorings. He wandered, tramped, explored, visited the insane, cast horoscopes, gathered esoteric knowledge, collected plants, stones.

'There is a perfection in everything that cannot be owned,' he said. 'I see it in fragments of cut marble, I see it in worn pieces of wood. There is a perfection in a woman's body that can never be possessed, known completely, even in intercourse.'

He wore the flowing tie of the Bohemians of a hundred years ago, the cap of an apache, the striped trousers of the French bourgeois. Or he wore a black coat like a monk's, the bow tie of the cheap actor of the provinces, or the scarf of the pimp, wrapped around the throat, a scarf of yellow or bull's-blood red. Or he wore a suit given to him by a businessman, with the tie flaunted by the Parisian gangster or the hat worn on Sunday by the father of eleven children. He appeared in the black shirt of a conspirator, in the checkered shirt of a peasant from Bourgogne, in a workman's suit of blue corduroy with wide baggy trousers. At times he let his beard grow and looked like Christ. At other times he shaved himself and looked like a Hungarian violinist from a traveling fair.

I never knew in what disguise he was coming to see me. If he had an identity, it was the identity of changing, of being anything; it was the identity of the actor for whom there is a continual drama.

He had said to me, 'I will come some day.'

Now he lay on the bed looking at the painted ceiling of the houseboat. He felt the cover of the bed with his hands. He looked out the window at the river.

'I like to come here, to the barge,' he said. 'It lulls me. The river is like a drug. What I suffer from seems unreal when I come here.'

It was raining on the roof of the houseboat. At five o'clock Paris always has a current of eroticism in the air. Is it because it is the hour when lovers meet, the five to seven of all French novels? Never at night, it would seem, for all the women are married and free only at 'tea time', the great alibi. At five I always felt shivers of sensuality, shared with the sensual Paris. As soon as the light faded, it seemed to me that every woman I saw was running to meet her lover, that every man was running to meet his mistress.

When he leaves me, Marcel kisses me on the cheek. His beard touches me like a caress. This kiss on the cheek which is meant to be a brother's is charged with intensity.

We had dinner together. I suggested we go dancing. We went to the Bal Nègre. Immediately Marcel was paralyzed. He was afraid of dancing. He was afraid to touch me. I tried to lure him into the dance, but he would not dance. He was awkward. He was afraid. When he finally held me in his arms he was trembling, and I was enjoying the havoc I caused. I felt a joy at being near to him. I felt a joy in the tall slenderness of his body.

I said, 'Are you sad? Do you want to leave?'

'I'm not sad, but I'm blocked. My whole past seems to stop me. I can't let go. This music is so savage. I feel as if I can inhale but not exhale. I'm just constrained, unnatural.'

I did not ask him to dance any more. I danced with a Negro.

When we left then in the cool night, Marcel was talking about the knots, the fears, the paralysis in him. I felt, the miracle has not happened. I will free him by a miracle, not by words, not directly, not with the words I used for the sick ones. What he suffers I know. I suffered it once. But I know the free Marcel. I want Marcel free.

But when he came to the houseboat and saw Hans there, when he saw Gustavo arriving at midnight and staying on after he left, Marcel got jealous. I saw his blue eyes grow dark. When he kissed me goodnight, he stared at Gustavo with anger.

He said to me, 'Come out with me for a moment.'

I left the houseboat and walked with him along the dark quays. Once we were alone, he leaned over and kissed me passionately, furiously, his full, big mouth drinking mine. I offered my mouth again.

'When will you come to see me?' he asked.

'Tomorrow, Marcel, tomorrow I will come to see you.'

When I arrived at his place he had dressed himself in his Lapland costume to surprise me. It was like a Russian dress, and he wore a fur hat and high black felt boots, which reached almost to his hips.

His room was like a traveler's den, full of objects from all over the world. The walls were covered with red rugs, the bed was covered with animal furs. The place was close, intimate, voluptuous like the rooms of an opium dream. The furs, the deep-red walls, the objects, like the fetishes of an African priest – everything was violently erotic. I wanted to lie naked on the furs, to be taken there lying on this animal smell, caressed by the fur.

I stood there in the red room, and Marcel undressed me. He held my naked waist in his hands. He eagerly explored my body with his hands. He felt the strong fullness of my hips.

'For the first time, a real woman,' he said. 'So many have come here, but for the first time here is a real woman, someone I can worship.'

As I lay on the bed it seemed to me that the smell and feel of the fur and the bestiality of Marcel were combined. Jealousy had broken his timidity. He was like an animal, hungry for every sensation, for every way of knowing me. He kissed me eagerly, he bit my lips. He lay in the animal furs, kissing my breasts, feeling my legs, my sex, my buttocks. Then in the half-light he moved up over me, shoving his penis in my mouth. I felt my teeth catching on it as he pushed it in and out, but he liked it. He was watching and caressing me, his hands all over my body, his fingers everywhere seeking to know me completely, to hold me.

I threw my legs up over his shoulder, high, so that he could plunge into me and see it at the same time. He wanted to see everything. He wanted to see how the penis went in and came out glistening and firm, big. I held myself up on my two fists so as to offer my sex more and more to his thrusts. Then he turned me over and lay over me like a dog, pushing his penis in from behind, with his hands cupping my breasts, caressing me and pushing me at the same time. He was untiring. He would not come. I was waiting to have the orgasm with him, but he postponed and postponed it. He wanted to linger, to feel my body forever, to be endlessly excited. I was growing tired and I cried out, 'Come now, Marcel, come now.' He began then to push violently, moving with me into the wild rising peak of the orgasm, and then I cried out, and he came almost at the same time. We fell back among the furs, released.

We lay in half-darkness, surrounded by strange forms – sleighs, boots, spoons from Russia, crystals, sea shells. There were erotic Chinese pictures on the walls. But everything, even a piece of lava from Krakatoa, even the bottle of sand from the Dead Sea, had a quality of erotic suggestion.

'You have the right rhythm for me,' Marcel said. 'Women are usually too quick for me. I get into a panic about it. They take their pleasure and then I am afraid to go in. They do not give me time to feel them, to know them, to reach them, and I go crazy after they leave thinking about their nakedness and how I have not had my pleasure. But you are slow. You are like me.'

As I dressed we stood by the fireplace, talking. Marcel slipped his hand under my skirt and began caressing me again. We were suddenly blind again with desire. I stood there with my eyes closed, feeling his hand, moving upon it. He gripped my ass with his hard, peasant grip, and I thought we were going to roll down on the bed again, but instead he said, 'Lift up your dress.'

I leaned against the wall, moving my body up against his. He put his head between my legs, seizing my buttocks in his hands, tonguing my sex, sucking and licking until I was wet again. Then he took his penis out and took me there against the wall. His penis hard and erect like a drill, pushing, pushing, thrusting up into me while I was all wet and dissolved in his passion.

I enjoy making love with Gustavo more than with Marcel, because he has no timidities, no fears, no nervousness. He falls into a dream, we hypnotize each other with caresses. I touch his neck and pass my fingers through his black hair. I caress his belly, his legs, his hips. When I touch his back from neck to buttocks his body begins to shiver with pleasure. Like a woman, he likes caresses. His sex stirs. I don't touch it until it begins to leap. Then he gasps with pleasure. I take it all in my hand, hold it firmly, and press it up and down. Or else I touch the tip of it with my tongue, and then he moves it in and out of my mouth. Sometimes he comes in my mouth and I swallow the sperm. Other times it is he who begins the caresses. My moisture comes easily, his fingers are so warm and knowing. Sometimes I am so excited that I feel the orgasm at the mere touch of his finger. When he feels me throbbing and palpitating, it excites him. He does not wait for the orgasm to finish, he pushes his penis in as if to feel the last contractions of it. His penis fills me completely, it is just made for me, so that he can slide easily. I close my inner lips around his penis and suck him inwardly. Sometimes the penis is larger than at other times and seems charged with electricity, and then the pleasure is immense, protracted. The orgasm never ends.

Women very often pursue him, but he is like a woman and needs to believe himself in love. Although a beautiful woman can excite him, if he does not feel some kind of love, he is impotent.

It is strange how the character of a person is reflected in the sexual act. If one is nervous, timid, uneasy, fearful, the sexual act is the same. If one is relaxed, the sexual act is enjoyable. Hans's penis never softens, so he takes his time, with a sureness about it. He installs himself inside of his pleasure as he installs himself inside of the present moment, to enjoy calmly, completely, to the last drop. Marcel is more uneasy, restless. I feel even when his penis is hard that he is anxious to show his power and that he is hurrying, driven by fear that his strength will not last.

Last night after reading some of Hans's writing, his sensual scenes, I raised my arms over my head. I felt my satin pants slipping a little at the waist. I felt my belly and sex so alive. In the dark Hans and I threw ourselves into a prolonged orgy. I felt that I was taking all the women he had taken, everything that his fingers had touched, all the tongues, all the sexes he had smelled, every word he had uttered about sex, all this I took inside of me, like an orgy of remembered scenes, a whole world of orgasms and fevers.

Marcel and I were lying together on his couch. In the semidarkness of the room he was talking about erotic fantasies he had and how difficult it was to satisfy them. He had always wanted a woman to wear a lot of petticoats and he would lie underneath and look. He remembered that is what he did with his first nurse and, pretending to play, had looked up her skirts. This first stirring of the erotic feeling had remained with him.

So I said, 'But I'll do it. Let's do all the things we ever wanted to do or have done to us. We have the whole night. There are so many objects here that we can use. You have costumes too. I'll dress up for you.'

'Oh, will you?' said Marcel. 'I'll do anything you want, anything you ask me to do.'

'First get me the costumes. You have peasant skirts there that I can wear. We will begin with your fantasies. We won't stop until we have realized them all. Now, let me dress.'

I went to the other room, put on various skirts he had brought from Greece and Spain, one on top of another. Marcel was lying on the floor. I came into his room. He was flushed with pleasure when he saw me. I sat on the edge of his bed.

'Now stand up,' said Marcel.

I stood up. He lay on the floor and he looked up between my legs, under the skirts. He spread them a little with his hands. I stood still with my legs apart. Marcel's looking up at me excited me, so that very slowly I began to dance as I had seen the Arab women do, right over Marcel's face, slowly shaking my hips, so that he could see my sex moving between the skirts. I danced and moved and turned, and he kept looking and panting with pleasure. Then he could not contain himself, pulled me down right over his face, and began biting and kissing me. I stopped him after a while: 'Don't make me come, keep it.'

I left him and for his next fantasy I returned naked wearing his black felt boots. Then Marcel wanted me to be cruel. 'Please be cruel,' he begged.

All naked, in the high black boots, I began to order him to do humiliating things. I said, 'Go out and bring me a handsome man. I want him to take me in front of you.'

'That I won't do,' said Marcel.

'I order you to. You said you would do anything I asked you.'

Marcel got up and went downstairs. He came back about half an hour later with a neighbor of his, a very handsome Russian. Marcel was pale; he could see that I liked the Russian. He had told him what we were doing. The Russian looked at me and smiled. I did not need to arouse him. When he walked toward me, he was already roused by the black boots and the nakedness. I not only gave myself to the Russian but I whispered to him, 'Make it last, please make it last.'

Marcel was suffering. I was enjoying the Russian, who was big and powerful and who could hold out for a long time. As Marcel watched us, he took his penis out of his pants, and it was erect. When I felt the orgasm coming in unison with the Russian's, Marcel wanted to put his penis in my mouth but I would not let him. I said, 'You must keep it for later. I have other things to ask you. I won't let you come!' The Russian was taking his pleasure. After the orgasm he stayed inside and wanted more, but I moved away. He said, 'I wish you would let me watch.'

Marcel objected. We let him go. He thanked me, very ironically and feverishly. He would have liked to stay with us.

Marcel fell at my feet. 'That was cruel. You know that I love you. That was very cruel.'

'But it made you passionate, didn't it, it made you passionate.'

'Yes, but it hurt me too, I would not have done that to you.'

'I did not ask you to be cruel to me, did I? When people are cruel to me it makes me cold, but you wanted it, it excited you.'

'What do you want now?'

'I like to be made love to while looking out of the window,' I said, 'while people are looking at me. I want you to take me from behind, and I want nobody to be able to see what we are doing. I like the secrecy of it.'

I stood by the window. People could look into the room from other houses, and Marcel took me as I stood there. I did not show one sign of excitement, but I was enjoying him. He was panting and could scarcely control himself, as I kept saying, 'Quietly, Marcel, do it quietly so that nobody will know.' People saw us, but they thought we were just standing there looking at the street. But we were enjoying an orgasm, as couples do in doorways and under bridges at night all over Paris.

We were tired. We closed the window. We rested for a little while. We began to talk in the dark, dreaming and remembering.

'A few hours ago, Marcel, I entered the subway at the rush hour, which I rarely do. I was pushed by the waves of people, jammed, and stood there. Suddenly I remembered a subway adventure Alraune told me about, when she was convinced that Hans had taken advantage of the crowdedness to caress a woman. At the very same moment, I felt a hand very lightly touch my dress, as if by accident. My coat was open, my dress thin, and this hand was brushing lightly through my dress just at the tip of my sex. I did not move away. The man in front of me was so tall that I could not see his face. I did not want to look up. I was not sure it was he, I did not want to know who it was. The hand caressed the dress, then very lightly it increased its pressure, feeling for the sex. I made a very slight movement to raise the sex toward the fingers. The fingers became firmer, following the shape of the lips deftly, lightly. I felt a wave of pleasure. As a lurch of the subway pushed us together I pressed against the whole hand, and he made a bolder gesture, gripping the lips of the sex. Now I was frenzied with pleasure, I felt the orgasm approaching, I rubbed against the hand, imperceptibly. The hand seemed to feel what I felt and continued its caress until I came. The orgasm shook my body. The subway stopped and a river of people pushed out. The man disappeared.'

War is declared. Women are weeping in the streets. The very first night there was a black-out. We had seen rehearsals of this, but the real black-out was quite different. The rehearsals had been gay. Now Paris was serious. The streets were absolutely black. Here and there a tiny blue or green or red watch light, small and dim, like the little ikon lights in Russian churches. All the windows were covered with black cloth. The café windows were covered or painted in dark blue. It was a soft September night. Because of the darkness it seemed even softer. There was something very strange in the atmosphere – an expectancy, a suspense.

I walked carefully up the Boulevard Raspail feeling lonely and intending to go to the Dome and talk to someone. I finally reached it. It was overcrowded, half-full of soldiers, half-full of the usual whores and models, but many of the artists were gone. Most of them had been called home, each one to his own country. There were no Americans left, no more Spaniards, no more German refugees sitting about. It was a French atmosphere again. I sat down and was soon joined by Gisele, a young woman I had talked with a few times. She was glad to see me. She said she could not stay at home. Her brother had been called, and the house was sad. Then another friend, Roger, sat at our table. Soon we were five. All of us had come to the café to be with people. All of us felt lonely. The darkness isolated one, it made going out difficult. One was driven indoors – so as not to be alone. We all wanted this. We sat there enjoying the lights, the drinks. The soldiers were animated, everyone was friendly. All the barriers were down. People did not wait for introductions. Everyone was in equal danger and shared the same need of companionship and affection and warmth.

Later I said to Roger, 'Let's go out.' I wanted to be in the dark streets again. We walked slowly, cautiously. We came to an

Arabian restaurant that I liked and went in. People were sitting around the very low tables. A fleshy Arabian woman was dancing. Men would give her money and she would place it on her breasts and go on dancing. Tonight the place was full of soldiers, and they were drunk on the heavy Arabian wine. The dancer was drunk, too. She never wore very much, hazy, transparent skirts and a belt, but now the skirt had slit open and when she did her belly dance, it revealed the pubic hair dancing, the massive flesh around it trembling.

One of the officers offered her a ten-franc piece and said, 'Pick it up with your cunt.' Fatima was not at all disturbed. She walked to his table, laid the ten-franc piece on the very edge of it, spread her legs a little and gave a twist like those she did in the dance, so that the lips of her vulva touched the money. At first she could not catch it. While she tried to do this, she made a sucking noise, and the soldiers were laughing and excited by the sight. Finally the lips of the vulva stiffened sufficiently around the piece of money and she picked it up.

The dancing continued. A young Arab boy who played the flute was watching me intently. Roger was sitting next to me dissolved by the dancer, gently smiling. The Arab boy's eyes continued to burn through me. It was like a kiss, a burn on one's flesh. Everybody was drunk and singing and laughing. When I got up, the Arab boy got up too. I was not quite sure of what I was doing. At the entrance there was a dark cubbyhole for coats and hats. The girl who took care of it was sitting with the soldiers. I went in there.

The Arab understood. I waited among the coats. The Arab spread one of them on the floor and pushed me down. In the dim light I could see him taking out a magnificent penis, smooth, beautiful. It was so beautiful that I wanted it in my mouth, but he would not let me have it. He immediately placed it inside my sex. It was so hard and hot. I was afraid we would be caught and I wanted him to hurry. I was so excited that I had come immediately and now he was going on, plunging, and churning. He was untiring.

A half-drunk soldier came out and wanted his coat. We did not move. He grabbed his coat without stepping into the cubbyhole where we lay. He went away. The Arab was slow in coming. He had such a strength in his penis and in his hands and in his tongue. Everything was firm about him. I felt his penis growing larger and hotter, until the edges ʳubbed so much against the womb that it felt rough, almost like a scraping. He moved in and out at the same even rhythm, never hurrying. I lay back and thought no more of where we were. I thought only of his hard penis moving evenly, moving obsessionally, in and out. Without any warning or change of rhythm, he came, like the spurt of a fountain. Then he did not take his penis out. It remained firm. He wanted me to come again. But people were leaving the restaurant. Fortunately the coats had fallen over us and concealed us. We were in a kind of tent. I did not want to move. The Arab said, 'Will I see you again? You are so soft and beautiful. Will I ever see you again?'

Roger was looking for me. I sat up and arranged myself. The Arab disappeared. More people began to leave. There was an eleven o'clock curfew. People thought I was taking care of the coats. I was no longer drunk. Roger found me. He wanted to take me home. He said, 'I saw the Arab boy staring at you. You must be careful.'

Marcel and I were walking through the darkness, in and out of cafés, pulling aside the heavy black curtains as we entered, which made us both feel as if we were going into some underworld, some city of the demons. Black, like the black underwear of the Parisian whore, the long black stockings of the cancan dancers, the wide black garters of the women especially created to satisfy men's most perverse caprices, the tight little black corsets which set off the breasts and push them up toward men's lips, the black boots of flagellation scenes in French novels. Marcel was shivering with the voluptuousness of it. I asked him, 'Do you think there are places that make one feel like making love?'

'I certainly do,' said Marcel. 'At least, I feel this. Just as you felt like making love on top of my fur bed, I always feel like making love where there are hangings and curtains and materials on the walls, where it is like a womb. I always feel like making love where there is a great deal of red. Also where there are mirrors. But the room which excited me most was one I saw one time near the Boulevard Clichy. As you know, at the corner of this boulevard there is a famous whore with a wooden leg who has many admirers. I was always fascinated with her because I felt that I could never bring myself to make love to her. I was sure that as soon as I saw the wooden leg I would be paralyzed with horror.

'She was a very cheerful young woman, smiling, good-natured. She had dyed her hair blond. But her eyelashes were of deep black and bushy like a man's. She had a soft little bit of hair in her upper lip. She must have been a dark, hairy southern girl before she dyed her hair. Her one good leg was sturdy, firm, her body quite beautiful. But I could not bring myself to ask her. As I looked at her I remembered a painting by Courbet I had seen. It was a painting commissioned by a rich man long ago, who had asked him to paint a woman in the act of sex. Courbet, who was a great realist, painted a woman's sex and nothing else. He left out the head, the arms, the legs. He painted a torso, with a carefully designed sex, in contortions of pleasure, clutching at a penis that came out of a bush of very black hair. That was all. I felt that with this whore it would be the same, one would only think of the sex, try not to look down at her legs or anything else. And perhaps that would be exciting. As I stood in the corner deliberating with myself, another whore came up to me, a very young one. A young whore is rare in Paris. She spoke to the one with the wooden leg. It was beginning to rain. The young one was saying, "I've been walking in the rain for two hours now. My shoes are ruined. And not a single client." I suddenly felt sorry for her. I said, "Will you have a coffee with me?" She accepted joyously. She said, "What are you, a painter?"

'"I'm not a painter," I said, "but I was thinking about a painting I saw."

'"There are wonderful paintings in the Café Wepler," she said. "And look at this one." She took out of her pocketbook what looked like a delicate handkerchief. She held it opened. There was painted on it a big woman's ass, placed so as to reveal the sex fully, and an equally large penis. She tugged at the handkerchief, which was elastic, and it looked as if the ass were moving, the penis too. Then she turned it over, and now the penis was still heaving but it looked as if it had gone inside of the sex. She gave it a certain movement which made the whole picture active. I laughed, but the sight aroused me, so that we never got to the Café Wepler and the girl offered to let me go to her room. It was in a very shabby house of Montmartre, where all the circus and vaudeville people stayed. We had to climb five flights.

'She said, "You'll have to excuse the drabness. I'm just starting in Paris. I've only been here a month. Before that I was working in a house in a small town and it was so boring seeing the same men every week. It was almost like being married! I knew just when they would be coming to see me, the day and hour, regular as clocks. I knew all their habits. There were no more surprises. So I came to Paris."

'As she talked we entered her room. It was very small – just room enough for the big iron bed on which I pushed her and which creaked as if we were already making love like two monkeys. But what I couldn't get used to was that there was no window – absolutely no window. It was like lying in a tomb, a prison, a cell. I can't tell you exactly what it was like. But the feeling it gave me was of security. It was wonderful to be shut in so securely with a young woman. It was almost as wonderful as being already inside her cunt. It was the most marvelous room I ever made love in, so completely shut out of the world, so tight and cozy, and when I got inside of her I felt that the whole rest of the world could vanish for all I cared. There I was, in the best place of all in the world, a womb, warm and soft and shutting me in from everything else, protecting me, hiding me.

'I would like to have lived there with this girl, never to go out again. And I did for two days. For two days and nights we just lay there in her bed and caressed and fell asleep and caressed again and fell asleep, until it was all like a dream. Every time I woke up I was with my penis inside of her, moist, dark, open, and then I would move and then lie quiet, until we got terribly hungry.

'Then I went out, got wine and cold meat and back to bed again. No daylight. We did not know what time of day it was, or whether it was night. We just lay there, feeling with our bodies, one inside of the other almost continuously, talking into each other's ears. Yvonne would say something to make me laugh. I would say, "Yvonne, don't make me laugh so much or it will slip out." My penis would slip out of her when I laughed and I would have to put it back again.

'"Yvonne, are you tired of this?" I asked.

'"Ah, no," said Yvonne, "it is the only time I have ever enjoyed myself. When clients are always in a sort of hurry, you know, it sort of hurts my feelings, so I let them go at it, but I don't take any interest in it. Besides, it's bad for business. It makes you old and tired too quickly if you do. And I always have that feeling that they don't pay enough attention to me, so it makes me draw in, away from them somewhere in myself. You understand that?"'

Then Marcel asked me if he had been a good lover that first time in his place.

'You were a good lover, Marcel. I liked the way you gripped my ass with both hands. You gripped it firmly as if you were going to eat into it. I liked the way you took my sex between your two hands. It was the way you took it, so decisively, with so much maleness. It is a little touch of the caveman you have.'

'Why do women never tell men this? Why do women make such a secret and mystery of it all? They think it destroys their mystery, but it is not true. And here you come out and say just what you felt. It is wonderful.'

'I believe in saying it. There are enough mysteries, and these do not help our enjoyment of each other. Now the war is here and many people will die, knowing nothing because they are tongue-tied about sex. It's ridiculous.'

'I am remembering St Tropez,' said Marcel. 'The most wonderful summer we have ever had . . .'

As he said this, I saw the place vividly. An artists' colony where society people and actors and actresses went, people with yachts anchored there. The little cafés on the waterfront, the gaiety, the exuberance, the laxity. Everybody in beach costumes. Everybody fraternizing – the yacht people with the artists, the artists with the young postman, the young policeman, the young fisherman, young and dark men of the south.

There was dancing on a patio under the sky. The jazz band came from Martinique and was hotter than the summer night.

Marcel and I were sitting in a corner one evening when they announced that they would put all the lights out for five minutes, then for ten, then for fifteen in the middle of each dance.

A man called out, 'Choose your partners carefully for the *quart d'heure de passion*. Choose your partners carefully.'

There was a great flurry and bustle for a moment. Then the dance began, and eventually the lights went out. A few women screamed hysterically. A man's voice said, 'That's an outrage, I won't stand for it.' Someone else screamed, 'Turn on the lights.'

The dance continued in the dark. One felt that bodies were in heat.

Marcel was in ecstasy, holding me as if he would break me, bending over me, his knees between mine, his penis erect. In five minutes people only had time to get a little friction. When the lights went on everybody looked disturbed. A few faces looked apoplectic, others pale. Marcel's hair was tousled. One woman's linen shorts were wrinkled. One man's linen trousers were wrinkled. The atmosphere was sultry, animal, electric. At the same time there was a surface of refinement to be maintained, a form, an elegance. Some people, who were shocked, were leaving. Some waited as if for a storm. Others waited with a light in their eyes.

'Do you think one of them will scream, turn into a beast, lose his control?' I asked.

'I may,' said Marcel.

The second dance began. The lights went out. The voice of the band leader said, 'This is the *quart d'heure de passion*. Messieurs, mesdames, you now have ten minutes of it, and then you will have fifteen.'

There were stifled little screams in the audience, women protesting. Marcel and I were clutched like two tango dancers, and at each moment of the dance I thought I would unleash the orgasm. Then the lights went on, and the disorder and feeling in the place was even greater.

'This will turn into an orgy,' said Marcel.

People sat down with eyes dazed, as if by the lights. Eyes dazed with the turmoil of the blood, the nerves.

One could no longer tell the difference between the whores, the society women, the Bohemians, the town girls. The town girls were beautiful, with the sultry beauty of the south. Every woman was sunburnt and Tahitian, covered with shells and flowers. In the pressure of the dance some of the shells had broken and lay on the dance floor.

Marcel said, 'I don't think I can go through the next dance. I will rape you.' His hand was slipping into my shorts and feeling me. His eyes were burning.

Bodies. Legs, so many legs, all brown and glossy, some hairy as foxes'. One man had such a hairy chest that he wore a net shirt to show it off. He looked like an ape. His arms were long and encircled his dance partner as if he would devour her.

The last dance. The lights went out. One woman let out a little bird cry. Another began to defend herself.

Marcel's head fell on my shoulder and he began to bite my shoulder, hard. We pressed against each other and moved against each other. I closed my eyes. I was reeling with pleasure. I was carried by a wave of desire, which came from all the other dancers, from the night, from the music. I thought I would have the orgasm then. Marcel continued to bite me, and I was afraid we would fall on the floor. But then drunkenness saved us, the drunkenness kept us suspended over the act, enjoying all that lay behind the act.

When the lights went on everybody was drunk, tottering with nervous excitement. Marcel said, 'They like this better than the actual thing. Most of them like this better. It makes it last so long. But I can't stand any more of it. Let them sit there and enjoy the way they feel, they like to be tickled, they like to sit there with their erections and the women all open and moist, but I want to finish it off, I can't wait. Let's go to the beach.'

At the beach the coolness quieted us. We lay on the sand, still hearing the rhythm of the jazz from afar, like a heart thumping, like a penis thumping inside of a woman, and while the waves rolled at our feet, the waves inside of us rolled us over and over each other until we came together, rolling in the sand, to the same thumping of the jazz beats.

Marcel was remembering this, too. He said, 'What a marvelous summer. I think everybody knew it would be the last drop of pleasure.'

Contemporary ... Provocative ... Outrageous ...
Prophetic ... Groundbreaking ... Funny ... Disturbing ...
Different ... Moving ... Revolutionary ... Inspiring ...
Subversive ... Life-changing ...

What makes a modern classic?

At Penguin Classics our mission has always been to make the best
books ever written available to everyone. And that also means
constantly redefining and refreshing exactly what makes a 'classic'.
That's where Modern Classics come in. Since 1961 they have been an
organic, ever-growing and ever-evolving list of books from the last
hundred (or so) years that we believe will continue to be read over and
over again.

They could be books that have inspired political dissent, such as
Animal Farm. Some, like *Lolita* or *A Clockwork Orange*, may have
caused shock and outrage. Many have led to great films, from *In Cold
Blood* to *One Flew Over the Cuckoo's Nest*. They have broken down
barriers – whether social, sexual, or, in the case of *Ulysses*, the
boundaries of language itself. And they might – like *Goldfinger* or
Scoop – just be pure classic escapism. Whatever the reason, Penguin
Modern Classics continue to inspire, entertain and enlighten millions
of readers everywhere.

'No publisher has had more influence on reading habits than Penguin'
Independent

'Penguins provided a crash course in world literature'
Guardian

The best books ever written

PENGUIN ![penguin logo] CLASSICS

SINCE 1946